As with so many stories, *The Sixth Angel* was a long time in development. The plot originated inside Theodore Bohlman's head, and he brought it to me with the thought of turning that idea into a book. We met and stewed over ideas, then developed an outline and a title. Unlike my first two published works, resources were available to hire an editor, and we were able to consult with many professionals whose insight helped to frame the story. We are thankful to God and so many people who gave freely of their time to provide feedback as our characters and their world came into focus. Without their help, this story—like so many others—would still be rattling around inside our heads like so much debris.

I would like to thank my wife Heather and daughter Jessyka for so many years of support, laughter, and love. I would also like to thank Theodore Bohlman and wife Sue for three years of fun discussions and meals; Leslie Peterson of Write Away Editorial; Tim Woodward for his infusion of insight; David Nehen for a great deal of advice on legal procedure; and Thomas Detras, my long-time friend and reliable critic whose trustworthy literary opinions have helped shape the author's many stories.

With much thanks, Kenneth Scherer

* * *

The thought of writing a book had probably never seriously crossed my mind. Oh, I suppose at some time we all dream of putting our thoughts to words, to be like John Grisham or Michael Connelly. But really, me a writer? We all have random thoughts that come to our minds from time to time, like ... Wow! "That would be a good comedy sketch," or, "Wouldn't that make a good human interest story?" or, "How would that mystery plot play out in a story?" Turns out, I *have* had those thoughts over the years, and this one in particular became *The Sixth Angel*!

Remember my line about my writing ability? Turns out I'm not a writer; I'm a thinker, a dreamer, an organizer! Enter Kenneth Scherer. Several years ago I shared with him my idea for a book based on my silly brain wanderings. Kenneth, to whom I will forever be indebted, is a published author, and I liked his writing style. He suggested we collaborate on my idea and put those thoughts to words, while also adding his own twists to the story. Writing a book is no easy task—it's taken over 3 years —but alas, we are now ready to share these musings with the world.

I have many people to thank for their support of this endeavor! First of all, my loving wife Susan. She provided meals, support, and ideas for our project. Wow, what would I be without her? My granddaughter Paxton Smith who critically read the book and provided a critique. To Tim Woodward, a suburb local journalist, author, film writer and narrator, for his help with the story. Also to Tim's friend, Pat Carson, for her input. To dear friends Mike and Vickie Chaney for their support, and to Dirk Kempthorne—our in-house Josh—for his encouragement, thoughts and support. And to other friends who reviewed the manuscript and gave encouragement and ideas.

Theodore Bohlman

*　*　*

We give you *The Sixth Angel*!!!

The Sixth Angel

A Murder Mystery

Kenneth Scherer
Theodore Bohlman

ONE

Harney County, Oregon

Spring, 1980

Morning's first light glimmered through a half finger of un-finished bourbon, casting its caramel reflection across a worn table and onto the face of Josh Matthews. He squinted, re-senting the pesky intrusion. Uncomfortable and exhausted, he took an inventory of himself. For one thing, he lay crammed into the confines of a couch too short for his six-foot frame. He hadn't taken the time to remove his gun belt last night, and he groaned as he shifted and felt his handcuffs and holster digging into his side.

The movement brought an answering protest from his legs. His knees were sore, no doubt the product of much prayer before God over the past few hours. To top things off, his eyes ached from tears and lack of sleep. His fitful napping had been punctuated with the memory of screaming voices and the broken bodies of young people crushed by the weight of indul-gence.

In short, he'd seen better days—or nights.

Alone in his anguish, he was brought upright by the grinding bleat of the telephone hanging in the kitchen. His eyes tracked to the clock near the door. Six twenty a.m. Twenty minutes past his lifelong rising time of six o'clock.

He scanned the table and growled at the star of golden light pestering him through the bourbon. "I hate you," he groaned as he strained to take the call. It seemed an impossible distance from his lonely dent in the couch.

"Matthews," he said into the receiver in a voice cracking with exhaustion. He rubbed his eyes.

The voice on the other end held barely restrained excitement. "Sheriff, it's Linda." Linda had worked in the office for sixteen years and strove to keep Sheriff Matthews informed of any major development. "You're needed up at Marshall Creek."

Josh immediately straightened. "What's wrong?" he asked. He already knew it was important because Linda would never have bothered him at home unless it was. His home was his only place of refuge, and she knew it. Her call meant something bad, perhaps worse than last night. There could be no other reason.

"Max just called in. He's up there right now. Harry Grey called in bright and early to report finding a dead body. He says to tell you that it's pretty horrendous."

"Foul play?"

"Yes."

Josh stood silent while his thoughts raced back over the past several hours. The last thing he needed was another disaster, but it appeared he was not going to avoid it. "All right. Let me get a shower and some coffee. Does Max have anyone in custody?"

"No, not at this time." The woman's voice cracked. "Sorry, Sheriff. I know you're tired."

"Don't worry about it, Linda. Call Max and make sure he's got the scene roped off. I'll be up there as soon as I can."

"Yes, sir."

Josh rested the phone on the receiver and leaned on it while he scanned the room. He couldn't remember a time when the kitchen looked so unkempt. It was a struggle to keep up, and he wondered how his daughter had done it. With her gone from the home so long, he could do little more than care just enough to notice. She had been a force in his life, and he missed her more in that moment than he had since she'd left.

He got coffee brewing, climbed into the shower, and closed his eyes as the hot water washed over his aching muscles. Rinsing the stink of death and vomit from his skin, he felt a bit more relaxed, if not at least clean. He shut off the faucet, toweled himself, and pulled on a fresh uniform. Pausing as he looked at his badge, he forced back a shuddering lower lip and the anguish of the night's horrid events. An early morning automobile accident out on the highway had taken the lives of a close friend's twin sons and resulted in the arrest of the driver, a girl he had known from birth. A girl his very own daughter had babysat for ten years.

And now, with that hell fresh on his mind, had come the news that a body had been found deep in the woods. The deputy, Max Shafer, was young but seasoned and knew his job well. He wouldn't use a word like *murder* unless it was. However, Josh wasn't one to jump to conclusions. He would reserve judgment until he arrived on the scene.

With a quick cup of coffee that burned his tongue and a full thermos for later, he left the house and returned to his home away from home—a 1971 Chevy truck he'd been driving since new. It was a bit rickety and slow to start on a cold winter morning, and it was in need of paint and new fabric, but it was reliable and got him around the county in a pinch.

The drive up Highway 395 soon brought Josh back to the previous night as he rounded a bend in the road and crept past the accident scene. A tow truck had at last arrived and the driver was hoisting a crumpled VW Bug's carcass onto the flatbed. In the dawning light Josh saw the true extent of the damage, and he was amazed that the driver had walked away with barely more than a scratch. He also fully understood why the boys had been killed.

He waved politely at the tow driver and went on his way.

It was a cool morning, and the trees were dipped in dew, sparkling with a million tiny rainbows. The road twisted and turned, and Josh kept a steady hand on the wheel as he tried to focus his mind away from one death scene to another. He had no idea what he would find up in the mountains, and he wondered why a body might be found so far off the beaten path in the first place.

He turned right onto NFD 2820 and pulled over to refill his coffee cup, then waited for a logging truck to rumble by before continuing on. The dusty road wandered east in something approximating a straight line until the turnoff at 3935 to the north. Josh followed the road with a steady determination that echoed his patience in focusing on the task at hand.

A few minutes longer and he pulled the truck in behind Max Shafer's cruiser, turned off the engine, and stepped out onto the dirt road. He shivered in the shade of the pines and junipers as they cast their long shadows across a thin stand of trees hemmed in by banks of fog hugging along the ridges. Trunks with four-foot diameters and one-hundred-foot heights were not uncommon here, and he leaned against one to adjust a boot and straighten out his gun belt.

"Ugh," he groaned as he wiped a sticky bit of pine tar from his hand. He looked up into the dizzying heights but held his words. Cursing at the tree would do no good.

Two additional squad cars sat parked in a clearing, telling Josh he was late to the party. That struck him a hard blow. He was known for his punctuality and made it a habit to be where he was needed when he was needed. He did his best to look after the people who'd put him in the office and entrusted him with their safety. When he'd first run for sheriff some twenty-eight years ago, he'd done so on the promise that Harney County would be a safe, satisfying place to live, where a man could raise a family free from the fear that some wayward misfit would come calling yet still hunt and fish and raise a ruckus so long as he didn't bother anyone else. He had won that first election by just four votes. Every election since had been a landslide. That near unanimous voter confidence caused Josh to take pride in his job. He knew he was good at it, and that self-assurance reflected onto his deputies, who also took pride in their jobs.

From where he stood beneath the towering pine, and with the murmur of his men hunting through the brush, he reached deep for control. Some terrible force had unleashed itself within the boundaries of his county, and although he could not escape the feeling that he had seen this too many times before, he had to focus. Still, he could not shake the sense of betrayal that the county's quiet existence had been shattered.

"Not again," he said under his breath.

He paused again to check his attitude, collect himself, and then take a slow look around to commit the details to his mind. Tire tracks, footprints, the mist, shadows, a broken twig, and a red Mustang convertible parked opposite the turnout. Other than an accumulation of road dust, the Mustang was clean. There was a woman sitting in it watching him. Further down the road a man in uniform strolled along, occasionally disappearing behind a tree or a shrub, and Josh recognized the portly figure of Deputy Shaw.

The sound of a chainsaw echoed somewhere in the distance.

"Morning, Sheriff," came a youthful voice from somewhere behind a plug of sagebrush.

Josh turned to Max Shafer, his favorite deputy and protégé, and smirked at the way the young man wore his gun. Max looked as tired as Josh felt; the deputy had been with him into the early hours at the accident scene.

"Morning Max," Josh said. "Seems like I just saw you a few hours ago."

"Too much happening these days," replied the young man. "I didn't get much sleep last night."

"Neither did I. You okay for this?"

"Yes, sir."

"Well, then," Josh said as he eyed the red Mustang again,

"show me what you found."

"Yes, sir. Follow me." Max led the way along a trail through the trees and toward the creek. "We got a call this morning from Harry Grey. You know him, I think. He's the guy who's always hiking up here."

"Yeah, I know him," Josh answered.

"Well, apparently he was up here doing his thing, whatever that is. He said he just happened to glance down and found this." Max motioned to a blue tarp. "She's been here a few hours. I can't believe it's been much longer than that. Still pretty fresh. Coyotes haven't even gotten to the body yet."

"Did you tarp her, or was she like that?"

"I did."

Josh squatted down and pulled the tarp back, then covered his mouth and pulled away. "Her head's near cut off," he said with disgust. He dropped the canvas and rubbed his chin with his sleeve. "What insane person did this?"

"Wish I knew. I got here about an hour and a half ago. She's naked, obviously. Lots of blood. I can't see any sign of a struggle. She hasn't got any obvious scratches or bruises or anything like that. It's like she got taken from behind and got her throat cut before she knew it was coming."

"Anyone touch her since you got here?"

"No, sir. And I haven't touched her either. Just had a quick look and then covered her up. I couldn't leave her out there like that."

Josh moved around so he could see the woman's face. "Hey, isn't that, oh, what's her name? Works out at the mill."

"Sure. Lisa or something like that."

"Yeah. That's her. Lisa Martin, if memory serves." Josh looked around at the terrain and the body's proximity to the road. "What on earth was she doing up here?"

"No idea, boss. Haven't got that far yet."

"Did you find any clothes laying around?"

"She's wearing three-inch heels," Max said. "Other than that, nothing. We found some car tracks on the other side of the road. I've got that taped off. There's a car parked down near the bottom of the hill—a Datsun, I think. Shaw went down there and got some pictures. He thinks it's hers, but he's running the plates to make sure. I don't know if she came up here for a walk or to meet someone, or if someone brought her here. I had a walk around out to about fifty yards when I first got here, but I didn't see anything worth looking at. Shaw has been looking around a bit out over there." Max motioned out into the trees. "He's been down the road, over across the creek and such, looking for footprints, car tracks, and stuff. Near as I know, he hasn't found anything in the immediate area, although he says there's a camp of vagrants up the creek about five hundred yards."

"Let's make sure we talk to them," said Josh. He turned back to the creek and studied the far bank. "Make sure you get plenty of photos, Max. Turn the place into a studio if you need to."

"I'm on it. Jane is already on her way with the camera gear. I'm sure she won't miss anything."

"Married, isn't she?" Josh asked.

"Jane?" Max asked quizzically.

Josh shot a rough look at the young deputy. "No, not Jane. Her," he said as he pointed at the body.

"Uh, yeah," Max said with obvious embarrassment. "As far as I know, yes. Doesn't mean anything, though."

"Maybe not, but we'll have to talk to her husband." Josh looked over the ground near where he was standing. "All the blood is right here. She died right here."

"Yes, sir. There's no sign of her putting up a fight, either. I think she got it right here and didn't move. There's blood spatter over the bushes all through here. I mean blood went everywhere. There's very little right under where she's lying, though, so I think she might have been placed specifically."

"Doesn't look like she was dragged."

"Sure doesn't. There are some scuffmarks here, and boot prints by that bush." Max pointed at the marks. "Looks like the best one is right there."

"Yeah. Looks like he's wearing size eleven Redwings. That narrows it down to everyone in the county."

"I wear size tens," Max said.

"I'll mark you off my suspect list," Josh said as he paused to write a few notes. "So, if he was waiting for her, then he must have known she was coming. I cannot believe she would come to this place on her own, at least not during the night. Might be somebody she was familiar with."

"Or someone who knew someone she was familiar with. Maybe she was lured thinking it was someone else?"

Josh nodded. "That could be," he said as he turned to the sound of an approaching vehicle. Did you talk to Grey, find out what he was up to?"

Max stepped from the brush and back onto hard earth. "Yes, sir. His usual. Came up from the highway a few days ago and has been wandering around. Says he likes to be outside. If he did it, he found a way to clean himself up. There wasn't a trace of blood on him. Anyway, we took his statement and sent him on his way."

Josh nodded and turned his attention to the approaching vehicle. "Looks like the ME is here. Let's you and I step away so we don't tromp around too much. I want these prints preserved. Maybe we can plaster them and look for any unusual cuts or dimples."

Josh and his deputy moved away from the body, taking care to watch where they were stepping, as a graying man approached the scene and quietly went to work.

"What do you think, Don?" Josh asked.

The man looked up and spoke through smoke-stained teeth in a voice to match. "Rigor mortis is barely set in. This woman hasn't been dead for more than twelve hours, I should think."

"Seem odd to you she was found so quickly?"

"Lot of folks up here, Sheriff. I don't think I'm too surprised."

Josh winced as the older man shuffled about, kicking up

sand and dirt. "Don, watch that area of sand there. Got some footprints we need to preserve."

"I see 'em, old friend. Not to worry. Say," the gray-haired, heavy-set man said as he poked about, "how you making out since last night?"

"Didn't sleep much."

"Neither did I. Been a long time since I've seen anything like that. Parents doing okay?"

"As well as can be expected."

The medical examiner stripped the tarp away from the victim and put his hands on his hips as if contemplating. Then he casually plunged a thermometer into the victim's abdomen as Max covered his mouth and turned away.

"What's her temp?" Josh asked.

"Looks like twenty-five Celsius. She died no more than eight hours ago. I'd say sometime around midnight." The ME removed a syringe from his bag and looked at the men hovering over him. "If I recall correctly, you two don't much like this."

Josh took Max's arm and turned him so he was facing away from the victim. "He's right, son. You don't want to see this. Remember what happened when we found that plane crash last year? You got pretty sick."

"Yeah, I hate this part," Max said. "Maybe I'll stand over here."

"Yeah," said Josh, "eye fluid samples are a bit too much for me too. I about fell over the first time I saw it done. He just pokes that needle in and—" He made a slurping sound.

Max's face turned white as he cringed.

Josh turned with a smile, then started back up the trail and looked toward the red Mustang. "Who's in the Mustang across the way there?"

"The red one?"

"Only Mustang I can see, Max."

Max seemed to stumble at the obviousness of his question but got himself in order. "Uh, yeah. That's the new *Burns Review* reporter, Gail Cruz."

"Hmm. I've heard that name tossed about, but don't recall having met her yet. What does she want?"

"A story, I suppose."

Josh cocked a condescending eyebrow at his deputy. "Max?"

"Sorry, sir. She showed up right after Shaw, walked around a bit, but stayed out of the way. I talked to her and convinced her it would be best for her to stay with her car for now. Polite enough. She said she heard the call come in and drove up here."

"What time did you make the call?"

"Uh, six twenty, I think."

"She was up at six twenty listening to a scanner?" Josh smiled with admiration. "Now that's dedication. I better go have some words with her."

"Careful."

"Why's that?"

Max broke into a dirty smile. "She's quite the looker."

Josh shook his head and spat on the ground in front of Max's foot. "You sure have a one-track mind, son. Maybe you ought to save that for the wife." He winked at his deputy, then turned for the Mustang. He had no idea what to expect, and he wondered if he wanted to meet the woman in the red car as an official gesture or to satisfy his curiosity. After all, he liked a pretty woman as much as the next guy.

* * *

It wasn't the first time Gail Cruz had been told to wait for the right person to speak with, but she'd known that arriving early was no guarantee she wouldn't have to wait. When she'd first arrived on scene and shown her credentials, a nice young deputy had stopped her and told her she'd be best to wait in her car until the sheriff arrived. Only then would any questions be answered. So she'd waited with eyes closed and dreamed of sandy beaches and glorious sunsets.

Earlier that morning, she'd awoken before sunrise as usual and poured a cup of coffee, added her two teaspoons of sugar, and topped it off with milk. She'd stirred, sipped, then sat down on an old couch in the living room and closed her eyes a second before flipping the power switch on her police scanner and pulling her bare feet up, slipping a throw over her cold shoulders. For a while there'd been nothing but static from the scratchy speaker, but her spirits had lifted when an excited voice came over the scanner. She still couldn't believe what she'd heard.

She went back over the moments leading up till now ...

"Linda, you awake down there?" the man's voice on the scanner said, and Gail could sense the distress in his voice.

At first there was no response, and Gail watched the second hand on the clock tick away thirty seconds.

"Linda, it's Max, I've got an emergency." This time the voice sounded even more urgent, and Gail sat upright and alert. More seconds ticked by before a young woman's voice finally responded.

"Sorry, Max, nature was calling. What gives?"

There was a sigh and the voice choked. "Linda, I need the Sheriff out here right away. Harry's call was legit. He definitely found a body."

Coffee spurted from Gail's nose as she leaned forward and dumped her cup on the table, sending brown liquid across glass and onto the carpet. "Crap," she said as she fumbled for a pad and pencil.

"Max, you're up there on Marshall Creek, right?" asked the faceless woman.

There was static on the line, and then, "Yes."

"Okay, hon. What's your exact location up there?"

Gail listened carefully and wrote down the information as relayed between the deputy and the station. Then, foregoing her morning shower, she rushed from the house and drove through town as fast as she dared. As she approached the Highway 395 turnoff to the north, flashing lights in the mirror told her to pull over, which she did after checking her speed. She was well over the limit. She banged her head against the steering wheel as she sat there waiting. A ticket was the last thing she needed. But the lights grew closer, and then her car shuddered as the cruiser flashed by at what she guessed was eighty miles per hour. She knew then they must be heading the same place she was.

The cruiser's brake lights lit the surrounding darkness as Gail did her best to follow in its wake, but she eventually lost sight as it turned off the highway to the right and disappeared into the mountains. With her lights on high she followed a dirt road for several miles until she was convinced she was lost, then pulled to the side to look around. She got out, scanned the blackness to the north, and got back in when a flashing glow in the distance told her which way to turn.

A few minutes of careful driving later, she pulled alongside the cruiser, its lights still flashing and banging off the trees, then made a U-turn and parked the car out of the way. She checked her watch and noted that it had taken just over forty minutes to get from her house to this place.

With a sigh, she hung her press credentials around her neck, left the car, carefully looked around the area, and took in a deep breath of pine and juniper. The sun was beginning to peek in from the east, and the growing ring of reflected yellow along the rim slowly descended, bringing its warmth and light to the scene.

Two sheriffs' deputies milled about, and she did her best to stay well away from the place they seemed focused on, snapping several photographs and walking along the road for some ways before turning back. She watched her footing and stayed on the road lest she stumble on something and destroy some vital piece of evidence, thus bringing down the wrath of everyone with a badge. She wrote down a few notes, described what she could see with professional flair, and then returned to her car to await an opportunity, which came along abruptly.

"Ma'am?" asked a deputy.

She recognized the voice and knew immediately that this was the same deputy she had heard over the call. "Yes?" she said with a thick Jersey accent.

The deputy approached cautiously with his hand on his gun. "Ma'am, I need to know what you're doing up here."

Gail felt a nervous reaction to the deputy's cautious approach and put her hands up at shoulder height. "Oh, hello. I'm Gail Cruz with the *Burns Review*." Very slowly, she held her name-tag out for Max to inspect.

"I see," he said with distracted eyes. "Can I help you?"

"Sure, if you don't mind. A little birdie says you fellows found a body out here."

"A little birdie, huh? Okay," Max said as he looked back into the trees, "sorry, ma'am. You'll have to wait until the sheriff gets here. He won't be too happy if we go talking to the press before he knows what's up. He doesn't much care for little birdies, if you know what I mean."

"Oh, are you sure?" Gail asked with her best smile.

"Sorry, ma'am," the deputy said as he looked her over. "I can't. Sheriff Matthews will be here within the hour. You can ask him anything you want."

Gail smiled and said her thanks as the sun rose above the horizon. The wind blew softly through the trees, birds chirped and grey squirrels barked and danced among the branches as she got back into her car. With no coffee to keep her awake she slipped into a very unintentional morning nap …

She guessed a half hour had drifted by before the rumble of a truck brought her back to the world. She watched a handsome gentleman step from the vehicle, lean against a tree, and then worry over the scene as someone who appeared in charge. The sheriff, she guessed, and scribbled some notes. Another two hours passed before the man suddenly approached her. He took his steps in a rapid, polished gate like a gunfighter straight from a western movie. He appeared strong and lean, with a face she knew most women would call pleasing. His square jaw and dark, crow's feet-edged eyes were sunken enough to offset a small nose, and his slightly graying dark hair protruded neatly beneath a Stetson. His lips were firm, if not locked in a state of intense thought, and capped with a well-trimmed mustache. He seemed a strong, fit man with purpose, and she guessed him to be in his late fifties.

Suddenly he was knocking on the window, and Gail knew she had been studying him a bit too hard, perhaps even with unnecessary longing. After six months of chasing stories she considered trivial, meeting the Burns chief of police, the county commissioners, the mayors of both Burns and Hines, and many of the area's movers and shakers, she was finally face to face with the sheriff.

"Morning, ma'am," said the man in a smooth, baritone voice. "I'm Sheriff Matthews. I'd sure like to know what you're doing up here."

Gail motioned that she wanted to get out, and he moved away from the door, politely held it for her, and gave her room to step from the car. She looked him over and smiled inside. *Now that's a man*, she thought.

"Sheriff," she said with what she would have described as butterflies in her stomach, "I'm pleased to meet you. I'm Gail Cruz with the *Burns Review*. I heard on the scanner that a body has been found. Would you mind if I ask a few questions?"

The sheriff turned his gaze to the trees. "This isn't really the best time, Ms. Cruz."

Gail was persistent. "Maybe just a few? Please?" She smiled softly. "Just five minutes?"

"For the good of the people and all that?" he quipped.

"Sure. Or maybe just because I'm a nice lady and I drove all the way out here." Gail found herself absentmindedly twirling a lock of hair. She dropped her hand and wanted to kick herself for acting so girly. The last thing she had room for was a man, and she could not believe she had reacted so flirtatiously, almost as though she had lost control of her senses.

He looked at her with a raised eyebrow. "Okay, you've got five minutes. Make them count, nice lady. I've got work to do."

She took a notepad from her purse and noted that her writing hand was trembling. "Do you know who the victim is?"

"Yes."

She turned her head, but her eyes never left his. "So?"

"So, I can't tell you that until we notify the family."

She held her gaze and then asked the next question. "How did it happen?"

"We aren't really sure yet. We'll wait until the medical examiner has released his report, but I *can* tell you that she was murdered. There is no doubt about that."

"So," Gail said, wondering if the identification of gender was intentional or a slipup, "it's a woman?"

"Yes."

The short answer and the look in the sheriff's eye told Gail it was no slipup.

"When?" she asked. "I mean, do you know how long she has been dead?"

"The ME will give us a more detailed picture once he concludes his business. However, we think she died sometime late last night." He reached out to shake Gail's hand. "Okay, listen," he said, "I have other commitments. I'm sure we'll talk again."

Gail watched with curiosity as the sheriff turned and walked to his truck where the young deputy stood waiting. They spoke for some time before the deputy returned to the taped-off area and the sheriff climbed into his truck and sat talking on his CB for several minutes before getting out and rejoining his deputies.

Five minutes passed and another cruiser appeared around the curve. The car approached slowly, parked, and a woman stepped out. She was short, trim, and wore her fiery red hair in a ponytail. Gail thought her a fine-looking woman and noted the sparkle of a wedding ring. She dug in the trunk, collected several duffle bags, and walked past the Mustang with a polite smile.

Gail opened the door after the woman passed and took

several photographs of the huddled officers, more of the collection of police cruisers, still more of the surrounding forest. She watched with greater interest as the redheaded deputy took a camera from one of her duffels and began shooting the crime scene. From a distance she seemed quite thorough as she stepped gingerly around the body. Gail watched as she placed a ruler and photographed something on the ground, then held it in front of something Gail could not identify. Although she could not see clearly through the sage and grass, Gail assumed from the photographer's actions that the body must be at the base of a great, tall pine that jutted up from the creek bed. The deputy dipped below the undergrowth, rose, dropped back, rose again in a different place. Gail knew she was maneuvering around the body, trying to get the best shots with the most detail.

The activity had progressed nonstop for nearly two hours when, after herself having shot through five rolls of film, Gail finally gave up and started for the office.

TWO

N estled into something not much more than a hole in the wall on Broadway Street, Sam's Diner had been serving greasy food to a wide range of customers for more years than Josh could remember. Any number of owners had passed through while he and numerous deputies filled their bellies on an ever-expanding menu of good food. The place was a favorite in town for more than one logger, cowboy, and trucker who had called the place their home away from home for years. Fortunately for Josh and Max it was a slow day and their regular booth by the window sat ready and waiting.

They were barely in their seats when a waitress approached and began chiding them. "You two look like you been swimming in the log pond again."

"Nice to see you, too, Connie." Josh said as he got comfortable in the booth and smiled. "How's the bacon today?"

Connie leaned on the table and eyed him. She was short, wore her blonde hair in a long, braided ponytail, and kept her fiery red nails trimmed to a meager half-inch in length. Her nose was too large for her face, her eyes were too far apart, and she spoke through her nose as she habitually itched at her right collarbone. "Same as always," she said with a quick smile.

"How's that?" Max interrupted. "Still taste like coyote?"

The waitress smiled and flipped the mugs on the table. "A

bit stringy, kind of like a deputy I know." She poured coffee and then changed the subject. "Heard there was a murder up in the woods. That true?"

"How'd you hear about that?" Max asked.

"I've got my sources. So, was there? A murder, I mean?"

"There was," Josh said in a hushed tone. "And no, you can't have the details."

Connie put her hand on her hip and looked at Josh with a flirtatious sneer. "Already got the details, hon. Say, uh, how's things with the wreck from the other night?"

"Danny and Todd are dead," Josh said with a frown.

Connie looked down and fumbled with her fingers. "That's what I heard. It's all anyone has talked about since yesterday."

"Understandable," said Josh. "Anyway, Connie, we've got business to talk about. Would you mind?"

The waitress turned from the table and went about her duties.

"I'm having a hard time with something," Josh said.

"Which part?"

"Her walking."

"Me too. Long way in heels."

"Too far," Josh said.

"I agree, and that means her killer either rode up there with her and then drove her car back to the bottom of the hill or she met him at the turnoff and went the rest of the way in his car. Either way, we have boot prints at the scene that match every farmer, rancher, and logger in the valley. There are wide, heavy-lugged tire tracks along the siding from a vehicle that's probably a pickup, which also narrows it down to practically everyone in the county. Oh," Max said as if placing an exclamation point on his list, "and there are no eye witnesses and no murder weapon."

Josh stirred at his coffee and took a short sip. "Okay," he said as he watched the same red Mustang pull up in front of the diner. "Seems pretty obvious with all the logging up there that any number of trucks rumble up and down the road, so tracks are going to be tough to match up. Anyone could say they were just driving along. Like you said, almost everyone we know wears boots that'll match those prints, unless there's something unique about them. So it comes down to matching up the blood to a murder weapon or finding an eyewitness, neither of which appears likely. Doesn't leave us much to go on." He looked down at his coffee and leaned forward. "Seems we should be able to do better than that."

The mood changed when the door opened and Gail Cruz walked in. She wore tight jeans and a blouse and looked like she'd just stepped out of the shower. Her hair was damp but neatly done, her skin radiant, and her eyes bright with excitement and a thirst for adventure. She made herself comfortable at the counter, turned to smile at Josh, and then appeared to focus her attention on the menu.

Josh eyed the reporter for longer than he should have and averted his eyes only when she caught him looking at her. "So, what we have is nothing." he said, embarrassed to have lost his train of thought.

Max smiled, looked at the reporter, and then back at Josh. "Told you to be careful."

"Shut up, Max."

"Sorry."

"Yeah," Josh said as he played with his coffee cup. "Max, I want to know everything about this girl. We know she worked over at the mill, and we know she worked part time at The Sawyer. We know she was married and had a kid. I want to dig in a little further." He paused and then reminded Max of the victim's humanity. "Kipp Martin was pretty distraught yesterday."

"Didn't go well?"

"Well, I did learn a few things." Josh tapped the table and wondered just how much he wanted to say. It was too early to speculate, but his deputies needed to know. "Seems our victim was a bit busy with other men."

"Oh," Max said.

"Seems she may have been a little too close to Robert Carter and that dude Sam Reynolds. And, get this," Josh said with a pause, "Sam Reynolds and James Hodges got into a fight the other night over at The Sawyer. Apparently they were squabbling over our victim."

Max slowly nodded his head. "Robert Carter that owns the mill?"

"Yeah," Josh said as he shook his head. "Anyway, Max, I want you to go out to the mill and rifle around a bit, and then get over to The Sawyer. I don't much like that place, so I'll leave that to you. See what you can stir up. Tomorrow I'll drive back up to Marshall Creek and get another look around. There has to be something we missed." He took another sip from his coffee before letting his eyes wander back over the reporter.

The waitress returned and leaned on the table. "What are you boys gonna have? Coffee, tea, or me?"

"Are you ever going to learn a new line, Connie?" Josh asked with a smile.

"Ain't got any need to, Sheriff. When a man knows what he wants, he knows what he wants." She winked at him and rolled her chewing gum between her teeth.

"Damn certain he does," Josh said, "and this one wants bacon, two eggs over easy, and a side of browns."

"And a brave man he is, if he's having that."

"Burger and fries," Max piped in.

"For breakfast?"

Max smiled. "My gut wants grease. May not get any the rest of the day."

"Y'all are original," Connie said as she turned to walk away. "I'll give you that."

Josh watched after her. She wasn't the finest catch in Burns, Oregon, but he did think she looked good walking away. "Brave one around here is Sam," he said in jest. "Why he keeps you working is beyond me."

Josh sighed deeply, closed his eyes, and listened to the background noise as the diner's patrons discussed the recent accident and newly discovered rumors of a dead woman found in the woods north of town. Max fidgeted in his notebook and flipped through pages while Josh pondered the random speculation as it relayed from table to table.

Several minutes passed before Connie brought their food. "Good luck, boys," she said. "Fresh from the grease trap."

"You know, Connie," Josh said, "the way you talk about the food here, I wonder if you ever eat it."

"Oh, no, not me," she said with a playful smile. "I need a paycheck, not indigestion."

Max laughed out loud as he dug into his burger.

"You sure know how to make it appetizing." Josh stabbed at his meal and took a bite. "Good as always, Connie."

"Yeah, well, I hear your taste buds lose sensitivity with age, so enjoy." She smiled and walked away to flirt with a table of loggers.

"She'll be a fine catch for someone, I'm sure." Max said.

"Man would have to be looking for a brawl to take interest in that one," Josh replied. He ate quickly, although he hated to do so. He would rather relax and share information with Max, but there was too much to be done on this busiest of days, and he couldn't bring himself to enjoy the meal. "I'll see you later," he said after finishing up. He then slipped from the booth and excused himself.

As he passed the counter, Gail Cruz turned in her stool and reached for his arm. "Sheriff," she said politely.

Josh stopped and looked at the soft, feminine hand tugging at his elbow. "Yes, ma'am?"

Gail stood and gazed at him with her emerald-green eyes. "I hope I didn't cause you any trouble yesterday. I know you had a rough night."

He smiled as he took in the sunlight dancing in her dark hair. She was beautiful, and he could barely stop himself from staring. Then, like a weight, the reality of the past two days dropped back into his mind and he found himself thinking first of the boys, then of Melissa Reed, the driver. "Hard to watch kids die like that," he said as he pulled away and pushed the front door open before turning back to her. "You were no trouble, Ms. Cruz. I hope to see you again."

Josh had started thinking, and he left the cafe with just one thing on his mind. He was no stranger to James Hodges, a vagrant known to his associates as Jimmy Wiggles. Hodges had moved into town in 1967 with his family after his father was hired on at the R. Carter and Sons Mill in Hines. James was generally a good kid until he and his girlfriend began experimenting with drugs when they were both still in high school. That same year, the girlfriend had overdosed and died before she could receive care. James blamed himself and left home in '71, and then returned six years later just months before the body of a woman named Eryn Rogers was found face down on the bank of a creek along an oft-used Forest Service road. Things had gotten interesting when Josh and his deputies found James washing his socks not five hundred yards down the road. The subsequent interview revealed that James had taken to vagrancy and traveled between Portland and Salt Lake City using Highway 20 as a conduit. He spent time in Bend, Burns, and Ontario begging at the local markets before disappearing off into the woods for weeks at a time. No evidence ever tied James to that murder, but Josh's suspicion had never subsided.

Over the past three years James had been in and out of the Harney County jail on charges of loitering, public drunkenness, and shoplifting. The most recent episode had occurred at The Sawyer, a local bar popular with the loggers and cowboys common in the county. Unknown to Josh at the time, James had been putting the moves on the weekend bartender and gotten into a scuffle with another suitor who had also laid his claim on the wayward woman.

Josh knew nothing of Sam Reynolds, but thanks to Kipp Martin he knew where to find him. The Square Nines Ranch was well south of Burns near Lake Malheur, and Josh would be paying him a visit.

*   *   *

"Howdy, stranger," Gail said as she moved into the booth in front of Max.

"Hello," he said with a big smile. "Are you here to grill me?"

"Now, why would I do that?"

"Why wouldn't you?"

She winked. "Because the sheriff would get mad at both of us."

Max stirred his coffee and lay a few dollars on the table to cover the tab. "Something tells me that isn't why."

"Oh, come on, Max. I know there are some things you can't talk about. I'm not here for that. I have other motives." Gail noticed Max's hands. He was spinning his wedding ring on his finger with his thumb, something she recognized as a nervous habit. She leaned back against the seat, hoping the distance would help him relax.

The deputy stared out the window and Gail wondered what he was thinking. "It's not very often you find a body," she said, more to soften him than fish for information. "Are you okay?"

Max looked at her and leaned forward. "To be honest, I'm pretty upset about it, but I'll get over it, I guess."

"You know," she said, "I've spoken to a few cops who have been through this. None ever just 'get over it.'"

Max could only nod.

"Don't hold it in, okay? Talk to the sheriff, talk to your wife, talk to anyone. Just don't bottle it up, or it'll eat at you forever." She hesitated before patting his hand.

"This isn't the first time it's happened around here," Max said with a frown.

"What do you mean?"

"You don't know?"

"Know what?"

"This is number five."

"Five," Gail said, letting it hang out there before cocking her head.

"Five," Max echoed as he finished his coffee.

Gail fumbled in her purse for her notebook. "Five murders? Recently?"

"No, not recently, but over the last—" He thought a moment. "—I don't know, like fifteen years, I think. All women."

"Are you sure?"

"Yes."

"So the body you found was the fifth in fifteen years?"

Max nodded.

"Let me make sure I've got you straight. You had four confirmed murders prior to this one?"

"Yes."

"And you've solved them all?"

He shook his head. "Well, not really."

"Four *unsolved* murders?" Gail was aghast. Four unsolved murders in a larger city could be expected, but in a rural place like Harney County? She scribbled furiously. "There are less than ten thousand people in the entire county," she said.

"Yeah," Max said. "Tell me about it. Still, it's pretty common knowledge around here."

Gail paused and looked at her notes.

"I'm surprised you didn't know," Max said.

"Why would I?" she asked.

"I don't know. I guess I thought that was your job."

"If you say so." *Four other murders*, she thought. "How long ago did you say?"

"There was one in seventy-seven, another in seventy-three, and the first two were in the sixties. I don't recall exactly."

Gail returned the notebook to her purse and slid from the booth. "Max, thank you so much." She shook his hand and pointed at his wedding ring. "You make sure you talk to her, okay."

"I will," he said.

Gail smiled and left the diner. There was work to do. She walked to her car and stood at the door as she fumbled for the keys deep down in her purse.

Gail's office was too cold and there wasn't enough light. Dust had long settled on the edges of the bookshelves, and dead flies littered the windowsills. Still, it was tolerably comfortable, and at least more comfortable than the office in Newark where her window had looked down into a dark alley rather than out onto a small parking lot and the steady shuffle of traffic out on the main street.

Gail moved from one filing cabinet to another and thumbed through old articles. The drawers were arranged by year, and she spent over an hour searching through five drawers' worth to find the old newspapers she was after. She removed several, returned to her desk, and started reading. The details were scarce, especially concerning evidence and motive. The only photos concerned road signs and a younger, but not less handsome, Sheriff Josh Matthews. Gail paused to admire the man's aging process and decided he was getting better looking with time.

A different reporter had penned each article, leading Gail to believe turnover at the small-town paper had been an issue, although the same owner had remained in control of it for thirty years. She decided that those people must have gone the opposite direction she had—off to bigger and better things rather than cleaner and quieter. The big city was a draw to those looking to make a name for themselves, but for Gail the big name was no longer a priority. She wanted to enjoy her work, and this small town atmosphere *was* enjoyable. No stress, no rush, clean air, a low crime rate. Yet, here before her was an indicator that things may not have been as peaceful as they seemed, and she wanted to know why.

Gail wrote down the details as they came to her. Each

article spelled out a small tale of wasted human life. All of the victims were women who had been found out in the woods or the desert. The murders were gruesome, but there was no indication of sexual assault. Their ages were varied, but within twenty years of each other; they shared similar build, hair color, and weight. All four had been killed in a different manner, though, and no clues linking the murders had ever been discovered. The investigating bodies, including the FBI, Oregon State Police, and the Harney County Sheriff's Department, had unanimously concluded the attacks were random acts of violence committed against random women in random locations. There were no identifiable connections.

The victims included a vagrant, a housekeeper, a widow, and a prostitute. Now a housewife had been added to the list.

A light knock sounded against her wall and Gail started at the intrusion.

"What are you doing in here?" asked a pleasant, reassuring voice.

Gail turned to her boss and smiled. "Hey, Sandi. Just reading through some of these old articles." She held up the stack for proof. "And I have a question for you."

Sandi, a very thin woman in her late sixties and graying, leaned against Gail's desk. "Yes, dear?"

"Well, you said you've owned the paper for thirty years, right?"

"Started thirty-one last month. Why do you ask?"

Gail crossed her legs and twirled a pencil from habit. "Someone told me the bodies of four other women have been found in the county over the last fifteen years, not including Lisa Martin."

Sandi's smile became a frown. "Honey, that's well in the past, but yes."

"Do you remember anything?"

"Hard to forget that sort of thing." The old woman moved to a corner chair and sat down.

"What can you tell me?"

"I don't recall the details," Sandi said while plucking at her nails. "But you check the filing cabinets, you'll find all the information we had when it happened."

"Yeah, I've been reading the articles. There isn't much in there."

"There was so little to tell. We never were able to get much information from the sheriff."

"Why do you think that is?" Gail asked.

"Honey, I have no idea. All I know is he never took too kindly to the press and never gave us more than he had to. Good luck getting anything out of him. Speaking of which, have you learned anything yet?"

"Not yet. The sheriff's office isn't releasing the details."

"Yes, well don't expect them to." Sandi removed herself from the chair and stepped quietly to the door. "I tell you, honey, that man is about as unfriendly as they get, so don't expect much. Listen, I'm heading over to The Sawyer. You want to tag along?"

Gail shook her head and turned back to her desk. "No, thanks. I'm going to keep digging."

THREE

Deputy Jane Smith knocked lightly on the faded door and stepped back. The department's only female deputy was new, inquisitive, and determined, although Josh thought she knocked like a girl. She was a short, attractive thirty-year-old, with medium-length red hair and a fresh, sweet face lightly dusted with freckles. Best of all, she was the sharpest investigator Josh had ever worked with.

Her first knock returned nothing but silence, so she stepped forward and knocked again. When there was still no answer, Josh stepped to the door and banged hard enough to shake the windows.

Another moment passed, and then came the muffled sounds of two people speaking. Josh banged again. "Harney County Sheriff!"

"Sounds like he has company," Jane said.

The door opened and a handsome face appeared in it.

"Sam Reynolds?" Jane asked.

"Yeah," the face said in a gruff, impatient tone. "Who wants to know?"

"I do," Josh said as he leaned closer. "I don't suppose you have a minute?"

Reynolds stepped through the door and closed it behind him. "This about that Hodges fellow? Because I already talked to the cops about that."

"It is," Jane said, "but it's not about the fight. We'd like to ask you a few questions about Lisa Martin."

Reynolds's face lit up at the name. "Sure, yeah. What do you want to know?"

"First of all," Josh asked, "were you aware that she was married?"

"Like I care. She wanted a little love, so I gave her a little love. That isn't illegal, you know."

"No, it's not," said Jane. "When was the last time you saw Lisa?"

Reynolds seemed to be studying his memory while his eyes wandered over the deputy's form. "Seems to me it was about a week ago."

"And that was before or after you and James Hodges had your disagreement?"

"Before."

"What was the fight about?" Josh asked.

"Hey, isn't that a city matter? Seems to me you're a bit out of your jurisdiction, Sheriff."

"It might seem that way," Josh said in a heavy tone, "except that we found Lisa Martin's body up in the hills, and word has it you were the last person who saw her alive."

The expression on Sam Reynolds's face fell dramatically, and in that moment Josh knew the man facing him was as unlikely a suspect as anyone in the county. The news hit the man hard, and he staggered back against the door, dropped to his haunches, and hung his head. "How did she die?" he asked through clenched teeth.

"She was murdered, Sam," Jane said.

Josh looked around the ranch and took in the smell and the sounds of baying animals in the distance. He didn't much care if the news was difficult for the drifter cowboy to take. The man was messing around with another man's wife and deserved nothing short of a good beating for it, at least as far as Josh was concerned. "Where were you on the night of May 14," he asked.

"Hey, man, I didn't kill Lisa. I would never hurt that sweet petunia."

"No one is saying you did, Sam," Jane interrupted. "We're just covering the bases."

Reynolds gave Josh a threatening look. "I was here," he said. "Right here. One of the bulls punched a hole in the fence, and we spent the whole night putting the place back together. The foreman can vouch for that."

"I'm sure he can," Josh said as he turned to Jane.

Jane quizzed Sam for several minutes, asked details of the fight, the following night's stay in jail, where he'd gone afterward, whether or not he had seen James Hodges since. Then she followed Josh to the truck.

"You want me to ask the foreman to verify his story?"

"Yep," Josh said. "You do that while I look around."

Josh watched Jane carefully as she approached the barn where Sam Reynolds had indicated the foreman could be found. Satisfied, he turned and walked toward a tool shed. He had no probable cause to go inside, nor a warrant to justify any search, but the door was wide open, and he felt obligated to peek in. Numerous tools hung from racks and hooks along two walls. In the back, a machete lay on an old whiskey barrel. A dark substance coated the length of the blade. He stepped forward for a closer look.

It was blood.

For a solitary moment, Josh thought he had found what he was looking for, but the discovery of a chicken head laying on the ground near the barrel put an end to his excitement.

The drive back was quiet. Jane studied her notes, made more, looked out the window, and seemed far away. Josh had nothing to say. There had been nothing useful discovered while speaking with Sam Reynolds. He had a solid alibi, as a quick check with the Square Nines foreman had proven. Yes, he'd had a quick, meaningless affair with the victim, and yes, he had been in a fight with James Hodges. However, he was fully accounted for over the following week, and there was no way he could have been anywhere near the victim at or around the time of her death. What Josh and his deputy did have was Reynolds's statement that James Hodges had made some very disparaging remarks toward the victim, and that he could be found at the homeless camp up on Marshall Creek.

Forty-five minutes later they pulled into a turnout on the north side of National Forest 3935 and just west of a long *U* the road followed as it crossed over Marshall Creek, and parked just a few yards north of the spot where Harry Grey had stumbled upon the body of Lisa Martin. The body had been removed on the afternoon of the fifteenth, yet two days later an odor of death still filled the air, and coyotes had been busy rooting over the scene, scratching at the dried blood in search of a meal.

Josh and Jane stepped over a long ribbon of yellow police tape and walked down a path toward the creek, which ran high with spring melt.

"What are you looking for?" Jane asked as Josh began rifling through the sage and rabbit brush.

"Tracks," Josh said as his mind pondered the possibility.

"Well, I'm not finding anything, boss," Jane said. "We've been over this area with a fine-toothed comb."

"I know," Josh said as he plucked another sprig from the undergrowth. "We're not looking hard enough. There's just no way he could be that thorough."

Josh hunted through the brush for another hour, kicking rocks here, rolling logs there. He tromped and stomped and looked at the trunks of every tree and the dirt and the shrubs and the flowers. When he finally quit looking, there was nothing new. Just a patch of dirt stained with blood and coyote prints and scratches and bugs scouring for the last remnants of the victim's body fluids.

"Jane," he said, shaking his head, "let's go home." He turned and hopped back across the creek to take one last look around and, just as his foot came down in the soft earth at the edge of the water, he found what he was looking for. A deep footprint right on the bank of the creek. He stopped and nearly fell as he struggled to change his stride mid-step. Turning to the print, he stooped down and gave it a good going over. Although it appeared to match those found next to the victim's body, it was the direction it led that Josh was interested in.

"Jane!" he called. "Get over here, and watch your step." Using practiced caution, Josh followed the line of the print. "See here, he's following the creek upstream. I think he was walking in the water to hide his tracks and lost his balance right here. Look how deep this print is, and sliding a bit."

"Looks like it's a couple days old, doesn't it?" Jane asked as she surveyed the woods.

Josh looked downstream. "Yes, and our murder scene is a couple days old too." He looked back up the draw and immediately knew what waited in that direction. "Let's go," he said as he hurried along the bank.

He and his deputy moved carefully along the creek, one on each bank, eyes vigilant for other clues. A cool breeze rustled through the pines and junipers. Water bubbled over a log. Soon, the sound of voices could be heard from upstream. As they drew closer, Josh recognized the open space from which the voices carried. "That's the vagrant camp Shaw found when he and Max first got up here on the fifteenth," he murmured as Jane jumped across to his side of the creek. "And if Sam Reynolds is telling the truth, James Hodges might be there. And if he is ..." The sheriff's voice trailed off.

Jane peered through the shrubbery and nudged Josh. "Quite a few in there, Sheriff."

"Shaw interviewed three of them the other day."

"Should we have another talk?"

"Oh, we will."

Josh stepped from behind cover and walked out into the clearing as Jane covered him. They walked slowly, eyes darting to and fro, until the first of the men they were watching spotted them and stood from his chair. The man had sandy-brown hair and a harsh, wrinkled complexion that indicated too many cigarettes and too much time in the sun.

"Howdy, officers," the man said. "What brings you up here this fine day?"

Josh looked at the crusty man. "Any of you been downstream recently?"

"How far downstream?" the man asked.

"Where the creek crosses the road," Josh said.

"You mean where that lady was found? No, not recently. We went to town a week ago, but haven't been out of camp since. Well, maybe to do our business, but not that far south. Got no reason to. Besides, we take the road here. Easier to travel."

Josh looked the man over, and then studied the camp and two other visible inhabitants.

"Your deputy asked a bunch of questions the other day," the man said as if he needed to remind them. "Sure is too bad about that nice lady. Still, if you're looking for whoever did that to her, you won't find him here. We aren't the best people you'll meet, but we aren't killers."

"Who said it was a he?" Jane asked as she studied a rusting trash barrel.

"Don't know one way or the other, ma'am. Seems unlikely a woman did that."

Josh watched as Jane peeked behind an old barrel and kicked at a pile of sticks.

"How old are your boots?" she asked.

The man lifted a foot and showed her. "Mine are the newest. Got them, let's see, ten years ago, I think. Not much tread left on the fool things, though. They've seen more miles than your car, I bet."

"All right." Josh then said to Jane, "let's just take a nice look around."

"Yes, sir." Jane did as told and turned her attention back to the barrel.

Several of the camp's inhabitants began to stir about as Josh and his deputy moved to and fro, their levels of excitement or aggression varying from one to another. Two men refused to budge, another quickly disappeared into his tent, and two others stood as if to run, but seemed to think better of it.

"Jane," Josh said, "if James Hodges is up here, I want you to have a quick look around his stuff. Remember, we don't have a warrant, so don't go peeking through his things unless it's in plain view. We get suspicious, I'll get one."

The deputy investigator acknowledged the order and went back to the barrel as Josh paced from tent to tent asking for James. At the third tent an old, thinning gray-haired man pointed the way to a juniper tree spreading its branches over a fading tarp. "Thank you," Josh offered as he turned for the tent, if one could call it that. "James," he spoke calmly. "You in there?" There was some rustling from inside the tent. "James, come on out here. It's Sheriff Matthews. I need to have a word with you."

More rustling and a shadowy figure appeared inside the tent's unzipped entrance. "What'd I do?"

"Don't know that you did anything, James." Josh stepped away from the entrance and motioned for deputy Shaw to come over. "Go ahead and come out anyway."

"Sheriff?" Jane interrupted.

Josh turned toward his investigator, but kept a steady eye on Hodges. "Yeah?"

She was digging around in the barrel with a look that told the sheriff it was important. "When you have a minute," she said with a tone of urgency in her voice.

Meanwhile, James Hodges crawled from his battered tent and stood up on unsteady feet. He was wobbly and appeared hung over from a hard night of drinking. His face was crusted with dirt and a beard more like a pad of steel wool than whiskers, and he stank of body odor and alcohol. He wore an old shirt and jeans that had never seen a seamstress and hadn't been washed in too many weeks. His bare feet, dirty and blistered, protruded from tattered pant cuffs.

"Sheriff, sir, what I can do for you?" James asked with a burp. He smiled as his buddies cheered.

"I see you're taking care of yourself," Josh said with sarcasm.

"Always. Had me a bath just three or four weeks ago." There was more laughter from the riffraff.

"All right, enough of that. Can you tell me where you were on the fourteenth around midnight?"

"Seriously?" James asked with a tone that denoted his distaste for all things regarding the law.

"Yes, seriously."

James wobbled and caught himself. "Do I look like a man that can tell you where I was any day of the week?"

Josh stood patiently.

"Okay, okay. Let me see. The fourteenth. Midnight. Um. No, I ain't got no idea, but I think I was right here. Probably. But I don't know."

Josh turned to the hooting campers and bellowed. "Any of you want to vouch for that?"

There was a moment of silence, then an older, scratchy voice answered. "He was here."

Sure he was, Josh thought to himself. Yet he knew the man's voice and turned to it. "What's your name, again? And can you prove that?"

"Dusty Stevens. The boys up here call me Dirt."

"Dirt?"

"Yes, sir. Dirt. You know—Dusty, Dirt."

"I get the reference," said Josh. "Dusty, you said James was with you, here in this camp, all night on the fourteenth?"

"Yeah."

"What about the morning of the fifteenth?"

"Yeah, man."

Josh sighed. "Don't go anywhere." He turned his attention to Jane and spoke in a lower tone. "What've you got?"

She returned his quiet manner. "Look right here on the rim of this barrel. See here?" And she pointed to a dark, reddish stain near the rim. "That's blood."

"Could've come from anyone, right?"

"Sure, even an animal. But you never know. Maybe one

of these guys got lonely, took a little walk down the trail, found a woman walking alone." Jane shrugged her shoulders and pinched her lips. "Then he came back here and tossed the evidence into this can."

"Sounds plausible," Josh said, knowing full well he had nothing else to go on.

"The trashcan is empty otherwise," Jane said as she stripped a soiled glove from her hand. "It's been cleaned out recently, and they burn in it from time to time."

"All right, listen, the judge isn't going to sign a warrant based on unsupported suspicion. Get a sample and let's go." He turned back to the campers and took note of their faces. "Jane," he said in a hushed tone, "I want you to post a cruiser on 395 at Poison Creek and another up at Gravel Ridge just in case any of these boys decide to hightail it out of here."

"Okay, Sheriff," she said

"As of right now," Josh said, "the fingers are all pointing here. I want to type that blood, and then make a decision where to go from there. I'd rather have one warrant, one search, and one arrest. Let's keep it as simple as possible." Josh turned and looked toward James Hodges. "I have a feeling we won't be looking much further."

* * *

Gail Cruz pulled her car into a vacant spot at the end of Lottery Lane and shut off the engine. It had been too long since she'd taken the time to watch the sun set, and there was no better time than the present. She opened the trunk and took out a folding chair, a bottle of wine and a glass, set herself up with a good view, and pulled on a sweater.

With plenty of time to enjoy the sun's final warmth, she opened a fading copy of the *Burns Review* and scanned through an old article for the fifth time. She read and reread the details of a previous murder, yet could find no mention of any suspect being named or even considered. Sheriff Matthews was working on it, his men were doing their best, every avenue was being explored, and no stone was left unturned. Eryn Rogers's murderer would be found, and the people could count on it.

In another article written three weeks later, nothing had changed. The trail was still cold, there was no new evidence to speak of, nothing else to consider. Although a person of interest had been spoken to, there was nothing revealed that would bring justice to the woman's untimely death. No names, nothing to report.

Gail laid the old papers in her lap and drank some wine. She savored it, turned the fluid over with her tongue, and moaned softly as it drained down her throat. Another drink and she slowly repeated the process until the glass was empty. She set the glass down while deep in thought, thumbed through the paper again and again, then thrust it to the ground in frustration.

She took another paper from a stack and read all about the sheriff's lack of action. The article had been written almost five years earlier, and the author clearly did not care for him, painting him as a crusty, bitter man incapable of completing the task he'd been elected to perform. Where were the answers the community was seeking? Why had nothing been done to bring a killer to justice? Why should the community put its trust in a man whose promises were empty, if not void altogether?

The paper was dated October 1975, nearly two years prior to the murder of Eryn Rogers. Gail knew the reporter was talking about crimes committed even earlier, as the article alluded to the murders of three other women in the county. As these articles progressed through time, the ever-changing authors seemed miffed that Josh Matthews had been reelected, and the vitriol began anew when another heinous crime was committed on his watch. Harney County had been peaceful before the sheriff came along, the reporters said—almost as if penned by the same author under different names—and now it was no longer. Was the sheriff even doing his job, they asked?

A shrieking whistle sounded at the mill, and Gail looked in that direction with approval. She had no idea what the whistle meant, but it was a beautiful sound to her ears. The shrill echo crossed the flats and broke the silence for a brief moment, just long enough to remind her that industry wasn't far away. Burns was a sleepy, quiet town, but it was alive and breathing.

She sniffed deeply at the pungent air full of bark and sawdust and wood smoke and waste and weeds. It was beautiful.

She poured another glass and swirled the red liquid in the sun's orange rays. She drank longingly and wondered about the past. Far away the mill belched smoke and steam and reminded her that life still hummed along. For a moment, as the sun continued its eternal vigilance, the pangs of loneliness began to rear up within her. She was happy to be away from the circumstances back in Newark, but six months on and she had still not made any friends in her new home. Sitting there watching the sunset, she longed for someone to share it with, someone to talk to and spill out the details of her day.

Gail refilled her glass and wiped a lonely tear from her cheek.

* * *

Josh Matthews pulled the old Chevy into the parking lot and squeaked to a halt. Jane got out and said her goodbyes, and Josh made the long drive home to sulk on the back porch. With his favorite whiskey in hand, he lit a Dominican and studied the rubicund skies. There was a fire burning somewhere north of Riley, and the smoke drifted toward Burns, bringing with it an expanse of red-orange radiance.

On an evening just like this in 1947, Josh had shared a final sunset with a young wife he loved dearly. Alyson was the only woman he'd ever been with. They'd met in 1942 and married just before he shipped out to fight the Germans in Africa. He'd been in Sicily with Patton's 7th Army when a healthy baby girl, Meredith, was born in a fashion typical of the time, where Mom was home alone and Dad was a million miles away fighting for the cause. Alyson waited patiently for him through the lonely nights while her knight fought for the liberation of Sicily and France.

Josh eventually realized that he and Alyson had not had much time to grow together. He loved her, but it was youthful love. Their relationship had progressed too rapidly, they were married too quickly, and then they were separated by years of war. While overseas he dreamed of being with her every night, and could barely stand the loneliness. However, he wondered if his physical needs, rather than the more powerful force of genuine love, had driven his desire for her. It never quite felt complete, and he had hoped to build a stronger foundation.

When he finally came home in 1945, she was waiting with open arms. Then, two years later tragedy had struck their young love while enjoying the honeymoon they had not yet taken until then. It had been Alyson's idea to go for a hike, and Josh was eager to follow her lovely, feminine form wherever she went. She was wearing a loose-fitting sundress speckled with flowers, and her hair was done in curls. He remembered her soft, white skin and the loving touch of her hand sliding across his . . . turning to a panicked clawing as she slipped over an embankment and fell twenty feet onto a rotting log. One old branch had thrust through her abdomen and it had taken every ounce of his strength to pry her loose and carry her limp body to the car. Josh forsook their belongings and for forty miles pressed his hand to Alyson's wound. His efforts were for naught. His patient, beautiful wife died in his arms three miles from town while their only child cried in the back seat.

His discharge papers came two months later. Josh had transitioned from the army to civilian life by taking a job with the Burns Police Department. In November 1952 he ran for sheriff and won by just four votes. He'd taken to his new job with absolute commitment and found a way to juggle his time with his daughter and put money away for her future. Meredith grew up with him and around him and learned more about the legal system than her daddy did. She studied and read and committed herself to a law degree, then changed her mind at the last minute and went to nursing school instead. She wanted to help people who were sick in the body, not in the mind.

Then, in 1965, the discovery of a woman's dead body began a series of unsolved murders. He poured life and limb into the investigations and left no stone unturned, no shrub unsearched. Yet each time he had failed the community as surely as he felt he had failed his wife.

Josh finished the bourbon in his glass and took a long pull on the cigar. Alyson had once chastised him for working too much, for drinking too much, and for smoking too much. To appease her he quit smoking cigarettes and took up cigars, and he tried to limit his drinking to a single glass of whiskey a night. The bad habits were hard to break, but he loved her and wanted her to be happy, so he'd tried, although there was little he could do about working too much. His wife seemed satisfied with the gesture and ceased her nagging.

Finally giving up, Josh went to bed just as lonely as he had done for the last thirty-three years. With the windows open and a soft, spring breeze flooding the room, he drifted away thinking of his empty life.

* * *

Gail Cruz placed the phone on the hook and went to the window. It was a beautiful morning. The birds were chirping, a squirrel danced on a clothesline, little clouds puffed their way across the sky. She opened the window and smelled the sawdust and felt reassured that the mill was still there. There was talk of a closure, there had been strikes, and there was uncertainty about the future of both Burns and Pine, Oregon. Too many people relied on the mill, and yet the mill was struggling. The sawdust and the whistle meant things were humming along, if only for the moment. The phone rang and she took the call.

"So," she said to the couch as she replaced the phone receiver on its hook, "the sheriff wants to have coffee." She wondered why? What was he up to? Did he intend to fill her in on the murder? Ask her to look at the evidence? Invite her out? What should she wear? Heels or flats? *Does this pink thing go with that black thing? No!*

Shower, coffee, toast, and she was out the door. She waved to a neighbor, smiled at the mailman, petted a wandering dog, and removed an errant beer can to the trash. There was a skip in her step, and she felt flush in her cheeks as she pranced down the sidewalk to her car. She wiped off a bit of dust and cursed the birds, then wheeled away like she was on a Sunday drive.

The office was still too cold and the lights were still too dim, but she admired it approvingly and placed the stack of old newspapers on her desk before pouring another coffee. She added two spoons of sugar and a touch of milk and went back to whacking at the typewriter for a few minutes to polish off her editorial on the last week's car accident, shuffled a few stories needing attention, and made a phone call.

Routine. If it weren't for her coffee date, she would think it was just another day of unbroken ritual.

She read the Rogers article again, and again she came away empty. A good night's sleep and the blanks were still blank. Nothing.

Gail turned her attention to the story at hand and wondered who the victim was. Was she pretty? Did she have a family? What had she been wearing? Why had she been out in the boondocks? How did she die? Who would want to kill her?

What was her favorite color?

The woman, whoever she was, certainly had some humanity. Regardless of her past, there was a human being in there somewhere, and Gail wanted to find her. That woman had had ambitions, goals, love in her heart, a favorite place to eat, perhaps children. Gail would write the typical article relaying the facts, but there would also be a column about the person, and she wanted answers to these things before she could delve into that part of the story. No death was meaningless.

She checked her watch and decided there was time to walk over to the diner rather than drive. On such a beautiful morning she couldn't find a reason not to get out and enjoy it. The air was fresh and real. It smelled of natural things with just a hint of humanity.

She stepped outside and started walking.

*   *   *

Josh Matthews focused his attention on the world outside the diner window and silently wondered if it was time to hang up the hat. He hadn't felt so tired since the days of war when he slept for only an hour or two a night. At that time his body had been in excellent physical condition, and he'd felt like he could conquer the world all by himself. Those days were gone now, and his muscles were tired, his eyes were tired, and his mind was tired.

He took a drink of his coffee as the front door opened and his guest joined him.

"Good morning, Sheriff," Gail Cruz said with a beaming smile.

"Morning, ma'am," Josh said as he stood from the booth and motioned to the opposite seat. "Fine day, isn't it?"

"Beautiful. I cannot get over the way the sun comes up over those mountains. And with the smoke in the air, mmm, I just love it. A sunrise through that is just amazing." Gail smiled and closed her eyes.

"Did you know that one day a year you can drive the straight toward town and the sun will be rising behind you and the full moon setting right in front?"

"Oh, really? I'll have to look for that."

Josh smiled and studied the creases at the corners of her

mouth and then, when she opened her eyes and caught him staring, turned his attention to the sugar dispenser. "In the fall," he said. "Late September or early October."

"I'll remember that," she said as she stirred a freshly arrived cup. "So, you wanted to talk to me?"

"Yes, but I haven't got a lot of time right now. I figure this will work best if I only have one reporter to deal with." Josh adjusted himself in the seat and took a serious tone with her. "To be honest, I don't much like the press, and I'd rather not have to deal with a mob. I just haven't got time to answer the same questions over and over."

Gail's face lit up and a twinkle sparked in her eyes. "I can handle that. I did some time with a big-city newspaper, so I know the drill."

"Okay. I've got half an hour. What do you want to know?"

The look of surprise on her face told Josh she wasn't prepared for this. "Uh, well, I kind of thought you were going to tell me to stay out of the way. So I, uh, okay. Maybe we should start with the victim's name?"

"Lisa Martin. Know her?"

Gail shook her head. "No. Was she married?"

"Yes, with one child, a little boy."

Gail turned and rested her hand in her palm. Josh noted the sadness in her eyes. "How did she die?" she asked.

The sheriff looked at her sympathetically and then out the window. "Well, there just isn't any easy way to say it." He held the hot cup of coffee in both hands and cleared his throat. He wished there were a manner in speaking to a woman about such things that could break the news gently, but he had never discovered it. "She was decapitated."

The look that appeared on Gail's face told him why he'd had that thought.

"What?" she demanded.

"Well, almost decapitated. Her throat was cut very deeply. There just isn't any way to soften it up. Her spine was the only thing attaching her head to her body."

"Should people be worried? I mean, this isn't the first murder you've had, right?"

"Listen, I don't want to get into that. Not yet. Right now we don't have any connection to any other crimes, okay?"

"Okay. But should people be worried?"

"Yes, they should. But this is Harney County. There are a lot of armed folks around here. They know how to take care of themselves."

Gail scoffed. "It sounds an awful lot like Lisa Martin didn't know how to take care of herself."

"Maybe not." Josh paused long enough for Connie to refill their coffee, smiled while she rambled on about the day's breakfast special, then politely excused her.

"Do you have any suspects?" Gail asked.

Damn, she's beautiful, Josh thought to himself. In the thirty-three years since Alyson's death he had been propositioned no less than ten times. There'd been several widows, a school teacher, a woman thrice divorced, Connie—which had caught him completely off guard—and one married woman looking for a little action on the side. Some had made their moves within three months of his loss, some politely waited for a year, Others, like Connie, were much more recent. None were successful. He believed he had moved too quickly with Alyson, and would never repeat that mistake.

So, why is this one different? he asked himself. *What makes her so special? Is it her eyes?* He stopped thinking about it when she caught him staring again.

"You all right, Sheriff?"

"Yes. Sorry," Josh said while clearing his throat. "No, we have no suspects to speak of. Not yet, although we're looking at some things, and we've ruled a few people out."

Josh noticed that Gail seemed to be scrambling to come up with questions, and her eyes kept drifting out the window. "I've been in town for six months," she finally said, "and written about rodeos and mustang roundups and hunting and fishing. Nothing seems to happen around here. Now this." She shook her head. "Have you established any possible motives?"

"I cannot go into that right now."

"Can I ask you about the accident the other day?"

"Talk about changing the subject," Josh said as he leaned back and pushed his coffee away. "Sure, I suppose that would be okay."

"People don't seem to want to talk to me about it," she said.

"That's because you're new in town. They don't trust you."

"Do you trust me?"

"I haven't decided yet."

Gail smiled lightly. "I don't bite, you know."

"I don't care. This place isn't big enough to hide. Even a little nibble can ruin your reputation around here."

Gail nodded that she understood the comment, and then got to it. "So, what I want to know is why do you think it happened?"

"Well," he said, "there's this spot up north where the kids go to party once in a while. They're pretty sneaky about it and they usually wait until Friday night. Sometimes we catch them and break it up, and sometimes we don't."

"So what went wrong?"

"They were up there on a weeknight. That never happens, and I didn't have anyone patrolling. I have no idea why they were up there. They got to drinking too much and they messed up." Josh paused as he tried to bury the emotion welling up inside him. "Two kids I've known since they were babies died, and another is going to jail."

"So," Gail asked as she looked intently into his eyes, "what happened?"

Josh looked out the window and clasped his hands near his mouth. "I can't give you too many details," he said. "There are minors involved. You already know the details of the accident, so I won't get into that. We can't be everywhere, and we can't always catch underage kids when they do something stupid. They and their parents have to own up to that."

"And you knew these kids?"

"Yes," Josh said, "all three of them. I've known the girl her entire life. Her granddaddy and I served together in the war. I came home and found this job; he came home and couldn't sleep. He really struggled with civilian life and had a hard time getting his head wrapped around girls and all the attention he got from them. I mean, he was a pretty good-looking fellow, and the women swooned all over him. He just couldn't handle the attention, so he re-upped and went back into what he knew best.

"When the Korean War ended, he came home and finally figured out how to put the brakes on and get himself settled down. When he contacted me about a job, I invited him out here and he stayed with me while he hunted for work. The mill was hiring at the time, so he went to work for Carter & Sons. Then he met his wife at a town social, and Melissa's daddy came along eleven months later. He grew up around the loggers and millworkers and learned to identify trees for the cutting and eventually wound up on Jacob Powell's crew. If you don't know Powell, he runs a pretty big logging outfit called Powell Forestry. Anyway, he met a girl and got married, and those two had a little girl they named Melissa. They were both working and needed help with babysitting, so my daughter, Meredith, volunteered to help them out. Melissa practically grew up in our home."

Josh teased at his coffee and sat back in the seat. "It couldn't have hit me any worse if she were my own. I was in the waiting room on the day that little girl was born, and her granddaddy and I shared a cigar. I remember kissing her mom on the forehead. She grew into quite the young lady, she did." Josh shook his head and trailed away for a long moment. "And the boys, they've never known another town. Their dad has been one of my biggest supporters."

Gail waited patiently as Josh took a breath and exhaled slowly. "Were any charges filed?" she asked.

"Yes. The girl has been charged with vehicular manslaughter and driving under the influence." There was a pause as Josh relived the nightmare. "That poor girl," he said, "she just kept screaming '*No, no, no!*'"

"Why do you think she was doing that?"

"Because I told her the twins were dead."

"They were twins?" Gail asked.

Josh studied the reporter's face and saw the sense of discovery in her eyes. "Yes, but you didn't hear that from me. And not a word about Melissa's name. You're not supposed to know that yet."

Gail reached across the table and rested her hand on his. His better senses told him to pull away, but he couldn't bring himself to do it.

"I'm sorry," she said before removing her hand, "and you don't have to worry about the name. I'd never set you up like that."

Josh continued on. "She's due in court today."

"And the kids that died?"

"I've known their pop for twenty years. I didn't have a relationship with those boys like I did with Melissa, but I knew them well enough."

Gail was reaching forward to console him again when the door sprung open and Max walked to the table and sat down.

"Hello, Max," Gail said.

"Ms. Cruz. Sheriff. How's everyone."

"Max," asked Josh, "something you need?"

"Oh, sorry. The ME wants to see you. I couldn't find you at the office, so I came over here."

Gail didn't seem surprised. "It seems this is a regular spot for you boys."

"Let me put it this way," Josh said. "If you want to get lost in this town, don't come to Sam's Diner. Ms. Cruz, I am very sorry, but it looks like I'm going to have to cut things short."

"Oh, not at all. I'll take care of the check."

"No, you won't. Max, make sure she doesn't touch that

check."

"Yes, sir."

"And I'll see you at the office." Josh tipped his hat. "Ms. Cruz, thanks for the talk. We'll do it again."

Outside, the day was overcast, but the air felt fresh and cool, with a smell of rain coming. The medical examiner's office was only a short walk from the diner, and Josh made it in good time. He found the hospital entrance and made his way to the examiner's office, checked in with the assistant, and took a seat to wait. There followed several minutes of silence, interrupted occasionally as nurses and doctors passed in and out of the cramped room. Finally, Josh was greeted by the familiar voice of Don Jackson.

"Howdy, Sheriff. How are ya?" he asked in a scratchy southern drawl.

Josh stood and took the man's hand. "Been a bad week, Don. What've you got for me?"

"Time of death," he said as he handed a piece of paper to Josh. "I put it between 11:00 and 1:00 a.m., so either very late on the fourteenth or very early on the fifteenth. I can't pin it down exactly."

"Seems to me that's about what you guessed up on the hill."

"As you know, I've been doing this a long time. Anyway, the cause of death is obvious. There is minor bruising under the chin, which suggests he took hold of her chin from behind to force her head back and slit her throat with a sawing motion. Looks like at least ten long back-and-forth strokes with a very sharp blade. There are knife marks on the C2 and C3 vertebrae, which is incredible when you think about it. The cut severed the esophagus, trachea, all the major blood vessels, all the way back to her spine, which is the only thing that kept her head on. She bled out in, oh, two minutes at most, but she was likely unconscious in a few seconds, so she didn't suffer much. The angle of the cut tells me her attacker is right handed because the first cut was pulled through in that direction. There is a substantial amount of blood in her lungs, which suggests her heart continued beating for some time after her throat was cut. Most of her blood was pumped out through the carotid arteries and the jugulars, and is either on the ground at the scene or collected in her lungs and stomach. Other than that bruising beneath her chin, there are absolutely no other marks on her body. There was no struggle, and she died fast."

Josh rubbed his chin. "Don, is there any indication this woman recently had sex?"

The ME shook his head. "No. We did a vaginal exam, and that came back negative."

"Is there anything else?" Josh pleaded.

"No."

Josh thrust his hands to his hips and turned from Don Jackson. "No hair? Skin under her nails? Anything at all?"

"Sorry, Sheriff. Squeaky clean."

Josh had but one final order of business. "I know Jane got you a blood sample. Any word on that yet?"

"Not yet. Hopefully in a day or two."

"Okay," Josh said as he turned to leave. "Thanks, Don. I'll look forward to your call."

"I understand Miss Reed is due in court today?"

Josh paused at the door and turned back to the ME. "Yes. Preliminary"

"I'm sure it will work out."

"I hope so, for her sake. Mike Gordon will have instructed her to plead innocent, and then after the jury finds her guilty Judge Parker will hammer her to the wall. Anyway, I'll be seeing you."

FOUR

G ail left the county court house and rushed to her office and dropped a sheet of paper into the typewriter. She knew precisely what she would be doing through the afternoon. She never would have guessed the weary teenager would make such a courageous decision, and now the entirety of her thinking was completely swept under the rug. She had to come up with a new story, and quickly.

"What's going on?" Sandi asked from the door.

Gail turned to her. "Melissa Reed pleaded guilty."

"She what?" The owner gasped as she covered her mouth.

"Yeah. Guess we didn't see that coming, did we?"

Sandi leaned against the filing cabinet and picked at her nails. "I suspected that girl would get off without so much as a slap on the wrist."

Gail didn't bite into the argument. "Pleading guilty is throwing yourself at the mercy of the court. That's a very brave thing to do."

"Yes, yes, I suppose it is," Sandi said as she let out a long breath that seemed to be a long time coming.

"Judge Parker gave her ten years."

Sandi's mouth hit the floor. "Ten years?" she asked incredulously.

"Parole in one year if she behaves herself."

Sandi shook her head, appeared disappointed, and left the room.

Gail struck out for the story she was digging for and began typing. "Local Teen Takes Responsibility" was the new headline. She paused and looked out the window to watch a pair of sparrows bickering on the sill, then went back to typing. "The court was stunned this week when, despite legal advice, a Burns teenager on trial for the tragic deaths of two friends took responsibility for the horrific accident on Highway 395. The teen, Melissa Reed, was expected to plead not guilty to manslaughter and impairment charges filed by the Harney County prosecutor. However, in a striking turn of events, the young woman pleaded guilty to all charges filed against her."

Gail inserted the confession and acceptance of responsibility near the end of the article and gave kudos to Judge Parker and more kudos to Sheriff Matthews for his impartial actions in making the arrest of a beloved family friend and then calling for a stiff penalty.

With that article finally finished, she turned her attention to the pile of old papers on the floor. A photograph beckoned to her from the top paper and she picked it up. "What are you telling us?" she asked. The article titled "Tattoo Artist Remembers Victim" told of the artist's personal friendship with one Gina Bergmann, a single mother who'd been the third in this string of murders. The woman's body, found along Narrows Princeton Road at the very southern tip of Malheur Lake, had been staked to the ground. Cause of death: a gaping axe wound to the head.

"Why were you left there?" Gail wanted to know.

Gina Bergmann had been forty-two, a brunette, widowed by the Vietnam War and struggling to make ends meet. She'd led a simple, solitary life with few friends, although she was known to frequent The Sawyer, just as the most recent victim, Lisa Martin, had done. But Gail was unable to sew together any connection between the two women or their normal acquaintances. Interviews with a number of regulars at the seedy bar had revealed that Gina Bergmann drank gin and tonic, liked to dance, and usually left with a man not known to her before that evening.

"How long did you know her?" she'd asked one of the regulars.

"Oh, not long," responded the scantily dressed woman. "She kind of kept to herself."

Another person, a man who said he had known Gina for just one night, said, "She was a real nice lady. I'd like to have known her more, but she never said another word to me. I must not have made a very good impression on her."

Gail gathered the Q and A and tried to make something out of it, but it revealed no motives and added nothing to the case file. She decided it was no wonder the sheriff had given up. According to a report she'd been able to scrounge from the lawman's secretary, Josh Matthews had once speculated that Gina Bergmann's loose ways turned up so many dead ends that the department had quietly slipped the case file into a dark drawer and closed it shut. She was a cold case from the beginning, and no sleuthing was going to change that.

* * *

The sun was just peeking over the tops of the pines when three squad cars and the old truck rumbled into the clearing where seven vagrants were making their summer home. Sheriff Matthews mowed down a young juniper and skidded to a stop not twenty feet from a fading tent as its occupant stumbled into the clearing. Josh was out of the truck and striding for another dilapidated tent in the far northern corner of the camp even before the other three cars had come to a rest.

"I need your attention please," he hollered. "This is the Harney County sheriff, and I have a warrant to search this site. Everyone come out, right now."

There was a long moment when no one did. Josh looked

around and scowled until Dusty Stevens, as if acting as the leader, crawled from beneath an old tarp and stood almost at attention. Soon, a second man appeared, then three more. James Hodges, appearing confused and inebriated, appeared from the confines of his tent and lay down on the ground with his head resting on an arm that was peppered with needle tracks.

Josh motioned to a place beneath the shade of a Juniper where Max Shafer and Deputy Shaw were gathering the camp's residents. "James, I need you to come over here and sit with these other men," the sheriff said in a voice that told everyone who was in charge.

James got to his knees and slow-crawled over to the spot and lay back down under the watchful eye of the deputies.

Josh showed his warrant, secured from Judge Parker barely an hour earlier. "James, we're going to have a look through your things."

"Why?" he asked.

"A woman was killed just down the road, and her blood was found on that waste barrel next to your tent."

James's eyes went wild with fear. "It wasn't me. Go ahead, though. I ain't got anything to hide."

"Okay. Well, I'm going to read you your rights just in case, all right?"

James nodded as he looked around at his buddies. "Like I said. I ain't done anything wrong."

Josh produced a card from his breast pocket and read the Miranda rights. "Jane," he then said, "come over here and let's have a look through this stuff. And watch yourself. I have no doubt we're going to find needles." He turned back to Hodges. "James," he asked, "is any of this stuff trash?"

"No, sir. It's all mine."

"All of it?"

"Yes."

Jane stepped over and handed Josh a pair of rubber gloves, then began rummaging through the pile of dirty clothes and food wrappers. There was an old wool blanket, a pair of rotting boots, three shirts filled with holes, a sock. Old liquor bottles and empty beer cans littered the area immediately around the tent. Several plastic bags were stacked behind and Jane went to work on them, dumping each into a neat pile in the sunlight.

"James," she asked, "is this your stuff behind the tent here?"

"Yeah. Why you doing this?"

Jane ignored the protest and instead picked a needle from the ground and held it up. "Seems to me that shooting heroin isn't exactly a legal activity."

"Hey, man," James said, "that ain't mine."

"You just said all this stuff was yours," Jane countered. "So is it or isn't it?"

"Yeah, but those needles ain't mine, man."

As James turned to Josh to plead his case, Josh noticed a bulge behind his back. At first he wondered if the vagrant would dare to carry a firearm, but then decided it didn't matter if he dared to or not. Even the possibility turned his stomach over upon itself and his thoughts went straight to the safety of his crew. "James," he asked with a stern, intimidating look, "you packing a weapon, son? Because if you are, you better let me know right now, or we're going to have ourselves a real problem."

James gave Josh a guilty look, stuttered, and then reached behind his back as if to fumble for something hidden in his shirt.

Josh's hand immediately dropped to his holster, but before he could pull the .45 free of the stiff leather, the sound of a firing hammer clicking stopped all parties in their tracks. Josh looked at James, who stood empty handed, and saw James looking back with the same intense, adrenaline-stoked fear. Neither moved a muscle as deputy Shaw inserted himself behind Hodges's back, his sidearm at the ready and dead to the vagrant's head.

"Don't move a muscle," Shaw said as steady as if he were ordering a burger.

Josh let the wind escape from his tense lungs and released

the death grip he held on his own weapon, still lodged securely in its holster. "What do you have back there?" he asked with deadly serious accusation.

"Just a knife, sir. Nothing but a knife. I weren't going to use it, I swear. You asked if I was packing, and I was going to get it out and show you. That's it."

Deputy Shaw reached forward and moved James's left arm up, placing it on his head, then repeated the process on the right. He then lifted the filthy shirt and turned Hodges so his back was to Josh."

Tucked neatly into his faded jeans, James Hodges carried a knife with a beautiful ivory handle and a blade polished to a mirror shine. Josh produced a handkerchief from his pocket and gently took the knife from James's waistline, careful to hold it by the rear bolster so as to preserve any prints. The blade slipped up out of the jeans, and from the stains present along the knife's spine Josh knew what he had found. "This yours?" he asked.

"Yeah, it's mine," said James. "I found that the other day."

Jane stepped over and gently took the knife from her boss. "Is that blood?"

"I believe so," Josh responded.

"Look here, in this detail," said the deputy investigator. Then she pointed to James's pants. "Looks like blood's been wiped on them. See the legs?"

"Sure enough," Josh said as he turned back to Hodges. "James?" he asked.

"Yeah."

"Where'd you get the knife? Seems a bit rich for you."

James searched the campground for answers and seemed to find them in the trash barrel Jane had rifled through at the last visit. "I found it in that trash right there. Got it out of there the other day."

"He's telling the truth," Dusty said, as if Josh had needed the input.

Josh wasn't convinced. "You mean to tell me you found

this knife in that trash? How'd it get there?"

"I don't know," James answered.

"I do," Dusty said as he stepped forward. "A man come through here the other night and threw it in there."

"And why didn't you mention any of that when we last spoke?"

"You never asked."

The response made Josh mad, but he contained himself because, well, he hadn't. "You didn't think we might like to know?"

Dusty stood dumfounded. "Hey, man, I saw what I saw."

"James," Jane interrupted. "The pants you're wearing—they're yours, right?"

"Yeah," James said with a scowl. "You think I stole them?"

Jane eyed the man before going back to digging through his things. Before long, she shot upright as if a snake had crawled out of a plastic bag. "Sheriff," she said.

"Yeah, Jane?" Josh stepped over to her. Before he gave her his full attention he motioned for Deputy Shaw to do what he didn't need to be told to do.

"I've got him," the deputy said with a smirk.

Josh smirked back, and then turned to his investigator.

"Found some women's clothes here," she said. "There's a lot of blood on them. Looks like they match the victim's last reported attire. Yellow skirt, green blouse."

"Great, Jane. Good job." Josh turned back to the campers. "Shaw," he said, "give me a hand, would ya?"

Deputy Shaw wasn't one to need a breakdown. He might have been the slowest and biggest deputy on the squad, but Josh trusted him to know what to do with little more than a look, and he did. The portly deputy pulled Hodges's hands down around his back, and then produced a pair of handcuffs with practiced efficiency.

"James Hodges," Josh said as the cuffs rattled in the thin mountain air, "you're under arrest for the murder of Lisa Martin."

Deputy Shaw locked the cuffs to James's shaking wrists with a sound like a fork grinding the serrated edge of a steak knife.

Dusty looked up from his agitated state to reassure his friend. "It's okay, Wiggles," he said. "You'll be all right, man. We got your back."

Not being one to let such a comment pass by the wayside, Josh made a mental note to include Dusty's comment in his report. "We got your back" seemed a bit too convenient to him, and he wondered if it wasn't intended as a promise to come to their friend's rescue, to say whatever needed to be said. Whether or not it actually was seemed immaterial.

After James Hodges was comfortably packed into the back of a squad car like an unsatisfied sardine, it took the crew a solid two hours to tidy up. The evidence was collected, bagged, and cataloged. There were a pair of old boots, a faded pair of men's Levi's, a woman's skirt and blouse, the knife, and the clothing James was wearing. Miscellaneous evidence included used needles, a small bag of marijuana, and several empty liquor bottles. Each was tucked neatly into a paper bag, and then marked with name, date, and location.

"Sheriff," Shaw asked, "you ever seen a man shake like that?"

Josh had also taken note of the way James's hands shook. "Pretty sure he's having withdrawals. From the needle marks, I'd say he's been shooting heroin for several years, and I won't be surprised if toxicology comes back positive."

"No, man," Dusty interrupted, "he's got Huntington's. He shakes and jerks like that. Gets worse when he's real nervous. Just go easy on him, okay?"

Josh accepted the man's opinion with a grain of salt. Dusty Stevens seemed to know James well, but Josh also had no trust for either of them.

The crew loaded their haul and left the vagrants to their camp, less one. Josh felt an overwhelming sense of accomplishment, and for the first time in fifteen years he felt as if he had gotten to the bottom of a terrible crime. It made him feel good, and he could barely contain his smile all the way down the hill and back into town.

As they approached Burns, he got on the radio and called forward to Max's car. "Max," Josh said, "let's take James over to the hospital real quick. I want to have him checked. That shaking business bugs me, and I don't want any mishaps without the docs signing off on him first." *Huntington's disease. Really?* Josh asked himself. He rested his chin on his chest. For a brief moment, he wondered how a disabled Hodges might have controlled his struggling victim while sawing through her flesh, but he had witnessed the young man efficiently gutting and skinning fish on more than one occasion, so he put the thought away. If he had the motor skills for the one thing, he could do the other. Besides, Dusty Stevens had indicated the symptoms came and went.

When Josh finally left the office he sat in the truck staring at the speedometer. He had no idea why that particular instrument caught his attention, but it did and he gave it the fullest. Dusty had mentioned someone came through camp and threw a perfectly good knife into their trash barrel. While Josh did not believe the statement, he knew he would have to look into it. The footprint they found near the crime scene had indeed led from there to the camp, but he could not bring himself to believe that the murderer would jeopardize being seen just to use their trash. The risks would be too great.

* * *

Gail wasn't anything if not inquisitive. It would be a very cold day in hell when she wouldn't want to have her nose inserted into the dark crevasses of a good case. The who, the what, the where, when, and why. All questions in need of answers. In many cases the answers were left dripping from the surroundings as plainly as the victim's blood. In others, not the least taste of evidence was left lying around, and the inquisitive were forced to rely on cunning and stealth to locate the forgotten tidbits.

She chose to start at the very beginning; by doing what the law had initially prevented her from doing, if only to pre-serve evidence. However, that evidence was now collected and Gail wanted to see the scene from close up.

The tree behind which the victim had been found was in full view of the road, and Gail found it the second time far easier than the first. Surprisingly, there was no pile of leaves, no shal-low grave. In fact, there appeared to have been absolutely no attempt to hide the body. Gail took a picture of the tree, took a bite of her banana, and then took another picture. She got sev-eral angles of the patch where the body was found, and several more looking back toward the road.

She noted that Harry Grey had seen the victim's head from a path just on the other side of the road. She went there, and sure enough the base of the tree was plainly visible. She went out to the middle of the road, and it was visible from there as well. She jotted the finding in her notepad and wondered what it meant. Not only would the victim have been visible from the path, but also from the road to anyone who happened to glance that direction. She walked further along the road where it turned to the south and could still see up the draw well enough. If the murderer was trying to hide the body, he hadn't thought it through very well.

"Was he trying to hide her?" Gail asked out loud.

She pulled a newspaper from her pocket. Gina Bergmann's body had been staked down like bait, the article said, right at the edge of the water. She had already decided Bergmann's body hadn't been staked down for the purpose of baiting. Ra-ther, it was staked down to prevent it from moving should the water rise with the spring snowmelt. Gail believed that Gina Bergmann's killer had wanted to make sure the body remained where he placed it. "But why?" she asked of the birds and the wind. And she immediately knew the answer to her own question. "So the body *would* be found!"

She took more pictures and walked up the draw back to the tree. *Why was Lisa Martin here?* she thought to herself. *No sign of a struggle means she knew her attacker. But was she brought here, or did she meet someone here?* Gail wondered if those questions had been asked and answered. She felt she wasn't thinking outside the box.

Of course she was brought here, she thought. *Her car was at the bottom of the hill.* Gail took some more photos. *She didn't walk for miles up a dirt road to meet someone when she could have driven to the same spot in a matter of minutes. And at midnight, with bears and coyotes and such.*

Gail suddenly looked over her shoulder and scanned the trees for wild vermin. A mild panic came over her as she realized for the first time that she was miles off the highway, by herself, surrounded by thick forest and maybe, possibly, almost certainly, hundreds of hungry critters. She swatted at a cloud of marauding insects and choked on the dying body of one such beast as it made a suicidal attack on the back of her throat. Gail quickly returned to her car and drove down the hill. She had been scouring for over an hour and nothing turned up. The scene was dead cold. It had been cold for the sheriff and his deputies, and it was cold for her.

Also, she had a late-afternoon interview with a teacher. And there were wild beasts. And she felt icky.

❊ ❊ ❊

Josh stepped through the door of Sam's Diner and slipped into the booth overlooking Broadway Avenue. He waved at a passerby and turned his attention to the most recent copy of the *Burns Review*. James Hodges's mug shot took center stage next to the headline "Murder Suspect Arrested" and over the subtitle "Is this the face of a killer?"

"Yes, it is," Josh muttered out loud as he accepted a cup

of coffee from Connie. He ordered breakfast and began reading, grumbling here, smiling there. Gail was a good writer and showed restraint in the details before she returned her reader's attention to the possibility that James was not the brutal man he was made out to be. "While there was ample evidence found in Mr. Hodges's possession," she wrote, "a confidential source had a very different account of how it came to be there." Her article contradicted the official story, and Josh knew straight away that she was referring to Dusty Stevens as her "source." Further along in the article, Gail noted that James's tenth-grade teacher painted him as a "sweet and caring young man" if not "a bit confused."

Josh smiled at this last. "Confused!" he muttered under his breath as if someone had just jabbed him in the ribs.

As he worked his way to the end of the article, he learned that Mike Gordon had been appointed public defender. Gordon wasn't exactly a successful attorney, but he was a good one. He had represented James no less than four times in the past, and gotten him off once—on a warrant technicality, a lesson Josh had learned the easy way, thanks to missteps made by the Burns Police Department.

Josh laid the paper out on the table and dug into his eggs.

He turned the page and read another article written by Gail, which detailed the outcome of Melissa Reed's hearing. He read it with admiration, as the facts were accurate and there was no bias presented. The young defendant was painted as being mature and responsible and terribly grieved at the outcome. Gordon's name was mentioned only in passing, which Josh thought humorous, while assistant DA Carl Franklin presented a number of comments on behalf of the state. "The defendant was smart," he was quoted as saying. "An admirable young woman who has saved the people of Oregon a great deal of time and resources."

Josh liked Gail's simple explanation. The article was concise and left him feeling good about the result of the sentencing —far better than he had before he sat in the crackly vinyl seat he now occupied. There was substance to her writing, but nothing overblown or dramatic. She stated the facts and left her opinions to the op-ed section, where in past issues she'd let loose on a number of topics, including the beauty of central Oregon's majestic sunsets, the pungent odor of men producing valuable lumber products, wild horses gathered and sold at auction, and the dysfunctional nature of the hospital's waiting room. This week she'd nattered on about rain and alfalfa and the high school's lack of funding, draped colorful comments upon the backs of the working stiffs, hollered aloud about the county's shortage of deputies, and then turned her attention to politics.

The *Burns Review* contained twenty-seven articles on that fine day, and Gail was responsible for five of them. Josh wondered where she had time to eat and sleep, and then smiled at a recent memory of her stumbling over the foot-high curb across the street from the diner. Her heel had caught as she lifted a dainty foot, her slightly-too-tight skirt had rebelled, and she couldn't quite get the elevation she needed to scale the cliff that was Burns' solution to a poorly constructed section of downtown's main thoroughfare. She'd caught herself and generated a laugh-worthy moment for the man she had no idea was secretly watching her.

Josh mused over that memory for a moment, wondered what it meant, and then returned to his eggs. He chewed vigorously, swallowed some orange juice, and then reflected on the thought that Gail Cruz had very nice legs.

FIVE

G ail sat on the couch and stared at a large whiteboard. Taped there were articles covering the five murders, photographs of the victims collected by the paper over the years, details of each crime as relayed by reports from the paper, as well as what little information she'd been able to obtain from the sheriff's department and citizens with any memory of those events.

Scattered amongst the publicly known details were locations, dates, family interviews, loved ones longing for closure, and dead ends. Fingers pointed randomly at the growing homeless population traveling through the area between Eugene and Boise, lonely loggers looking for company, and drifter-cowboys under the influence of too much alcohol.

Of further note was the lack of physical connection between the victims or the evidence. None of them knew each other, although all were living in the county at the time of their murders. The cause of death was different from victim to victim, the bodies were left in different locations under different circumstances, no fingerprints were found, footprints in the area were unreliable, car tracks were driven over, eyewitnesses were nonexistent, and there were no consistent markers.

Gail had spent much of the day speaking with people the paper had interviewed in the past. Many still lived in the area, although a few had moved on and become unavailable. An old woman remembered Annette Walker, a young man remembered Eryn Rogers. News came to her that there were two old duffers who used to fish at the southern tip of Malheur Lake who had discovered the body of Gina Bergmann. They found her in the shallows of their fishing hole and commented how unfortunate it was that the attention given her murder had negatively affected their floundering bait business. Gail would get ahold of them somehow and ask the questions that may not have been asked.

After Gail returned to the office she carefully placed her camera and notepad on her desk and dropped into her chair. The office lights flickered and rain tapped lightly at the window as she turned to her typewriter and pored over the details.

"Three weeks after the body of Lisa Martin was found in the woods near Marshall Creek," she began, "a single suspect, James Hodges, has been arrested and charged with murder in the first degree. The Harney County Sheriff's Office released their report detailing the progress of the ongoing investigation. Many details are still under wraps, although we have learned that a murder weapon and the victim's clothing were found in Mr. Hodges's possession."

Gail leaned back and turned her gaze to the window. She had spent the last few nights nearly sleepless worrying over the murder, and the anxiety was getting to her. Something amongst the evidence told her it was all a little too neat, as if it had been packaged up, gift wrapped, and presented to the Sheriff's Department like a brand-new birthday bicycle. The proximity of the suspect to the victim and the evidence found on him were just a bit too convenient for Gail's intuition to accept.

The rain increased with a steady pitter-patter, sounding its drone against the window as Gail gathered her jacket and made for the door. With her hair matted down and her face dripping with precipitation, she made her way to a cup of coffee and then returned to the office to continue her article. "Assistant District Attorney Carl Franklin is convinced that evidence collected by the state will be sufficient to convict James Hodges and, at the very least, send him to prison for the remainder of his life.

"The *Burns Review* has made several attempts to speak with defense attorney Mike Gordon, but he has thus far refused to comment on his strategy, nor has he agreed to speak publicly regarding his client other than to say that James Hodges is innocent of Lisa Martin's death."

Gail paused and sighed, cracked her knuckles, sipped her coffee, and rested her feet on the desk. She waved off a fly, thought deeply, and then returned to the typewriter. "The trial is expected to begin within a week, and a twelve-member jury will decide the question. Of note, the defense has already filed an official protest of the rapid advancement of this case, stating that not enough time has been given to prepare an adequate defense."

Gail spun the article from the typewriter and laid it on her desk. She would read and edit it later, after she had time to let her mind rest. She needed a break. There was too much going on these past few days, and she had barely been able to think, let alone rest adequately.

❋ ❋ ❋

A telephone call from the district attorney's office brought Josh out of his chair. He had been waiting impatiently for the call, although he knew he had no right to expect such a quick decision. In times past, The DA's office had been slow to move on anything larger than an inappropriate hiccup. Yet, the case against James Hodges had matured so rapidly that even Josh was surprised.

"The evidence is sound," said Carl Franklin, "and I'm confident we can go straight to trial."

Josh gathered the pertinent paperwork and left his office, walked the short distance to the prosecutor's office, and found the assistant district attorney waiting for him. "Afternoon,

Carl," he said as he took a seat across from the grim-faced man.

"Howdy, Sheriff," came the response in a cool western drawl. "That was quick."

"Let's just say I've got a fire under my seat," Josh said.

Franklin produced a tall stack of papers and dropped them on his desk, then reached for a coffee cup that Josh knew was spiked. The assistant DA was average in height and build, balding across the back of his scalp, pale as a ghost and as dark-haired as any man could be. He had a thick beard surrounding red cheeks and a pointy nose, wore glasses too large for his face, and spoke with a mellow, cool confidence that had wooed several women Josh believed were out of his league. "I want to be absolutely certain," he said, "that we've got all the loose ends tied up."

Josh kicked his feet out and rested his head back against his folded hands. He had it in his mind that there might actually be some loose ends, but he didn't believe they were necessary to move the case forward. "We still haven't sorted out what Lisa Martin was doing up there. We *do* know she liked to go for long walks, and her husband says she would stay out for hours, but why she would do so way up there makes no sense. Near as we can tell," Josh said as he pointed to a map, "she parked here and rode with the assailant the last few miles. Her tracks break away from the path right about here and lead to a tree beside the creek, where the suspect attacked her. Anyway," Josh said "we had a conversation with Kipp Martin and he let on that his wife was pretty busy on the side. Apparently she's been seeing several men."

"Just playing, or was she working?"

"I don't think she was 'working' in that sense. We spoke with several regulars at The Sawyer and none of them indicated she was. It seems like she was just in it for the fun."

"Maybe she was lonely?"

"I don't know about that. Kipp Martin doesn't seem like the kind of man that would ignore his wife like that. I do know they didn't have a lot; I can witness to that. But why she did what she did only she knows."

"You talked to these men she was seeing?"

"There are only two that we know of for sure. One is Robert Carter out at the mill. She worked part time in the office as his 'assistant.'" Josh used his fingers to sign quotation marks. He had spoken with enough people in the office and gathered enough personal opinions that he felt it was safe to conclude that Lisa Martin did not have the skillset to work as anybody's assistant, let alone the owner of the most important industry in the town.

"Mrs. Carter's going to be plenty upset to hear that," Franklin said as he shook his head and made some notes. "Good church lady like her won't sit still for that kind of activity. Any connection between her and the victim?"

"No. She didn't have much to offer us other than cold looks. Robert Carter denies any involvement, of course, but there are witnesses who will swear they've been caught kissing in his office. However, I don't think Gordon will be able to show the jury anything more than a fling. Carter certainly isn't a murderer."

"Either way, Gordon is sure to put him on the stand."

"Oh, I'm quite certain of that." Josh shook his head. "As much as it pains me to see it happen, I understand the process."

"Reasonable doubt," said Franklin. "Gordon will try to show there are people who might have wanted Lisa out of the way."

"Of course he will. But if he thinks old Carter was able to get himself up there and cut a woman's head off, he's going to be sorely disappointed."

"He doesn't have to prove it, Sheriff. You know that. If he can get the jury confused, it won't matter. As far as I know, Gordon will try to show that Carter hired a hit man."

"The jury should see through that," Josh said in disgust. "Max hunted that angle and there's nothing evident."

"I believe you on that. I've dealt with Carter on a number of occasions and cannot, in this life or another, see him involved in anything of the sort." The assistant DA shuffled papers and continued scanning his own notes. "And what did you think of this Sam Reynolds fellow?"

"We learned from Kipp Martin that he works at the Square Nines. He's a cowhand, drifter, you know the type. Jane tells me he's pretty rough around the edges but nice to look at, and he spends his money right. Most Friday nights he's over at The Sawyer. He tips well and buys the ladies lots of drinks. According to Nick, anyway."

"Chief Anderson?" Franklin interrupted.

"Yes. Reynolds has been in the city tank twice for fighting, including a big one with James Hodges, which is what got all this started. Turns out James had a thing for Lisa Martin and was hitting on her at the bar. Reynolds didn't like something he said and they got in a scuffle. They both spent the night in jail, then Nick let them go home."

"No charges?"

Josh shook his head. "No. They took it out into the parking lot and knocked each other around good. No damage to property, so Anderson let them sober up and kicked them out."

"He's a better man than I."

"Yeah, well for what it's worth, Reynolds has a very strong alibi. Along with him, we spoke to three witnesses from the bar that all swore Lisa had some harsh words to say to James. He was good and mad when the police got there and had to be restrained. According to their report he was really cussing her out."

"So, the motive is he wanted to get even with her for shooting him down in public like that?"

"That's what it looks like."

"Pretty open and shut, if you ask me."

"Sure looks that way."

"You got anything that ties him to Eryn Rogers?"

Josh rubbed his chin. "Just his location at the time, which hasn't ever been enough. I went back through the case file and tried to build something more concrete than we had, but there is absolutely nothing I can use to connect Hodges to Eryn Rogers other than his proximity, and you know as well as I that we cannot build a case on that alone."

"Okay, Sheriff," Franklin said, "great job on this. We have enough to proceed, and I'm confident we'll get a conviction. I don't know how a jury can look at all this and not see that James is guilty. Once we get a conviction we can dig deeper into the Rogers case. Let me know if you stumble onto anything."

"Will do. So, then, we're ready?"

"Yes. I still have to interview a few more people, but I don't foresee any problems."

"And Robert Carter?" Josh asked.

"The man is far too old and creaky, Sheriff. I have no doubt it will come to nothing."

"Well, I'll leave that to you, then."

Carl Franklin leaned forward and rested his elbows on the edge of the mahogany desk. "Josh," he said, dropping his usual formal salutation, "there's one more thing."

"What?" Josh asked with an air of concern.

"Try to keep it together on this, okay?"

Josh narrowed his eyes. "What?"

Franklin sighed long and hard before revealing the news. "Gordon turned over his preliminary witness list this a.m., and Melissa Reed is on it."

Josh knew the look on his face must have caused the ADA a great deal of concern.

"Take it easy, Josh," Franklin said as he held his hands up. "It gets better."

"How so?"

"Connie is on the list too."

Josh muttered something under his breath that even he did not understand, placed his hands at his sides, rummaged through his memories of the two women, and wondered why on this green Earth either would be showing up on the defense's witness list. "See you later," he said as he stood to leave. "I've got work to do."

As he walked down the hall he was surprised to find Gail Cruz seated in the lobby.

"Sheriff," she called as Josh exited the hallway. "Do you have a few minutes?"

He looked at his watch. "I suppose I do. What are you doing here?"

Gail stood and greeted him with a handshake. "I just finished an interview and heard your voice, so I thought I would wait for you."

Josh was flattered but hoped it didn't show. "Very kind of you. Coffee?"

"Of course. Let's walk, shall we. It's beautiful outside."

"If you say so," Josh said as he popped an umbrella open. The sky was a light gray—the color of crumpled, dirty bed sheets—and drizzle pelted the ground and danced in a thousand puddles. It was cool, going on cold, and a light breeze blew from the west. Where Gail wasn't at all concerned and plodded ahead with a smile, Josh was more prepared and shielded himself from the rain. "I'm beginning to wonder about you," he said with a grin. "You know, you have some funny timing. I was just heading for Sam's. I needed to get out of the office."

"Too much paperwork?" Gail asked.

Josh nodded his head. "We're buttoning things up. Carl wants to go to trial as soon as possible."

Gail looked down as rainwater dripped from her hair.

"Get in here out of the rain," Josh said as he held the umbrella out for her and took the rain on his shoulder.

"Thank you."

"You call this beautiful?"

"There's too much ugly in the world to get lost in gray skies. I try to see the beauty in things. The clouds shelter us from the heat of the sun, the rain brings life to the crops, and because of that I can smell alfalfa on the wind. There's really not much here, but I love it. It's so clean and peaceful."

"We are talking about Burns, right?"

She laughed. "I'm a Jersey girl. Any place west of Newark is clean and peaceful."

"We just watched a seventeen-year-old girl go to prison and we're in the midst of a murder investigation. You call that peaceful?"

"You know," she said as she forced Josh aside to skirt a puddle, "where I come from it's not at all uncommon for a seventeen-year-old girl to be sentenced for a lot of reasons, or for a murder to happen right down the street. So, yes, this is peaceful."

Josh held the door to the diner and led Gail to the usual booth.

"Coffee, hon?" Connie asked as she approached the table in fly-by fashion.

"Yes, please," Gail answered. "It's Connie, right?"

"You guessed it. Good thing I'm wearing this here name tag."

"Oh, Connie," Josh barked, "will you mind yourself for once."

"Can't do it, Sheriff. The men like me feisty. Don't want to go and ruin my reputation, now do I?" She winked and bumped him with her hip.

As the waitress walked away in a hurry, Gail leaned forward. "What's her problem, anyway?" she asked with a teasing smile, clearly less offended than amused.

"She's just mean. You'll get used to her. Besides, she's mad that I won't go out with her."

"Are you serious?"

"Yes. Last year she sort of... well, don't ask." Josh winked and leaned on the table.

"Okay. Uh, you do know that you can get coffee where people aren't mean."

"Been coming here twenty-eight years, Gail. Seen a lot worse than Connie go through the place. Besides, she's a pretty good lady. It's mostly an act. The loggers like it."

Gail shrugged. "It's your time."

"So, what can I help you with on this beautiful day?" he

asked sarcastically as he looked outside.

"Well, I was curious if you were surprised the other day. It sounded like Melissa Reed kept everyone in the dark about her plea."

"Caught me off guard. Caught her family off guard. Gail, that girl even caught her attorney off guard, and that's hard to do with Mike Gordon. The man's a fink. Good attorney, but he's still a fink."

Gail laughed. "Do you think she'll be okay?"

"No, I do not. That girl's been pampered all her life. Never gone without anything, so far as I know. Got her pick of the boys, cheerleader, homecoming queen, straight As, dad is a foreman on Jacob Powell's big crew working up north and has been for some time. Family is doing well."

"I heard she was offered a scholarship at U of O?"

"Oregon offered her an academic scholarship. Hard to get." He sipped his coffee. "No, she isn't going to be okay. The pen over in Salem isn't the worst in the country, but it's still prison. Some of the women over there are just horrible people. I know; I've put some of them in there. I can say one thing, though: she got off light. Parker is fair, but he could've nailed her ass to the wall. Pardon my French."

Gail laughed and pointed to herself. "Uh, Jersey girl, and my daddy was a Marine. There isn't a four-letter word in the dictionary I haven't heard."

"Marines, huh? When and where?"

"World War II, the Pacific. First Marines. Guadalcanal, Iwo Jima, Okinawa. You know, all those places."

"I know the places, but I was on the other side of the war from there."

"You served then?" she asked.

"Fought under General Patton in Africa, Sicily and France."

"Oh, wow. I bet that was—what's the word I'm looking for?"

"'Terrifying'?"

"Umm, I was going to say 'adventurous.'"

"Oh, it was an adventure, all right," Josh said as his mind drifted away for a moment. "One I'd rather not repeat."

"Of course. Sorry. Anyway, back to Melissa Reed."

Josh recovered and got his head around the current reality. "Melissa is a good kid. But good kids sometimes make bad decisions, and she made a whopper. Now she has to pay for it. I'm not happy about that, but the law is the law, and in my county the law stands."

"Her parents seemed quite unhappy with you."

"They'll get over it in time. I'm more worried about her granddaddy, but he seems to be okay. He comes from the old school and knows she did wrong. For now, her parents need someone to blame, and no one ever wants to blame their kids for something like this. They want their kid to get a little slap, some tough words, and a bad look or two. What they don't want is to see their legacy shipped off to prison. But she has to pay."

"I thought it was very touching of her to apologize to the Johansens."

Josh nodded. "It was. I've known Melissa long enough to say she meant every word of it. She's repentant. Those boys were her best friends. She knows she did them wrong, and their parents wrong. Now she has to live with it."

Gail lightly touched his hand. "And how are you doing with all this?"

Josh leaned forward and stared into her eyes. "I'll live. By the way, are we going to order lunch or what?"

"I thought we were just getting coffee?"

Josh laughed and opened his menu. "I'm so hungry I could eat a coyote," he boomed with gusto.

"Came to the right place," came Connie's retort from across the dining room.

Gail smiled and opened her own menu. "I guess I could go for something to eat."

"Good," Josh said with a smile. "Have whatever you want."

"I feel like something greasy," she said with a half-joking tone.

"Don't know there's anything on the menu that isn't greasy. Hell, even the salad is greasy. But the burgers are always good."

"I'll take your word for it. Nothing like a big, greasy burger."

Again Josh laughed at her.

"What, can't a girl enjoy a burger?" Gail asked.

"You go right ahead. I'm just having a salad."

She looked at him quizzically. "You serious?"

"Trying to watch my girlish figure," he said with a wink.

"You're making fun of me."

"Not at all."

Connie returned to the table, took their order, then disappeared. Gail turned her attention to the weather, spoke about how much she enjoyed it, and raved more until their food came. They ate, mostly in silence, with her occasionally interrupting to get some new detail from him.

"Have you ever considered completely revisiting every murder scene?"

"Done that a hundred times," Josh said.

"With just your own eyes, or with someone else along?"

"My own. Naturally there were other investigators on scene, most of whom predate my current staff. I know a couple of OSP folks who've been back, but nothing ever comes of it." Josh sighed and called for Connie and the check. He noted that Gail seemed skeptical, but to her credit she said nothing as she gathered her belongings.

The walk back to the courthouse was swift and quiet. Ugly clouds continued to hold the blue sky hostage and the rain fell harder. Gail walked under the umbrella while Josh relied only on his hat. He saw her glance up at him.

"Something on your mind?" Josh asked.

Gail stopped walking and Josh turned to her. "It's just that," she said with trembling lips, "well, I've been going through the *Review*'s old articles, and I found something that makes me a little jumpy."

"Oh?"

"All the murder victims are women, brunettes between twenty-five and fifty-five. I've seen the pictures, and they could almost be related."

"You've been doing your homework."

"Yeah, and, so, well I'm five-five, fifty-five, a hundred and thirty, and I'm a brunette. I'm a little worried, okay?"

"It's not like a woman to tell those things to a man she doesn't know."

"Well, don't go spreading any of that around."

"No, ma'am. I've no intent to do anything of the sort. Gail," he said with a gentle tone, "it is my duty to see to it that every citizen in this county is safe. I spend my time, both on and off the job, doing just that. Twenty-eight years I've been sheriff of this County. I wouldn't be here that long if I weren't doing my job. Now, I understand your concern. I only hope you'll see that we aren't going to stop until this matter is finished."

"I guess I'll take your word for it," she said as they arrived at her car. "I hope to see you around, Sheriff."

Josh tipped his hat. "You will. Sunday."

"Sunday?"

"My place. A few of the deputies and their families are coming out for dinner. If you're hungry, come on out. You do eat meat, right?"

"Oh, ha, ha. I think I just ate half a cow."

"Good. Come out if you want to."

"How do I get there?"

"Easy. Follow the noise," said Josh as he smiled and walked away.

That same afternoon, Josh returned to the diner, but with a different purpose than was his norm. Having learned that Connie was on the defense's witness list, he wanted to know why. When he asked her to sit with him, she at first resisted, noting that her customers needed her attention.

"Please? It's important." Josh said.

She looked at him, puzzled. Then, as though a light had gone off, her demeanor changed, her eyes widened as a flirtatious smile broke across her face, and he realized she thought he was going to ask her out.

"No, it's not that," Josh said as she leaned on the table and gave him her best sexy eyes. "But I need you to sit with me, and not because I want coffee." He was firm with her, and didn't like it. The diner was his home away from home, and he hated to drag the waitress into anything business related. Still, he needed answers, so he waited patiently as Connie made her rounds. When she seemed satisfied that all was well in the little world that was her domain, she brought two cups of coffee to the booth and sat opposite him.

Josh had been in the valley long enough to know that Connie Newcastle, like so many of Burns' residents, had never left the sleepy, eastern Oregon town. She'd graduated from Burns High School, worked in various restaurants, dreamed of leaving, but never did. What Josh did not know until this day was that there had been a relationship between her and the victim, and it wasn't a pleasant one. Connie relayed the details, and the revelation caught Josh by surprise.

"Connie, I swear, girl," he said with disappointment hanging in his voice.

"I'm sorry, Sheriff. I had no idea it would ever be important."

The middle-aged blonde was nearly in tears and Josh felt sorry for her. She was in a very difficult spot.

"Why didn't you tell me this?" Josh asked. "You know we've been discussing this here, right?"

"How was I supposed to know it would mean anything?" Connie protested. "That was high school, like, twenty years ago almost."

"Maybe so, but you threatened the woman just a few months ago."

Connie's eyes dropped to her coffee and she started to cry.

Josh sighed. "Connie, we're fighting to put a murderer behind bars."

"I'm really sorry, Sheriff."

Josh breathed deeply to relax himself before squeezing Connie's hand. "Tell me how you and Kipp Martin met," he said.

Connie sipped her coffee and refused to make eye contact with him. "We were still in high school. Kipp was on the football team. I think he was on defense. He stopped the receiver from catching the ball, I think. I thought he was real cute, but he wasn't popular with the girls. He was smart, you know, kind of nerdy, and I was prettier then, not like now."

Josh looked around the room nonchalantly. Connie wasn't the county's most attractive woman, but she wasn't ugly, either, and he could understand why the riffraff liked her. Her rear end certainly attracted a lot of attention.

Connie looked down and scratched her forearms before continuing. "This one day Kipp caught me staring at him and he asked me out. We dated for, like, two years. Then we started living together after high school. He didn't get a scholarship, so he took a job on a logging crew. He was real buff and handsome when he was sweating and covered in sawdust. I loved that about him. He was a real hard worker, and he was good to me.

"Least, until Lisa came along. We went to high school together, but I never knew she had a thing for Kipp. He and I were having a rough time—money was tight and we were arguing a lot. I went to stay with my parents because I thought we could use a few days apart, just to think, and I took a job so I wasn't a burden on Kipp while he cooled off.

"I guess that's when Lisa made her move. She was always butting in on other girls in school, always trying to be the center of attention, but she never butted in on me and Kipp at all, at least not then. I think because Kipp wasn't the quarterback or popular. But while I was gone, Kipp went down to the Retread in Hines. That's where Lisa was working at the time. I guess she put her moves on him. He was feeling sorry for himself and wanted company, and he strayed on me. I've always blamed Lisa for that. She knew he was my man, but she muscled in anyway.

"Me and her fought plenty over it. Whenever we met, in the store or at the bar, wouldn't make any difference, we always got into it. About three months ago I was in The Sawyer having a drink with a friend, and me and Lisa got into it again. She told me she did Kipp real good, you know, like a woman and all that. Treated him like a man should be treated. Ha, that's a laugh, like treating your man right means screwing half the town. I may not have been the best girlfriend, but I treated Kipp good. He never went without.

"Anyway, some people in there heard me tell Lisa I was gonna kill her one day. I was good and drunk. I didn't mean anything by it, Sheriff, honest I didn't. She made me real mad and I just reacted." Connie paused as if in thought. "I'm real sorry. I hope I didn't screw things up for you."

"Connie," Josh said, "It's okay. I appreciate your honesty."

"Can I go now?" Connie asked.

Josh nodded. "You be careful, young lady," he said as he stood to leave.

"Why?" she asked with a look of surprise.

"I think Gordon will try to paint you as the killer."

"What?" Connie demanded. "I would never do that."

"I know that, Connie, but a jury might not."

SIX

The dismal gray and its incessant dripping finally took a break for the first time in days, and the sun shone brightly in the afternoon sky. A few billowing clouds trailed in the wake of the recent storm. For Josh it was perfect weather for a Sunday barbecue, and there was a respite and an opportunity for Josh and his hard-working employees to let off some steam.

"Need any help, Sheriff?" asked Max.

"Indeed I do. See that cooler right there?"

"Yes, sir," Max said as he let his children loose into the backyard.

"There's a cold beer in it. Get one and drink it."

Max turned to the cooler and dug around. "You want one."

"Yes, please."

Josh accepted a beer, clanked Max's bottle, and took a long, cool draw. "Nothing better than a cold beer on a day like this," he said with a contented smile.

"You might want to rethink that," Max said.

"How's that?"

Max motioned toward the driveway.

Josh turned and felt his jaw drop when he saw a woman walking up the path. "Is that Gail?"

"Sure is."

"Mind yourself, Max," Josh said with a nudge. "Wouldn't

want Brenda smacking you this early in the day."

"How old did you say she was?"

"I didn't, and you didn't hear it from me."

"Wow, she is a nice-looking lady."

Josh was surprised that Gail would actually take him up on his offer to come to his picnic, and he could not believe the way she looked. She wore a spaghetti-strap sun dress and short heels, her hair was untamed and flowing across her shoulders, and her face was made up more than usual. "I'll be a stuck badger," he said.

Max gave him a quizzical look. "'Stuck badger'? Don't think I've heard that one before."

"Me either. Just made it up. Seemed to fit the moment."

Before the reporter was close enough to say hello, Max's wife cornered her to make introductions. There followed a handshake, some giggling children, and then some giggling women.

"Brenda makes fast friends, doesn't she?" Max asked.

"She does indeed, Max. You have a good woman there."

"I do. Oh, hey, there's Jane. I needed to ask her something."

Josh knew exactly what Max was up to, excusing himself and thinking he was being nonchalant about it. He turned back to the barbecue and lit the charcoal. Soon smoke was drifting upward from the savory hickory chips, and the aroma of sweet, burning wood filled his nose. The sound of playing children and laughing adults filled the space behind him, and he smiled. These were good people, and it delighted him to entertain them.

"Afternoon," came a sultry voice from over his shoulder.

"You made it," Josh said as Gail approached him. He caught himself looking low and adjusted his eyes.

"Yeah," she said, "but someone forgot to give me directions to the place."

"No," he said shaking his head, "I didn't forget."

"Uh, yes, you did."

"Did not. I knew you would figure it out."

"I had to ask at the office."

"Yeah. You figured it out. You're a reporter. I guessed you would know what to do."

Josh was delighted to see her, he realized. In fact, he was a bit surprised that he had invited her in the first place. For whatever reason, though, the invitation had fallen from his mouth before he could stop himself. Now that she was here, he was exceedingly happy as her smile lit up the deck and his face.

"I see you met Brenda," he said.

"Yes. What a wonderful woman. And those kids, so adorable."

"You have kids?"

"Me? Oh, no. No, never got around to that. You?"

"Yes. A daughter. Meredith."

"I take it she's off living her life?"

"Yes. She's thirty-seven and lives in Bend."

"Oh, good. She's close." Gail looked at Josh's beer. "Got one of those for me?"

Josh realized that he was trying so hard not to stare that he'd forgotten to ask if she wanted a drink. He turned to hide his embarrassment and coughed to clear his throat. "Of course. Where are my manners?" He retrieved a beer and popped the top, handed it to her, and clinked his bottle to hers.

"Thank you," she said. "So, how often do you do this?"

"Drink beer?"

"No, silly. Cook for your people. How often do you do that?"

"Every Memorial and Labor Day."

"Always the same people?"

"No. If you work Memorial Day, you come over on Labor Day, and vice versa. Always a load of fun trying to get their schedules in order." He gestured. "These guys have been busting their butts, and they needed to get away. Been an emotional time for all of us."

"Indeed, it has. So," Gail then said with a puzzled look, "I have a question for you?"

"Should I be scared?"

"Of course not." Gail took a long drink and rested her beer on the barbecue. "Isn't it a bit unusual for a murder investigation to conclude so quickly?"

"I'd be a fool to say no, considering I've still got four unsolved sitting on my desk. We caught a break, and James has a right to a speedy trial. He'll get it. Unless, that is, his defense asks for a stay and gets it." Josh caught himself and looked into her eyes with what he hoped wasn't too serious an effort. "Are we off the record?"

"Of course," Gail responded with an intensity matching his. "I would never hijack you in your home."

"Good to know." Josh stirred the charcoal and put a lid on the barbecue. "Going to be ready to cook in a few minutes." He motioned to a chair near the door. "Want to sit?"

"No, thanks."

Josh shrugged. "Anyway, Lisa Martin's husband, Kipp, turned us onto a fellow named Sam Reynolds. Apparently, she went home and told Kipp about a fight James got into with him."

"Sam Reynolds. He's the fellow from the Square Nines?"

"You've been paying attention."

Gail winked at him. "It's what I do. So, what has this to do with anything?"

Josh turned his attention back to the grill. "How did you know about Reynolds?"

"I've been down to the Square Nines a couple times, talking to people about Gina Bergmann. His name came up."

Josh nodded his approval. "Well, James has been in a lot of trouble over the years. Between his interest in the victim and the fight with Reynolds, we've built a motive."

"Jealousy?" asked Gail.

"That's our best guess. Then, we considered he was living not a quarter mile from the crime scene, and it was all easy from there."

"Yes, I suppose so." Gail took a long pull from her beer as Josh smiled in appreciation. "Do you think he might be responsible for Eryn Rogers's death?" she asked.

"You're really playing on my trust, aren't you?"

She smiled.

"Well," he asked, "can I trust you?"

Gail leaned toward him and looked deep into his eyes. "Yes, you can. And, what kind of trouble has James been in?"

"Drug use, shoplifting, loitering, the usual stuff." Josh put burgers on the grill and sucked on his beer. "Also, while we were scouting around where Eryn Rogers died, we found James asleep about five hundred yards up the road. I never counted that as coincidence. At the time, I was certain he was involved. He has a solid criminal history, he's loaded more often than not, and he's unstable. But I have never been able to find anything concrete. And trust me, I looked."

"What about the other three women?"

"He's too young to have been involved," Josh said in a tone he thought expressed too much disappointment.

Gail appeared to catch onto that, but said nothing of it. "Considering all these women were similar in appearance, do you think you're dealing with a serial killer?"

"I have entertained that, but there's no calling card. Yes, the victims are similar, but it ends there. A visual similarity is just not enough, I don't think. After Gina Bergmann was found in seventy-three, we had a good hard look at that very possibility. We had an expert come in from the FBI and examine every scrap of evidence we had, and their report indicated a solitary incident. I have a stack of files on this stuff. They're cold as ice, but I have them."

"I'd love to get a look at those," Gail said with a glimmer of hope in her eyes.

"Don't get ahead of yourself," Josh said.

"So, back to Eryn Rogers," she said, "you're sure Hodges was involved, or you're sure he wasn't?"

"I'm not sure either way, but I am looking at it fresh. We've never been able to connect any of the other murders together. Five dead women, and the only thing consistent between any two is that James Hodges was found squatting within spitting distance of two of them."

"You know," Gail said as she stepped slightly closer, "if I can help in any way, I'd like to."

Josh looked intently at her. "You said you worked at a paper in Jersey. What'd you do there?"

"I was an investigative reporter."

"Did you like it?" Josh asked.

"I loved it."

"All right. I'll get you a copy of the files. I'll take all the help I can get."

She looked at him with joy. "Seriously?"

"Yes."

Her response was priceless, like giving a child a new toy.

Then, as was his habit, Max interrupted at a most inconvenient time. "You two talking shop up here?" he demanded in a playful tone.

"Max," Josh said with a growl, "I swear son, your timing is impeccable."

Max laughed. "Get on down here and join the party."

Gail didn't need to be told twice and was off in a spark of energy.

"Yeah, well, that's fine," Josh growled to their retreating backs. "But someone has to cook."

He returned to the cooler for a fresh beer and caught the sizzling aroma of meat wafting from the grill. The smell of it, the sound of children playing in the yard, the delightful appearance of the woman who had been standing with him were all better than the beer and the cigars and the sunset. The smell and sound of the barbecue told him someone was over and he didn't have to spend the evening alone and discontented. And Gail's presence was electrifying. Not since coming home to his dear Alyson after the war had he felt so alive. Gail was spectacular to look at, amazing to talk with, and sensational to smell. She was a fresh peach in a basket of sour apples.

Josh flipped the hamburgers, rolled the hotdogs, and then

turned to watch his deputies and their spouses play with their children. The children played on the swing set he'd bought for Meredith so many years ago. And swing they did, propelled higher and higher by hooting and hollering fathers and encouraged by loving mothers.

He caught Gail looking his way, smiled politely, and then turned back to the grill. He thought she seemed interested in him, but he was having a hard time with it. He wondered if she might just be fishing out a story, and yet she seemed more thoughtful than that. There was a genuine air of interest in her eyes, or at least he hoped that's what he was seeing. In that moment he thought of Alyson, and how much he was beginning to realize that theirs had been a young love. The days of war and the feelings of loneliness and helplessness had led them to marry—perhaps before they were ready.

Josh stacked the meat on a platter and headed for the picnic table. "Come eat, you little pigs," he said as he found a place at the long picnic table.

The children raced to the table, some of them leaping from their swings while still high in the air. Mothers exclaimed and fathers laughed as their children hit the ground rolling. The picnic table greeted the deputies and their families, with women taking up residence at one end and leaving the other to the men. The children provided a comforting, if noisy, barrier in between.

"So who belongs to whom?" Gail asked.

Jane took credit for a pair of boys, Deputy Shaw claimed the girl sitting on his lap and a son tucked neatly into the crease of an arm, and Max pointed to three girls and a boy.

"Wow," Gail said. "Four. That's a lot of work."

"You don't have to tell me that," said Brenda, Max's wife of eleven years. "I was ready to stop at one."

"Oh, you were not," chirped Max.

She laughed and rubbed a child's head. "They're our everything."

"Mom, stop it," cried the child.

"So, Gail," Jane asked, "what brought you to Burns, Oregon?"

Gail dropped her sloppy burger onto her plate and wiped ketchup from her chin. "I needed to get out of New Jersey. I have a sister in Portland who knows someone who knows this guy whose married to Sandi that owns the *Review*. I needed a job, so here I am."

"Are you married?"

"Oh, no. Not anymore. But that's a really long and angry story."

"Oh, do tell."

She cast a weary eye toward Josh. "Let's just say it didn't turn out well. I could tell you he was a jerk and I was innocent, but that would be unfair. We couldn't make it work. I'll leave it at that."

"And no children?"

She shook her head. The look on her face had more story to tell, but the words did not follow.

"So, you're a reporter, then?"

"Yeah, full time even. And that says a lot in a town this size."

"Is Burns too small for you?"

"No, it's just about right. Compared to Newark, let me tell you. I worked for a paper there and it was all 'so and so did this, and so and so did that.' Politicians and mobsters and corporate BS gone crazy. Just . . . I'm sorry, my mouth gets away from me. These poor tiny ears," she said as she covered a little girl's ears.

"Oh, with Josh around, there's nothing they haven't heard before."

"Is that so?" Gail asked.

The sheriff shook his head. "There's plenty of that to go around," he said in his own defense. "It's not all me. Although I'm sure a fair portion of it is. Anyone need another beer?"

Hands went up all around the table, but Josh refused the smaller ones.

"So," Jane continued, "what do you think of our little

problem?"

Gail looked to the sheriff for permission and got it. "I think it's really scary, but I have to admit it's taken the dullness out of the job."

"I bet you got a lot of that in New Jersey."

"Every day, and then some."

Max took a turn. "You gave up a big city gig for this hole in the wall?"

"Max, it's not all fun and games. Big city means lots of competition, lots of backstabbing. I was ready to get away from that. This job opened up, and I decided it was time to make a change. You know, take a chance and all that. I love the peace and quiet, and I cannot get enough of that sunrise."

"Have you seen the sunrise and moonset together?" Brenda asked.

"No," she said as she winked at Josh, "but I hear it's amazing."

Then it was Brenda's turn to grill. "Are you a Republican?"

Josh slapped his hand to his forehead.

"Oh, no," Gail said, "I voted for Jimmy Carter."

There was a full round of boos from everyone other than Josh.

"I did," Gail said with a pout. "So?"

"We're all Republicans here," said Brenda with a touch of self-righteousness.

"Not all of us," Josh said.

"Yay! I have an ally in the camp."

"No, ma'am. I'm no Democrat, either."

Max answered for him. "Josh is one of them Libertarians."

"Hey," Josh said, "I just want everyone to be happy under his own fig tree, that's all."

Brenda piped in again. "Mostly good Christians around these parts. Law and order is what we need."

Josh put a stop to the conversation before it could get out of hand. "Look, everyone, if there's one thing I'm sure of, the best way to lose a friend is to talk religion or politics. So lay off, okay? Let's enjoy a nice day in the sun. There are plenty of other things to talk about."

Brenda didn't want to let it go. "Like what, sports?" she asked sarcastically.

"No," Josh said coldly, "like the weather, or the crops, or what did little Becky do with those seeds I gave her?"

"I planted them and they spouted."

Josh smiled at the child's cute four-year-old word. "They did? Well that's just wonderful. I bet you'll have some delicious carrots in a few weeks."

"Oh, I will. And pickles too."

"Honey, those are cucumbers," her mother said.

"Brenda," Josh said, "if she wants to grow pickles she can grow pickles."

"Who says?" Max asked.

"I says, and that's all the says-ing that needs saying, right, pickle girl?" Josh said while digging in the child's belly.

Over the next four hours, Josh spent most of his time enjoying the camaraderie between his deputies and their families. There was volleyball, horseshoes, tag, and children playing on the swings. Fresh berry pies and whipped cream kept the smiles going. He especially admired the way Gail took so easily to the horde of children prancing about, and he wondered why she had none of her own.

Then, as the sun began to sink on the western horizon, the young families gathered in their chicks and said their goodbyes. Before he knew what happened, Josh found himself alone with Gail.

"You're going to be driving home soon, so I'm not sure about offering you anything else."

"Only had one beer," she said with a flirtatious smile.

"Well, I'm going to have a bourbon."

"Oh, I'll have one of those with you. But just a tiny one."

Josh poured her a drink and took it to her on the porch.

"Wow, that is a tiny one," she said.

"I would rather you get home in one piece."

"So," Gail said with a change of subject, "how is Melissa doing?"

"Good. I spoke with her on the phone yesterday. Considering she's on the defense's witness list, I had to ask her some questions."

"Any idea why?" Gail asked with surprise.

"Can't sort it out. Only thing I could patch together is that she and the boys would have driven by the turnoff sometime around or just before midnight."

"Turnoff? You mean to the murder scene?"

"Exactly. She's still struggling to put that night together. I suspect it'll come to her when her mind is right."

"Is she in Salem yet?"

"No, she's being held here until she turns eighteen, which is a few weeks away. Plus, she has to be here for the trial anyway."

"Have you been to see her?"

"No. That isn't a good idea right now. The DA will certainly talk to her face to face, but not me. I'll wait and drive over to see her in Salem once this thing is settled."

"I think she would like that. How are her parents doing?"

"Don't know. They won't talk to me."

"What about her grandpa?"

"He's having a rough go, and it'll take time. I'm content to let him work it out. He knows I'm around, so when he's ready to talk, I'm ready to listen."

Gail took a sip of her drink. "This is really good bourbon."

"Funny, you don't strike me as the bourbon type."

"Ha. You don't know me very well at all."

"That's true. But now I know you like bourbon, and that makes you all right in my book."

"Is that your bike?" she asked as she pointed at an old motorcycle tucked beneath a shed.

"Yeah. Forty-eight Harley Davidson Panhead. Just about time to get her out and cleaned up."

"It's beautiful."

"Thank you kindly. You ever been?"

"On a bike? Oh, no," Gail said as she shook her head.

"Afraid or never had an opportunity?"

"A little of both, I think."

Josh nodded. "We might have to correct both of those problems."

"You think I'm going to get on that thing?"

"I think you just might."

She shook her head again. "I don't know. It's getting kind of dark."

"Not tonight, you silly woman. Alcohol and motorcycles are not a good combination."

"Good choice, Sheriff."

As they talked, the sun sank closer to the horizon and the sky took on its characteristic red and orange tone. Drifting clouds shone bright yellow upon a purple background dark and foreboding. The smoke from the fire down by Riley was blowing north to south across the plain, and the sun's path took it through that brown and amber haze. It was like some great hand was shoving a glowing ball through strawberry syrup.

Gail seemed in awe. "That is so amazing. It's poetry in motion."

For Josh the moment was difficult, if not downright confusing. He had turned down every woman's advances for over thirty years, and now he found himself sitting in his favorite place just feet from this beautiful woman, and yet his mind would not let go of the past. He tried to look at her and enjoy her radiance, but he couldn't get Alyson from his mind. He felt as though she was there with him looking out over the distance with that far-off gaze she'd always had as the sun and the wine went down. He would love to tell this new friend all about it, but the words were locked up in that mysterious place where men's emotions go to die.

He stroked his glass and pulled a cigar from his pocket. He caught Gail smiling as he lit up. "You want one?" he asked jokingly.

"Yes, I do."

"Seriously? I was joking."

"Pass one over here."

Josh took another cigar from a box and handed it to her, then offered her a light. She bit the tip off, turned the cigar to the flame and puffed away. The thick Nicaraguan smoked and sputtered until she got it going. Smoke rolled from the corners of her lips and that was it: Josh could look at her and enjoy the smell of her perfume, and Alyson was gone.

At least for the moment.

"That's almost as good as pot," she said as smoke billowed from her mouth.

"Not the kind of thing you go saying in front of the county sheriff," Josh said with a smirk.

"It's all right. I think he'll let me live under the shade of my fig tree."

Josh chuckled, and then laughed out loud.

"Next time you come over I'll bring out the Cubans."

"Uh, not the kind of thing you go saying in front of someone who knows the sheriff," she teased.

They smiled at each other. The smiles turned to laughter, and the night echoed their enjoyment as the sun settled into bed. Once it did, Josh began to feel a bit uneasy with his new friend. He wanted to sit closer to her, but he could not find the courage to do so. Instead, he stood and politely indicated his need for sleep and offered to walk Gail to her car, an offer she accepted with what Josh thought was disappointment. While he did like her, he had no idea what to say or do. He knew he wanted to be with her, and he was confident she knew it, too, but he couldn't shake Alyson entirely. His wife was thirty-four years gone, and he was still childishly devoted to her.

Had things been different he would have felt safe taking Gail into his arms and enjoying her charms. However, old memories were rekindling, and he struggled to contain them. Alyson's death had left him feeling empty and unnecessary in a post-war world headed in new directions. Eventually, he'd felt outmoded on the job, and when Meredith went off to live her own life he was no longer needed on the home front.

That feeling of loneliness was even more pronounced as he gently closed the Mustang's door and watched forlornly as Gail drove away. The longing look she gave him told him she would have stayed if invited, but he let her go. He didn't know her story, but he sensed she was also feeling a need to express her love. Josh was sad to see her go, but would play his cards the way he had always played them: straight and narrow.

As the taillights faded away, he went to his home office, gathered several files and clippings, dropped them in a box with his collection of cold-case files and papers, and set them by the front door. He would get them to Gail the first chance he got. He needed her fresh eyes and her incredibly prescient mind. Her experience was in digging into the details where others never thought to look, even himself or the DA. Josh was entirely focused on the evidence that he needed to make an arrest, and he had done so as carefully as he could under the circumstances. Gail, on the other hand, could clearly get outside the state's investigation and dive headlong into the crowd without raising suspicion. She was just another nosey reporter looking for a story. People would talk to her differently than they would talk to him, reveal things under strict confidence that they were certain would never come back to bite them.

He hoped his hunch was correct.

* * *

Gail went to the door and smiled when she found Sheriff Matthews standing on her stoop holding a cardboard box. He calmly stepped past her when she invited him in. She watched eagerly as he looked around her tidy living room, smiled at her, then set the box neatly on the cheap coffee table next to last night's empty wine glass. His toned biceps attracted her eye, and she found herself incapable of turning them away. Something about the way his shirt fell over his torso that seemed very different to her. Or perhaps she was only noticing him differently. She wondered if the previous night had something to do with it.

"I have those files I told you about," said Josh as he turned to face her. "I hope you see something I can't."

"Wow," she responded. "That was fast. I didn't expect to see this stuff for weeks."

"Why?" he asked.

"Well, because you're a busy man. I didn't think I was much of a priority."

"You're right about the busy part," he said with a wink, "but wrong about being a priority."

"I'm flattered."

Josh blushed. "You're the only person in recent memory who really wants to see this stuff. There's nothing in there but old bones and lost trails."

"Sounds intriguing," she said as she knelt on the floor and began digging through the box. When she found an old photograph, she held it up. "Who's this handsome fellow?"

Josh smiled and took the photo from her dainty hand. "Wow. How the time flies."

"Nineteen sixty-five," Gail said with admiration. "You've aged well."

Josh's cheeks flushed, again. "Seems like forever ago."

Gail removed a folder and flipped it open. "Oh," she said as she put her hand over her mouth.

Josh took the folder from her trembling hands and looked at the picture. "Annette Walker," he mused. He handed the folder back and took a seat at the dining room table.

"How many times was she stabbed?" Gail asked.

"Twenty, if I recall correctly. I believe the ME determined the wounds were all aimed at the heart from slightly different angles."

"That's horrible."

Josh harrumphed. "That's nothing. Wait until you see the

photographs of Lisa Martin. Listen," he said, "I'd love to stay and chat, but I have work to do. I wanted to get these to you, and I sincerely hope you find something. Everything I have is in there."

"I'll do my best."

"I know you will," Josh said as he stood. "I've rummage around in there far too often, always trying to jiggle something loose. If you find anything, even if you have some ridiculous theory, I'd like to hear it."

"You'll be the first to know, Josh." Gail got up from the floor and led the way back to her front door. She nonchalantly stood in the doorway, forcing Sheriff Matthews to pass close to her on his way out, and she closed her eyes at the feeling of his muscular chest brushing past her shoulder. She smiled politely while trying to hide her passion and closed the door behind the sheriff, then turned back to the box. She could think of nothing better to do than rummage through the history it contained. Unfortunately, there wasn't much time.

Driving to The Sawyer was painful. Gail knew there was a treasure trove in those boxes begging for her attention. Certainly, there must be more there than there would be in the musty bar that smelled of fresh cigarette smoke and old beer, but she'd had yet to visit the place during the midmorning hours. She had heard from numerous patrons that a crustier gathering of folks paid their visits before things got hopping later in the day.

Immediately upon entering through the double doors, Gail espied a crowded table of old men seated near the back. She fixed her gaze on them and noted they were drinking whiskey or some equivalent. There wasn't a beer to be seen at their table.

"Morning gentlemen," she said as she sauntered over to them.

The men, who must have ranged in age from seventy to ninety, watched her approach with bated breath. Gail knew that the men were checking her out, but not with the shy, schoolboy energy she would have expected from the later crowd. Rather, they admired her in a slightly more gentlemanly manner, one she appreciated for its calm demeanor and a complete lack of concern for what anyone might think or say. They admired her because they could.

"You boys mind if I sit with you for a while?" she asked while pulling out a chair.

The men said nothing, but followed her every move as though a goddess had suddenly fluttered down from the sky to entreat them.

Gail then did something she hadn't done since her college days. She reached over, took the closest man's drink, and took a sip from it. "Not bad," she said with a fiery gleam. "What're we drinking?"

"Scotch," said the man whose drink was being shared against his will.

"Tastes like the house swill," Gail said, handing the drink back.

Another man piped in across the table. "All Pete ever drinks is that house crap."

Pete responded by taking apart his associates' rye. Soon, the table had devolved into a dreadful argument until the entire troop shared a collective senior moment and forgot why they were arguing in the first place.

Gail used that opportunity to introduce herself and bring up the subject of murder.

"Why, shore, I remember that lady," said the one called Pete in response to Gail's query regarding Gina Bergmann. "We found her not twenty feet from the dock."

"'We?" Gail pressed.

"Shore," said the old man. "Me and Tanner here," he motioned to a silent gentleman seated next to him, "we found that poor girl. Dreadfulest sight I ever did see."

"Where did you find her?"

The old man went on to describe the scene in detail Gail thought remarkable. He described the area at the very southern edge of Lake Malheur not far from their bait shack. They had been fishing and nothing was biting, so they'd moved a little closer to shore where the two men had seen her almost at the same time. At first they thought she was just sleeping, hoping beyond hope they had not found what they knew they had found. One of the men had rushed to the closest home and called for the sheriff while the other stayed to watch over the area.

They had been banished from the dock for over a month, but neither could stand to return even after the police stopped asking questions. The memory was too fresh, and they'd decided it was all very bad luck and took to fishing a different hole farther to the west.

"Not been back since," said Pete. "Just ain't the same since then. Can't hardly go down there without seeing that poor woman all naked and bloated."

"Did they ever find the killer?" Gail asked, already knowing the answer.

"Never did. Some say it was the same feller that got one of those other two ladies. Forget their names, though. Others say it was just a passer-by who got lonely."

"And what do you think?"

The man looked Gail dead in the eyes and leaned toward her. "Ain't nobody here that knows, Miss Cruz. Nobody. Whoever done it, they just vanished away into the night."

"Sure made ol' Powell mad," said the quiet man.

"What do you mean?" Gail asked with a queer look.

"Powell?" the man asked back.

Gail nodded.

The man smiled. "Ol' Powell donated that dock. Said it was a gift to us ol'-timers for all the work we put into logging these parts. Wanted to leave us a legacy, beings we liked to fish down there. Sure made it a darn site easier getting in and out of the boat."

"Sure did," said Pete.

"Sure did," muttered the table.

Gail made the notes in her book and closed it. "Thank

you, gentlemen," she offered.

As she left the table, she heard them whisper something about her fine behind. It made her smile.

SEVEN

Josh stepped into the hall, took a deep breath, and smiled at Gail. She sat waiting patiently after having been excused from jury selection due to her proximity to the case.

"Hello, Sheriff," she said with a brightly lit smile.

"Ms. Cruz. How are you this fine morning?"

"I'm well, thank you. Would you like to get a cup of coffee with me?"

"I would love to, but it'll have to be here. This thing's gonna start today," he said as he checked his watch. "In about an hour."

"Are you serious? Wow, that's fast."

"It's a big county, but there aren't many people. Judge Parker was raring to go on Friday."

"What stopped him?"

"This motion, that motion. Not enough time to prepare. It's all very unfair, you see."

"Of course."

Josh poured two cups of coffee from a dispenser. "Sugar and cream, right?"

Gail looked surprised. "Yes. How did you know that?"

"It's my job to know things."

"Ah, yes, of course. You've been paying attention."

"Don't read too much into it. I pay attention to everything."

"I'm not surprised," she said with a smile. "What's your prediction?"

"Off the record?"

"I'm not grilling you today."

A voice interrupted. "So, who's on the jury?" Max asked.

Josh shook his head at his deputy's propensity for finding his way into conversations. "Just a moment, Max," he said with a hint of perturbation. "I think," he said as he returned his attention to Gail, "that Hodges will be found guilty. There's too much evidence against him."

"I suppose," she said while looking at the floor.

"You disagree?" Josh asked.

She shrugged at him. "I've seen men walk with more evidence."

"Well," Josh sipped his coffee, "that may be. For now, though, we have to wait and see what those twelve folks have to say about it. Max, your timing is always appreciated, but to answer your question, you know it doesn't matter."

"Well, phooey on you."

Josh shook his head. "This isn't going to be some two-dollar trial, Max. Hodges isn't charged with swiping candy bars. For all we know it'll take two weeks for this thing to hash out. If Gordon has his way, it'll run on for a month. Let's you and I mind our business, okay? Who's on the jury doesn't matter a lick, and we need to remember that. We can't have a hung jury because the sheriff's office is biased."

"Yes, sir," Max said. "You think Gordon will get this clown off?"

"From what I hear," Josh answered, "he's so convinced of Hodges's innocence he's guaranteeing an acquittal."

"You still think the case is strong enough to convict him?"

"Hell, guys," Josh added, "we've got the murder weapon and her clothes in his possession, matching blood on both, and his clothes with her blood on them. The murder happened within spitting distance of his camp, and he was found with a bunch of boozed-up bums shootin' heroin and who knows what else. Witnesses will testify that he had an argument with her, then got into a fight with one of her lovers. The list is endless."

A man approached the trio and interrupted. "Sheriff?"

Josh turned to the man. "Yes."

"Sorry to bother you, sir. Judge Parker has ordered the trial to begin at one o'clock. We will have opening statements and the prosecution will call its first witness."

Josh wasn't surprised. "Well, good. Let's get this thing over with."

"Ms. Cruz," Max asked, "will you be covering the trial?"

"Are you kidding, Max? I wouldn't miss it for the world. I'll be in there every moment. This is the most excitement I've had in six months."

Josh chuckled. "You don't get out enough."

* * *

Only a few hushed whispers broke the silence that otherwise hung over the courtroom. Gail took a seat in the back row of the room opposite the jury box so she could watch the looks and expressions on the juror's faces. She was watching them closely when the bailiff interrupted her concentration.

"All rise," he shouted.

The bailiff stood almost at attention as the people continued a slow rise from their seats. "Department One of the Superior Court is now in session. The Honorable Judge Parker presiding. Please be seated."

The judge cleared his throat and looked down his nose at the participants. "Good morning, ladies and gentlemen," he said. "Thank you for being here. The Superior Court calls to order the People of the State of Oregon vs. James Hodges." Parker then turned to the jury. "All right. Will the clerk please swear in the jury?" The judge took a drink of water and leaned back on his black throne.

A woman stepped from the side and approached the jury box. "Will the jury please stand and raise your right hand?"

To Gail the jury seemed confused and out of sync as they fumbled through the oath.

"You may be seated," The clerk said as she returned to her chair and the room again went silent.

"Mr. Prosecutor," the judge asked, "are you prepared to give your opening statement?"

Carl Franklin stood from his chair. "Yes, Your Honor."

"You may proceed."

Franklin moved to the podium and cleared his throat. "Your Honor," he began, "and ladies and gentlemen of the jury, the defendant has been charged with the crimes of murder in the first degree and possession of a controlled substance. The evidence the state will introduce will clearly and without doubt prove that Mr. Hodges is guilty and will show that late on the night of May the fourteenth or very early in the morning of the fifteenth, nineteen hundred and eighty, he lured an innocent woman into the woods and did, with forethought and malice, kill her and leave her body in the woods. We will show you that Mr. Hodges stripped the victim naked and took those articles of clothing into his possession. We will also show you that the defendant did have in his possession the drug heroin, which is a controlled substance within the state of Oregon. While the defense will try to paint Mr. Hodges as a sweet, lovable boy, we will show that he is nothing less than a cold, calculating murderer. The evidence presented by the state will prove to you that the defendant is guilty as charged." Franklin thus ended his sermonette and took his seat.

Gail scribbled furiously in her notebook and watched with great interest as the different members of the jury expressed pleasure or discontent depending on their immediate satisfaction with the prosecution's opening remarks. The jurists ranged from the steely-eyed calm of Mr. Jacob Powell, local and beloved businessman, to the animated head jerking of Maggie Johnson, an older woman from Frenchglen whose religious antics were seen as nothing more than self-righteous sermonizing.

"Thank you, Mr. Prosecutor," Judge Parker said as he motioned to the sleepy-looking Mike Gordon. "Is the defense ready to give its opening remarks?"

Gordon rose from his leather-padded chair and turned to the jury box. "Your Honor and ladies and gentlemen of the jury. Under the laws of our great nation, my client is presumed innocent until *proven* guilty. During the course of this trial, you are going to hear 'evidence' that my client, Mr. James Hodges, took the life of an innocent person. However, what we intend to show is that my client is nothing more than the wrong man in the wrong place at the wrong time. You will be presented with the truth: that while James was, in fact, near the scene of this grisly crime, and that while some evidence was indeed found in his possession, that this evidence is circumstantial at best. He is not the culprit. Ladies and gentlemen, my client, James Hodges, is not guilty." He paused. "Your Honor, I return the floor to you."

Gordon took his seat and leaned over to talk with his client. Water was poured at both tables, assistants shuffled papers back and forth with their attorney bosses, and whispers were exchanged.

It was Judge Parker who broke the silence. "The state may call its first witness."

"Thank you, Your Honor. The state calls Mr. Harry Grey."

Judge Parker ordered Mr. Grey to the stand.

Gail leaned back on the bench. Some of the jurors looked uncomfortable, and others appeared right at home. Two in particular stood out to her. Jacob Powell sat calm and relaxed. He was nice looking, clean shaven, and poised. He wore a suit she presumed he'd paid top dollar for. From an earlier interview with him, she knew him to be somewhat cold, calm, less than friendly, although always ready to entertain, and he seemed to be a master of the details.

The other jurist she took special note of was Maggie Johnson, who was a stately woman approaching sixty, and who looked irritated and nervous. She bit her lip, fumbled with her fingers, and looked as though she was prepared to write down every word of testimony. Perhaps the most animated character Gail had ever witnessed on a jury, Johnson's head bobbed, twisted, nodded, and shook depending on her apparent state of understanding.

As Gail scribbled in her notebook, a gentleman moved into the aisle and approached the witness stand. He was young, short, and stocky. He raised his hand, took the oath, then moved to the witness stand and sat down.

The prosecutor stood up. "Mr. Grey, now that we all know who you are, will you please tell the court where you were earlier on the morning of May 15 of this year?"

"Oh, uh, yes. I was up on Marshall Creek."

"And where is Marshall Creek?"

"Oh, see, yeah, it's about, oh, twenty miles north of Burns. You take, uh, 395 and then you turn right—"

"Thank you, Mr. Grey. The specific directions are not important. You say you were at Marshall Creek."

"Yes, sir."

Carl Franklin grilled the hunter for almost an hour. He asked for details of his whereabouts, whether or not he had a relationship with the victim, and then asked the emotional man to describe exactly what he had found and when. Grey struggled to explain the details. Not, Gail reasoned, because he could not remember them. Rather, his emotion declared that he had been suffering tremendous stress after finding Lisa Martin's body, and he struggled to replay the events without breaking down somewhat. Franklin mercifully ended his questioning, but Gail knew worse was to come.

Mike Gordon walked to the attorney's podium and leaned on it nonchalantly. "Mr. Grey, can you please tell the court what time it is right now?"

Gail followed Harry's eyes as he looked to the courtroom clock over her head.

"It's two thirty."

"Why'd you look at the clock back there?"

"Objection," the prosecutor called out. "The defense asked for the time."

Mike Gordon chuckled. "Your Honor, if the court will indulge me for a moment."

Judge Parker looked over the rim of his glasses. "You did ask Mr. Grey for the time, counselor."

"Yes, I did. Please, Your Honor."

"Make it quick. Overruled. Mr. Grey, please answer the question."

"Okay. Well, you see, I don't wear a watch."

"How do you tell the time?"

Harry Grey stared into space. "I just know."

"You just know?"

"Yes."

"Mr. Grey, you gave very specific times. I believe you said you arrived at the location at four in the morning."

"That's correct."

"Yet, you have no timepiece to confirm that."

"I don't ever need one."

"So, you expect us to just take your word for it?"

"Yes, I do. I'm no liar."

"No one is calling you a liar, Mr. Grey. However, is it possible that you arrived at Marshall Creek earlier than 4:00 a.m.?"

"How much earlier?"

"Oh, I don't know. Fifteen minutes?"

"I suppose that's possible."

"Then, is it possible you arrived thirty minutes earlier?"

"Yes, I guess it's possible."

"An hour?"

"No. I don't think so. I've been getting up at the same time as long as I can remember."

"Yet you're not really sure what time it was."

"I know within a few minutes."

"Objection," called Franklin. "Your honor, Mr. Gordon seems intent on confusing the jury with a bunch of nonsense. If Mr. Grey's time recollection is off by even an hour, it does not change the facts of the case."

"The defense has no further questions, Your Honor." Gordon returned to his desk and whispered something inaudible to his assistant.

* * *

Josh Matthews made his way to the foot of the ridge and started up. Although he couldn't remember exactly where the body of Nikki Rhodes had been found, he knew it was right along this ridge. He pushed himself through the thick underbrush until he came to a rocky outcropping and stopped. It had been very near here, he recalled. Up the way, just above the rock ledge, sat an old water tank. He remembered that. The tank stood upon wooden legs that showed their age with graying lines, jagged cracks, and splinters showing through fading white paint. The tank had been built many years prior to the murder, installed by Powell Forestry as part of a massive thinning contract brokered with the Forest Service in the mid-1960s. The Forest Service didn't want clear cutting, preferring instead to thin out the old, diseased, and fallen trees. The logging outfit used the tank to supply water from a spring to thirsty loggers on that job, and for the overheating radiators of their equipment. Now, it stood as a stark reminder of the ghastly murder of a woman known among the logging camps as a freewheeling prostitute.

Josh stepped over a downed tree and fought away the limbs as they snagged his jacket. He wasn't even sure why he'd come up here. What was there to be seen that he had not already seen many times before?

Josh remembered that three of Powell's surveyors had been returning from the ridge after spending the week marking trees for removal. One of the three men had stepped behind some rocks to urinate when, according to the report, he let out a disgusted yell. When his companions came to see what the commotion was all about, the decaying body of a naked woman had greeted them. She was laying face up, one hand at her side, the other stretched out perpendicular to her torso. Maggots feasted on her decaying flesh and, as an autopsy would later verify, an animal had been gnawing at her left leg. One of the three men rushed to their company car and went straight to the sheriff's office to report the finding while the other two remained behind and flagged down a Powell supervisor. By the time Josh arrived on the scene a small number of Powell's loggers had established something of a "camp" centered by a canopy-covered table with maps laid out, food and water at the ready, and a number of men guarding the area to keep other employees away. Josh's team had been most thankful for the consideration, as the covered table proved very useful when an uninvited afternoon shower drenched the area.

All present swore on Bibles and lost relatives that not a soul had ventured near the body since the gruesome discovery.

Josh and his deputies had taped the area off further, called the Oregon State Police, and begun their initial investigation. Nothing was recovered that pointed to the assailant, and there was no visible evidence or eyewitness testimony regarding vehicles, people, or strange happenings. As had been the case previously, there was nothing incriminating. The medical examiner did note, however, that the woman had likely died where she was found. There was no evidence she was killed elsewhere and dumped where she lay. He also learned that the woman was most likely struck by an axe as she lay on the ground. She had not been raped, nor had had sex in the twenty-four hours prior to her death. Considering her past, it could only be surmised that one of her tricks had gone south on her, or that he intended to kill her from the start. No matter the reason, it was murder, and Josh pursued it as such.

Interviews were conducted with multiple loggers, the surveyors, and several area ranchers. Every man they talked to had an alibi. No witnesses, no guesses, no usual suspects to sift through. The case went cold three months after it was opened.

Josh returned to the truck with nothing new to go on, and headed back to town.

＊ ＊ ＊

"The state calls Max Shafer," said the prosecutor.

Gail wrote a note on a page labeled *Max Shafer*: *Looks like he's having fun with this. Always seems happy. Can't get him down for anything.*

Deputy Shafer sauntered to the witness stand, affirmed the oath, took the stand, and answered questions for thirty minutes. He was the most relaxed witness Gail had ever observed.

"Thank you, Mr. Shafer. Your witness, Mr. Gordon."

"Max—can I call you Max?" asked Mike Gordon in his friendly style.

"Sure. Just don't call me in the morning," he said with a grin.

Scattered laughter filled the courtroom until the gavel slammed home. "Mr. Shafer, could we keep focused, please?"

"Sorry, Your Honor."

Gordon leaned onto the podium and rubbed his eyes. "Deputy Shafer, I want to talk to you about a few things, if you don't mind."

"Sure."

"On May the twentieth—that's the day Sheriff Matthews first visited what you call 'the camp' in person—you stated that you were not with him. Is that correct?"

"No, I wasn't."

"Would you please tell the court what you were doing."

"Well, I was chasing leads."

"Deputy Shafer, what leads were you chasing?" The question was absolutely direct and left no room for interpretation.

Max looked around the room trying to find his boss. When he couldn't, he appeared desperate, and Gail believed she knew why.

"Deputy Shafer?"

"Uh, well, uh," he stumbled and coughed.

Gail noted that Judge Parker didn't seem to be in the mood for stalling. "Mr. Shafer, will you please answer the question."

"It's just that, um, I don't want to embarrass anyone."

"We're not here to dillydally. Answer the question, please." The judge raised his gavel as if to slam it, and Max understood the warning.

"Yes, sir. Uh, Mr. Martin—that's Lisa Martin's husband—he told the sheriff that Lisa might be messing around with another man."

"Just one?"

"Two, actually."

"Who?"

Max sighed heavily as he clasped his hands. "Sam Reynolds, and Robert Carter."

The courtroom whispers rose to a crescendo, and once again Judge Parker had to silence them.

Gordon continued. "And you considered these men to be leads?"

"Yes."

"Now why on earth would you do that?"

"We were looking for a murderer. Anyone who had anything to do with the victim in the last few days was considered a suspect."

"So, Robert Carter—who, I might add, is a very respected man in town—was a suspect in your investigation?"

"Yes."

"And what did you learn."

Max shrugged. "Nothing. We stopped looking at him."

"Why?"

"Our investigation didn't turn up anything."

"Fair enough. No further questions."

Max reluctantly took his seat, and then it was Jane's turn.

Gail thought she was an attractive woman. She was svelte, alluring, and carried a certain charm about her. She was also very female and didn't play the rough, tomboy cop role. Her fiery red hair was done up in a ponytail, and her nails were painted emerald green, which Gail thought strange for a police officer. But she hadn't known many female police officers. Even in Newark most of the women at the local station worked in the office. But, times were changing and she loved seeing Jane take the stand.

"Mrs. Smith, how long have you worked for the sheriff's office?" Carl Franklin asked.

"Just over a year."

"And will you please tell this court what you do?"

"I'm a deputy sheriff's investigator. I investigate criminal behavior and assist the sheriff in bringing criminals to justice."

"And what roll, if any, did you play at the crime scene?"

"Well," Jane said in a firm, reassuring tone, "my primary rolls in this case involved acting as the forensic photographer and performing evidence collection and documentation. I took over two hundred photographs of the body and the surrounding environment, collected soil samples, tissue and blood samples, and assisted with evidence protection."

Franklin dove into a series of technical questions regarding photography, photo development, evidence handling, and finally, after droning on for some hours, he held up a plastic bag and got down to the meat. "Do you recognize this?"

"Yes," Jane answered matter-of-factly. "That is the murder weapon."

"Deputy Smith, what are your impressions of this knife?"

Jane shuffled and appeared to be collecting her thoughts. "It's a custom cutlery piece with detailed engravings. It has a three-degree primary bevel with a fifteen-degree secondary bevel angled at seventy-five degrees from the perpendicular. It is made of Japanese steel of a quality rarely seen in cutlery. The engravings are quite ornate and very detailed. We found blood on this knife that matches the victim's blood type."

"Your Honor," Franklin said as he turned to the judge, "the

state wishes to introduce this as people's evidence 9-A."

"Any objections?" the judge asked.

Mike Gordon shook his head. "No objections," he said without looking up.

Franklin turned back to Jane. "Mrs. Smith, do you know who made this knife?"

"No, I do not."

"Did you look into it?"

"Yes, I did. We could not identify a source."

"And what does that lead you to believe?"

"Well," she said matter-of-factly, "It is custom made, probably outside the country. Japan is my best guess."

"Thank you. Now, where did you find this knife?"

"It wasn't I that found it."

Carl Franklin turned to the jury. "Who did?"

Jane adjusted her seating position. "Sheriff Matthews found it on the defendant. He was carrying it behind his shirt."

Carl Franklin continued. "Naturally, Mrs. Smith, the defense will ask if it is possible that the knife in question actually belonged to someone else."

"I suspect that too. However, we asked Mr. Hodges if the knife was his and he said, 'Yeah, that's mine.'"

"Did he also claim to have found these?" Franklin held up other bags containing several articles of clothing.

"Yes, he did."

"Did he tell you why he needed blood-stained women's clothing?"

"We didn't ask. We only asked if they were his, to which he said 'Yes, they're mine.'"

"No further questions."

The defense asked for a short restroom break, which was granted, and Gail took the opportunity to stretch her legs. She got a coffee, schmoozed with a few people, scribbled notes, used the restroom, and then returned to her seat.

At the conclusion of the break, Mike Gordon took his turn. "Mrs. Smith, I understand all of these technical things are, well, very important, obviously, but I need to clarify something else. So, can we just forget that all this 'evidence' exists for a moment?"

"No, I don't think I can forget that at all."

Gail smiled. Most witnesses might have been tempted to play along, but Jane was too smart for that.

"Suit yourself. I'd like to talk for a moment about Sheriff Matthews."

"What about him?"

"You seem like a very honest woman, so we'll expect some honest answers."

"If you say so."

"Have you ever known Sheriff Matthews to hold a grudge?"

Carl Franklin stood from his chair in a rush of papers. "Objection, Your Honor. Relevance."

"Your Honor," Mike Gordon responded, "I intend to show that Sheriff Matthews has a vendetta against my client."

"Sustained," said the judge. "Opinion is not evidence, Mr. Gordon."

Gordon nodded as he turned to his desk and took a paper from it, made some notes, then returned his attention to Jane. "Deputy, have you ever witnessed Sheriff Matthews acting in a vindictive manner?"

"Vindictive? No. Although I can say that Sheriff Matthews has a very low tolerance for criminal behavior, if that's what you're asking."

"You mean to tell me you've never heard your sheriff speaking ill of my client prior to this incident?"

"I didn't say that at all."

"So you have heard him speak ill of James Hodges."

"Yes."

"Would you please explain."

"Objection, Your Honor. The sheriff's personal opinions are of no consequence to this trial."

"Oh, I do disagree, Your Honor," Gordon countered. "I intend to show this court that Sheriff Matthews has had a thing against my client for many years and that he intended to arrest Mr. Hodges even before any evidence was found in his possession. I will also show that the good sheriff dropped all other possible leads in this case the moment he had an opportunity to pin it on the defendant, regardless of evidence to the contrary."

"Overruled."

"Thank you, Your Honor," Gordon said as he confronted Jane. "Now, Deputy Smith, will you please continue. I believe you were going to tell us what the sheriff has to say about Mr. Hodges."

Jane seemed to lose her composure momentarily, but after a few deep breaths, she regained it and continued. "Where to start. Uh, well, the evening that James was caught urinating on the door over at Swenson's Candy, the sheriff called James an ungrateful piece of crap. Can I say that? Anyway, there was the time about six months ago when James was begging over at the mill and was calling people who refused to help him some pretty awful names. When we arrived on the scene, Sheriff Matthews had some choice words to say. Oh, and back at the office he called him a low-life loser who expected everyone to just give, give, give while Hodges did nothing to earn their respect.

"Is that the kind of stuff you were wanting to hear, or should I expand the list to include shoplifting, loitering, public drunkenness, assault, drug use, etcetera?"

Mike Gordon tried to dig deeper, and Jane continued to give examples of the sheriff's displeasure for James Hodges. In every instance, Gail noted that a crime had been committed or James was otherwise making a nuisance of himself.

"When," asked Gordon, "did Sheriff Matthews first mention the defendant as a possible suspect in the murder of Lisa Martin?"

Once again, Jane took a short moment to collect herself before answering with professional calm. "When he came back to the office after speaking with the victim's husband. That's when he learned that James Hodges and Sam Reynolds had been fighting over Lisa Martin."

"Wow. One might think the sheriff would know such things as they happened."

Jane folded her hands and spoke softly. "Crimes that occur within Burns city limits are not within the sheriff's jurisdiction —"

"No more questions, Your Honor."

"Hey," Jane half yelled, "you can't just cut me off like that."

"Mrs. Smith," Judge Parker interrupted, "you may step down."

"But—"

"Thank you, Mrs. Smith."

The situation appeared to have unraveled until Carl Franklin butted in. "Redirect, Your Honor," he said as he stood from his chair.

Parker motioned for Jane to remain seated.

"Objection!" Gordon said with his back still to the bench.

"On what grounds?" Judge Parker demanded.

"Prosecution is attempting to confuse the jury."

"Nonsense," said Franklin. "The defense brought up the notion of jurisdiction. The state has the right to redirect on this line."

Judge Parker appeared annoyed. "Granted. Mr. Gordon, please sit down. The witness will remain on the stand until this matter has been exhausted."

The prosecutor cleared his throat and returned his attention to the witness. "Since Mr. Gordon brought it up, Deputy Smith, would you mind elaborating on that last part? Something about jurisdiction?"

"Yes, thank you." Jane smugly looked over at the defense attorney. "That fight happened inside the city limits, which is the city's jurisdiction and something Chief Anderson's department is responsible for. The sheriff's department does not involve itself in city matters unless our assistance is directly requested by the Burns chief of police, the matter clearly *requires* our assistance, or a criminal investigation leads us inside the city's boundaries. It is neither the chief's responsibility to inform the sheriff's department nor our responsibility to ask. To infer Sheriff Matthews is derelict in this matter demonstrates the defense's ignorance."

"Thank you, Mrs. Smith. Nothing further, Your Honor."

Gail watched admiringly as Jane returned to her seat. She was strong, but the defense *had* ruffled her feathers, even if only slightly. Jane clearly respected the sheriff and wasn't going to be lured into betraying his trust. Still, the defense had a point. From early on Sheriff Matthews had commented on James Hodges's ways. The lawman had no respect for the drifter and might have allowed his judgment to become clouded by the defendant's rocky past. Either way, the defense had done little to clear Hodges's name.

"All right," Judge Parker said as he broke a long and penetrating silence, "we're going to adjourn. We'll meet back here at nine o'clock tomorrow morning. The jury will please move to the jury room for instructions." He smacked the gavel down.

"All rise," the bailiff called.

Gail stood, waited for the judge to exit, and then rushed through the door and out into the hall, where she waited patiently for the defense attorney. A number of people exited the courtroom and filed out before Mike Gordon entered the hallway with his assistant in tow. Gail immediately caught his pace and introduced herself.

"Mr. Gordon, I wonder if you might have time for a few questions?"

The attorney's pace never let up. "I'm sorry, Ms. Cruz, but I'm afraid that's not possible at this time." He bulled through the front doors and disappeared into the crowd.

Gail turned around and started up the steps in time to see the assistant district attorney flirting with a reporter from Portland.

As Gail was about to give up and go home for the night, Sheriff Matthews walked through the door and smiled at her.

"Afternoon, Ms. Cruz. Looks like your prey is escaping."

"Oh, shut up," she snapped playfully.

Josh winked. Gail adored that. The way his mustache framed his mouth, and how his crow's feet were a most handsome feature on his already handsome face. His eyes were tired, though, and she understood the pressure he was under.

"Gordon isn't going to talk to you," Josh said. "He never talks to anyone during a trial."

"He was actually kind of rude."

"If I were you, I wouldn't expect anything else. And forget about Carl. He has a thing for young blondes, so don't bother."

"She seems very young for him."

"She is. She has no interest in him, but she'll get his time one way or the other."

"What's a girl to do?"

"If I were you, I'd get a good night's sleep. Tomorrow will be a long day."

"Got any plans for dinner?" She almost stopped herself from asking. She had a feminine sense that he might not be entirely ready for a relationship, but she liked being with him. He was kind, honest, and nice to look at, as well as strong and masculine in an Old West kind of way. Still, she hadn't wanted to ask, because she thought he would say no, which is exactly what he did.

"Actually, I have to get over to the office and get caught up on paperwork, but thank you for asking. Maybe another time."

Josh very politely escorted Gail to her car and opened her door.

"I'm looking forward to reading your article this week," he said.

Gail smiled, lightly touched his arm, and then got into the Mustang.

The short trip from the courthouse to her apartment in Hines took only minutes, and she had a glass of wine in her hand almost as soon as she walked through the door. That in one hand and the bottle in the other, she stepped outside to take in the musty smell of soggy wood, alfalfa, and cattle. Soon she was reminiscing and wondering how it was she came to be in this place and wrapped up in the story of her life while simultaneously working through her unexpected attraction to Sheriff Matthews.

"What are you doing here?" she asked to the wind.

Gail's thoughts drifted back to the education and career path that had led her from her birth home in Cedar Rapids to Providence, Rhode Island, where she went to work for the *Newark Gazette*, and spent twenty years working her way up from freelance to senior investigative reporter. It was a good job with benefits, and she'd only needed another ten years to retire comfortably.

Then along came Hank. He was adorable, smart, funny, tall, handsome enough, a cyclist with nice, strong legs and a shining wit she loved, especially around other people, where he quickly became the life of the room. Unfortunately, he was also an alcoholic. At first his drinking was fun, if not downright entertaining. The vast majority of the time he was a fun, lovable drunk, and Gail was convinced he was little worse than a rambunctious drinker—until the first big fight convinced her otherwise. He'd been loaded and barely comprehendible when he told her so many ugly things that she wondered if their marriage was a whirlwind sham. As many do, they worked through it. Several times. Until one day when a cancelled flight to Cincinnati meant she returned home in a taxi and found him in bed with the neighbor's wife. Both were so drunk they laughed while Gail cried at the door in agony so complete she fell to her knees.

At first it was only a separation. She was hopeful that some time apart would get him thinking. Unfortunately, the only thinking he did involved tequila and loose women collected at a pub on the corner. The separation turned to divorce, and that to a fight over the house and the car. She got both, sold both, and moved into an apartment closer to work. After a year she grew tired of the loneliness and the boredom and put in her notice at the paper. The dart she threw had landed on Oregon and a job search turned up the *Burns Review* and its search for a new reporter and columnist. A close friend had arranged a telephone interview, and two of those had landed her the job. So she left Newark two weeks later for Burns, Oregon, and the small-town charm that she'd hoped would come with it.

The new job was slow, boring in comparison to what she'd been used to, and yet somehow very appealing. In the first six months she'd reported on the mustang roundup, the rodeo, and the county fair. There were concerns out at the lumber mill and worries over federal regulations and what they might mean for the county's loggers. A bad fight at the high school needed immediate attention while two stolen cars, a robbery, and a few drug busts made up the balance of serious crimes that needed reporting. There was an occasional arrest for loitering or fighting and several new babies to announce. Three weddings, one divorce, a bankruptcy hearing, the usual small-town gossip, and the bridge tournament all needed covering with varying degrees of effort.

Small potatoes.

Suddenly, a loud, penetrating whistle engulfed the patio with sound as the sawmill—half a mile away—announced quitting time. The mill wasn't visible through the trees, but the concrete smokestack was. A white, wispy vapor rose from its black top and away in the wind. At that moment, she knew two hundred sweating, hard-working men were filing away to their cars while the office cleared out, itself short one receptionist whose body now rested in the town cemetery.

Gail opened the case file. Seated at the couch with a fresh glass in hand, she thumbed through her notes, photos, and official public records. The case against James Hodges was as close to perfect as any case she'd ever seen. The defense had so little room to wiggle that Gordon was squeaking. Gail asked herself how he might be able to show that James had not killed Lisa Martin when James had had the murder weapon in his pants. Could he prove the weapon had been found? Should the jury take the word of Dusty Stevens, who admitted to being high the night he claimed someone stole into his camp and planted evidence in the garbage can? Would the defense be able to paint some other person as a possible suspect? And why on earth would young Melissa Reed be so vital to his defense strategy? What had she seen that fateful night? And, if anything, could the jury be expected to receive her testimony with anything less than contempt?

Of equal interest to her was the defense's pointless attack on Harry Grey. Naturally, the defense attorney's position was to discredit any witness whose testimony was contrary to the story he wanted to paint. However, Gail had personally spoken to Harry Grey and found him to be friendly, polite, and honest. Other than the sheriff, she had not met another man in the state whose record was so spotless. He was a retired Marine who split his time between a small home in Hines and the high-desert forests. He harmed no one, didn't drink or smoke, and had no criminal background, not even a parking ticket. A number of other witnesses could regularly put him at Marshall Creek, along with three other favorite mountain locations, and very regular hunting grounds. Two people said the man could look at the sky and tell the time of day within thirty minutes.

"What are you up to, Gordon?" Gail asked out loud to no one but herself and the night.

She smiled curiously as she turned her attention to a *Burns Review* story written some years prior regarding the jurist Maggie Johnson. According to the article, the old woman was a self-proclaimed advanced messenger sent by Jesus to warn the community of its sins. There was smoking and drinking and sex to be put down, too much labor on the day of the Lord, too many sinners to be called out. All this came from her typewriter and the comfort of her small home in the tiny, one-horse town called Frenchglen, some sixty miles south of Bend. Her reputation in the county was a mixed review of patron saint and fiery old badger whose nose was too far up in other people's business, and not close enough to her own. Some said she was a prophet preaching the Word to the heathen, others that she was as self-righteous as they ever came and would personally nail her Savior to the cross if He dared show His face in her presence.

In contrast, Jacob Powell was the most notable individual on the jury. Born in 1935 in Portland, Oregon, Powell had little public history prior to his founding of Powell Forestry in 1960. With a small loan and a never-quit work ethic, he'd built his one-man logging company into a small empire employing over a hundred people and supplying Robert Carter's mill with a lion's share of logs. He was a respected man within the community, although he was fairly reclusive and shy. His company exclusively sponsored the Burns Bridge Club and provided funding for the rodeo and wild mustang roundup, as well as donated extensively to the wild-land firefighters. Court records indicated he had served on juries in the past but had no ties to local law enforcement, the sheriff's department, Judge Parker, the defendant, or any other member of the jury or court officials.

A conversation Gail had had with Sheriff Matthews earlier in the day revealed that he had few nice things to say of juror number four, one Fred Lipton. However, Gail liked him and had said as much. He was friendly enough, a bit shrewd, and easily approachable. He ran Lipton Ford and had sold her the shiny red Mustang she currently drove. Like Jacob Powell, Lipton had been a local businessman for many years, although his was less well liked as a whole—not that that mattered under the current circumstances. Previous *Review* articles noted that Lipton's dealership was a bit underhanded, sometimes shady, and his salespeople operated beneath a competitive-pay structure the *Review* called "grossly burdensome and unfair." The same article noted, "Lipton stands behind the products he sells in the same manner a mouse stands next to a cat!" The article went on in its fire-breathing vitriol for ten paragraphs.

"I like Fred Lipton," she had said to Josh.

"Nothing but a squirrelly salesman, if you ask me," he had replied with a touch of fire.

"Oh, come on. He's nice."

Josh had rolled his eyes at her as if she had committed some terrible crime. "He tried to sell the county a bunch of Fords that were rejected up in Crook County. I sorted it out when Sheriff Kester over there turned me onto it. We met at the county line to talk about some things and he says to me, 'Such and such model has a bad transmission. Don't buy those.' When I went to Lipton he was recommending we buy these Fords. I called him on it and he denied the issue. Haven't been to see him since."

"That's too bad," Gail argued. "I got my Mustang there. He was very nice." She crinkled her lips and eyes and teased at him. "Maybe he just doesn't like cops."

"Or maybe he can't be trusted. Either way, he's on the jury, and I don't like him."

Gail returned to her notes and saw that another of the jurors, Diego Lopez, had come to the country in 1950 and fought in Korea before buying a few acres in the county's southern region to grow corn. Eventually, he turned his effort to alfalfa and found his niche, quickly becoming one of the most respected growers in the county. His alfalfa was known to be free of weed seed, dried to perfection, and reasonably priced. He also had a miraculous way with the ladies. He was known as a player, but a polite, gentlemanly player, and not for the purpose of bedding every woman in town. He liked their company, but respected them. The county women knew they could go out with him in complete safety and be treated as royalty for a few hours. Still, the rumors spread, but none was ever proven.

Of the remaining jurors, only Heather Boydega had enough public history within the county to shed any light on her character. She was a manager at the local food mart, having worked her way up from bag girl. Born and raised in Hines, she had never been out of the state. In fact, never once had she been further west than Bend, while Juntura marked the eastern boundary of her travels. However, within that small range she was practically famous for her work as a midwife, having taken part in the delivery of more children than the local hospital. She was godmother to a large handful of local kids, a volunteer at the grade school, and herself barren, having lost her ovaries to cancer as a teenager. No member of the jury was more loved or respected within the county.

Within the brief notes Gail was reminded that of the remaining seven jurors, there was a rancher, a nurse, a school-teacher, two unemployed mill workers, a cook, a gas station attendant, and a retired door-to-door salesman. Gail closed the book on them and resigned herself to learning what she could during court proceedings. There was no reason to waste time chasing rabbits down the never-ending labyrinth of personal stories whose drama went no further than "once won the county pie-eating contest at the annual fair."

Gail laid her list aside and thought of the trial. A few citizens she'd spoken with were concerned about fairness and whether or not James would get the kind of trial any other resident would receive. Some complained that the region's successful business and political leaders could practically get away with murder, while the hard-working surfs were regularly busted for spitting on the sidewalk. They even cited Melissa Reed as the spoiled daughter of rich parents who'd received a light sentence because of her privileged position.

It seemed that, in their minds at least, James Hodges could not get a fair trial in Harney County. He didn't have enough money to buy one. Oh, they were glad someone had been arrested, but they were almost unanimously convinced that were one of the better-connected residents on trial, things would go much differently.

Finally, Gail gave up and slipped into bed. She tossed fitfully and decided she would never get any sleep. At least not until her alarm sprang to life and jostled her from a peaceful dream. She ran through the usual morning routine and at eight forty-five slipped back into the courtroom bench and took out her trial journal. She referred to her notes and studied the names of each player, which she kept on separate, dated pages to keep track of important details. She had detailed notes for the prosecutor, the defense attorney and his assistant, and the judge. She even had a page on the bailiff, although there was nothing more than a name since the sharp-voiced man never seemed to leave his home other than to report to work.

The two competing attorneys couldn't be more opposite. Mike Gordon was short, fat, balding, a bit pretentious, and rude. He wore a cheap suit doctored with a colorful scarf and shiny cufflinks. His hair was messy, and he smelled of BO. Carl Franklin, on the other hand, was tall, awkward, sharply dressed, and exuded confidence. He was usually polite and friendly. In the course of her investigation Gail had learned that no love was lost between defense attorney Gordon and Assistant DA Franklin. Cases in the Superior Court of Harney County frequently pitted the two against each other, with a roughly even split of wins and losses. A clerk at the Safeway she'd recently spoken with said it was something of a game between them.

Perhaps.

A movement grabbed her attention and she turned to find Sheriff Matthews sliding in next to her. He seemed in good spirits and spoke softly.

"Good morning, nice reporter lady."

"Good morning, Sheriff. How are you?"

"Quite well, thank you. Anything interesting happen yet?"

"Not unless you think watching Mike Gordon pick his nose is interesting."

Josh laughed. "That might be considered a real event 'round these parts."

She smiled and leaned closer. "I hope there's more to the county than that."

The bailiff stepped forward and announced the usual court business to get things started. The parties were present and accounted for, the court reporter was busy click-clacking away on her stenograph machine, and Judge Parker seemed to be in a lousy mood.

"All right, let's get to it. The state will call its first witness of the day."

"Your Honor, the state calls Dr. Donald Jackson to the stand."

The Harney County medical examiner approached the stand, turned and took the oath.

"Please spell your last name for the record."

"J-A-C-K-S-O-N," said the examiner with deliberate enunciation.

"Thank you. You may be seated." The bailiff moved away as Don Jackson sat down.

"Dr. Jackson," Carl asked, "how long have you been the Harney County medical examiner?"

"I think it's been about nine years."

"Would it be safe to say that your experience in these matters is quite extensive?"

"You might say that."

"Would you please qualify that experience for the court?"

"I certainly would. After graduating high school in Biloxi, Mississippi, I attended Mississippi State where I earned a bachelor's degree in Biology. From there, I transferred to the Ole Miss School of Medicine and graduated MD. I did my pathology residency at OHSU in Portland, then remained there for thirty-one years. After I retired, my wife and I purchased an alfalfa farm southeast of Riley. Harney County needed a medical examiner, and though I had plenty to do, I took the opportunity. It's a small town, so I'm not terribly burdened."

"Thank you, doctor. I'd like to go through a few things with you, if I could."

"Of course."

Carl Franklin placed a transparency on the overhead and stepped back. "Ladies and gentlemen," he said, "the photographs you are about to see are very graphic. I'd like to ask each of you to take a breath and compose yourselves. I'll be very candid with this. These images depict a near decapitation and will be difficult for some of you." He turned to the projector and switched it on.

Gail noted that Maggie Johnson immediately buried her mouth in her sleeve. She counted eight jurors in a mild state of shock, two who seemed only somewhat disgusted, and Jacob Powell looking into his lap and showing no emotion. She wrote in her notebook that his previous jury experience would mean he might have seen such things before, or that his experience as a logger meant he had been exposed to serious injuries amongst his crew.

Franklin replaced the slide with another, and then another, each taken from different angles and exposure levels. "Now, Dr. Jackson, I think it's pretty clear what caused this woman's death."

"Objection," Mike Gordon shouted. "Prosecution is leading the witness."

"Sustained," Judge Parker said. "Rephrase your question, please."

"Dr. Jackson, during your examination of the victim, were you able to determine the cause of death?"

"Yes, I was."

"Would you please tell the jury what that cause was and how you arrived at your conclusion?"

Don Jackson crossed his legs and clasped his hands. Gail knew he had been in this position many times before and he was incredibly comfortable on the stand. "The murderer approached the victim from behind and, I believe, used a technique taught in the armed forces. He grasped her chin with his left hand and pulled up and back. This causes the neck to rotate backward and lifts the chin to expose the throat. In the same motion he pulled the murder weapon—in this case a very sharp knife—across the throat exactly at the point where the chin meets the neck and just behind the jaw. He used a great deal of force."

"How much force? Would you elaborate on that, please?"

"Yes, of course. Enough force that there are knife marks

on the inside of the C2 and C3 vertebrae. The victim's neck is a little more than four inches thick, meaning the knife cut through just over two inches of flesh. All four major blood vessels in her neck were severed, and she bled to death in perhaps two minutes at most, and was unconscious within fifteen seconds. The angle of the cut suggests the attacker is right-handed. He made multiple passes, which we were able to ascertain from the cut marks in and around the soft tissues, as well as the neck bones."

"Could the knife in question have made this cut?"

"Yes."

"Please explain."

"In order to make a cut of this nature, the knife would have to be long and very sharp. After examining the knife, I found it to be of extraordinary sharpness and long enough to accomplish its task."

"How were you able to make that determination?"

"Pork."

"Did you say 'pork'?"

"Yes. I used the knife on a pig carcass. I was able to simulate the cut on the throat of a pig."

Carl Franklin set his notes aside. "Would anyone have heard her scream?"

"No. The cutting technique used would have prevented any audible sounds from the victim other than gurgling. The trachea is cut within a fraction of a second. While the victim would have struggled briefly, she would have been unconscious almost before she knew what happened."

"Could she have fought back?"

"There are no signs of a struggle other than what happened in the few seconds she remained conscious. The blood on her hands is the result of panic whereby she reached for her throat in a reflexive action."

"Do you think that Lisa Martin understood what was happening to her?"

"Yes, I do. That reaction I just spoke of—she would have

125

known her throat was cut. She would have felt the wound and known she was going to die. She may have only known that for a few seconds, but she knew it."

"Thank you, Dr. Jackson. Nothing further, Your Honor."

Mike Gordon ambled to the podium like a man who had a secret. Even without seeing his face, Gail knew the secret was a good one, because she knew it as well as anyone who had the information.

"Dr. Jackson, just how thorough was the autopsy you performed on Mrs. Martin?"

"It was very thorough. I examined the body for bruising consistent with a struggle or with confinement and for the presence of foreign matter. I looked for prints, sores, cuts, abrasions, semen, and hair. We checked for pregnancy, lingering diseases, the presence of alcohol or drugs. You name it, we looked for it."

"Dr. Jackson," Gordon said as he turned to his desk for fresh notes, "let me ask you a question regarding the defendant, if you don't mind."

"Of course," replied Jackson, who appeared content to remain on the stand for as long as it took.

"Dr. Jackson, are you aware that James Hodges has been diagnosed with Huntington's disease?"

"I am."

"Are you familiar with his condition?"

"I am."

"Please explain."

Don Jackson did not seem to be a man who would shirk his duty and immediately dove into a long and detailed explanation of the disease James Hodges was said to be carrying. After the long expository, the county's senior medical officer finally weighed in on the question Gail knew was coming.

"Could James Hodges make this kind of cut considering his condition?" Gordon demanded.

"I think it would be quite difficult."

"No further questions," Gordon said as he took his seat.

The prosecution was no dummy and immediately sought

permission to redirect.

"Perhaps it would be difficult," Carl Franklin said with a crooked smile, "but would it be possible?"

"Yes," stated the always honest examiner, "it would be possible."

Carl finished with Don Jackson and then proceeded to parade three other professional witnesses across the stand, whose testimonies ranged from short and exciting to long and boring. More photographs and transparencies were presented. Then, just before lunch, Carl called Sam Reynolds.

"Now, Mr. Reynolds, you're something of a drifter, are you not?"

"I get around a bit. Right now, I'm working at the Square Nines as a ranch hand."

"How long have you been doing that?"

"About six months, I think."

"Exciting work?"

"Not really. Most days it's kind of boring."

"What do you do for excitement?"

"Oh, I don't know. I sometimes go down to The Sawyer."

"The Sawyer?"

"Yeah. It's over there on Broadway. Me and some of the fellas like to go in there and have a couple beers."

"Ever had any trouble in there?"

"Yeah. A few times."

"Tell me, Mr. Reynolds. Have you ever seen the defendant before?"

"Yes, sir. He's the cause of one of them few times I've had trouble."

"Would you please describe that incident?"

"What's that?"

"I said, would you please describe that incident?"

"Oh, yeah. See, I was in there for a drink and I was sitting at the bar. Lisa, she worked there, and me and her had a, uh, an understanding about certain things, if you know what I mean. She wasn't being taken care of at home, like that, and so we were getting things done."

There was a groan from Gail's left. She turned and watched as Kipp Martin slipped from the bench and left the courtroom. When she turned back to the witness stand, the look on Sam's face had changed. He was grinning from ear to ear and she knew he felt a sick sense of victory.

"So, anyway, this dude here come into the bar." He pointed at James.

Carl Franklin held his hand up to silence the witness. "Your Honor," he said, "if it please the court, may we have the record reflect that the witness has pointed to the defendant."

"So the record shall reflect," Judge Parker responded. "Mr. Reynolds, you may continue."

"Okay. So, Hodges sat down at the bar and started flirting with Lisa. Well, now, I don't take too kindly to anyone flirting with my girl, so I started to listen and I hear him say to her, 'You're gonna sleep with me tonight' like it's an order or something. I got real mad about that, so I went over there and got in his face about it."

Sam went on to describe the fight. James went outside, Sam followed. There was some yelling and cursing, and the bar's patrons yelled their support for this participant or that. First it was just words, then threats, then fists. Sam was stronger and came away victorious.

"So that was that. He ain't been in The Sawyer since."

Carl returned to the table. "Who threw the first punch?"

"Say that again?"

"I said, who threw the first punch?"

"Oh, I don't remember. No, wait, yes I do. James did. Yeah, it was him."

Gail noted that James kept his head down, and she wondered what he was looking at. His hands were in his lap, and they were shaking.

"No further questions, Your Honor."

A long period of silence enveloped the courtroom as the prosecutor retook his chair.

Eventually, with a little prompting from Judge Parker, Mike Gordon rose and approached the podium. He appeared frustrated, and Gail had no idea why.

"Mr. Reynolds," Gordon asked, "how often do you go to The Sawyer?"

Reynolds shuffled in the jury box. "I don't know, maybe once a month or so."

"Did you say once a month?"

"Yeah. Sometimes more, sometimes less."

"And you said you had 'a couple beers,' is that correct."

"Yeah. You know, I ain't much of a drinker."

"Oh, really. Well, Mr. Reynolds, would it surprise you that I have depositions here from three witnesses willing to testify that you, sir, are at The Sawyer *every* Friday evening, and that you drink until you have to be helped out of the bar?"

Reynolds remained silent as he scanned the room.

"Mr. Sawyer?"

"Well, sometimes I'm there a bit more, I guess."

"You guess?"

"Hey, man, it ain't like I keep track or anything."

"You don't keep track?"

"No, sir. Ain't got time to worry about that."

"So you just kind of make it up as you go along?"

"Objection," called Franklin.

"I'll rephrase," Gordon shouted. "Mr. Reynolds, you earlier said you don't drink very much. Would you say that is not entirely true?"

"I suppose."

"And now that there is proof to the contrary, would it be fair to say that you visit the Sawyer more than once per month?"

"I suppose."

There was mumbling from the jury until Judge Parker was forced to silence them.

Gordon continued to spar with the witness. "Kind of like the way you make up the details regarding the fight you had with my client?"

"Objection!"

"I'll rephrase," Gordon said as he squeezed harder. "Did you throw the first punch?"

"No."

"Who threw the first punch?"

"What?"

"Who threw the first punch?"

Carl Franklin rose immediately. "Objection, Your Honor. The witness has already answered that question."

"Who threw it?" Gordon demanded.

"Counselor," shouted judge Parker. "I have not yet ruled on the objection!"

"I did," said Reynolds over the yelling. "I mean, he did."

"Who?" asked Gordon.

The gavel slammed. "Overruled!" Parker bellowed. "Now, get yourselves in order!"

Gordon withdrew from his aggressive stance and Carl Franklin sank back to his chair, shaking his head in disbelief.

"Mr. Reynolds," Gordon demanded, "you seem to be having trouble with this, so I'll ask again. Who threw the first punch?"

Sam Reynolds sunk into his chair and Gail knew he was cornered. "Hodges started it. He was hitting on my woman. He deserved a good beating. Punched that clown right in the face, I did. And I'd do it again."

"So, you hit him first?"

"Damn right I did!"

"Yet you just told this jury it was James Hodges that swung first."

"I don't remember." Reynolds said as he turned his eyes from the jury.

"So, now you don't remember? If you don't remember what happened outside, how can you possibly expect this jury to believe you remember what happened inside?"

Reynolds leaned forward, but Gordon cut him off. "No

further questions." He strutted back to his seat and smiled as he wrote on the legal pad before him.

EIGHT

"Doesn't this booth ever get old?" Gail asked with playful contempt.

"What do you mean?" Josh responded.

Gail slid around on the faded vinyl and tried to get comfortable. "Same place every day. Same restaurant, same seat, same food."

"When you've been coming here as long as I have, it gets to feeling a bit like home."

"I've been to your home. It needs a little help, so I guess I can understand."

Josh laughed out loud. "Woman, you sure have a way about you."

Gail remembered the dented couch and the messy kitchen and thought he needed to put a little more time into it. Of course, she was comparing her immaculate little apartment and her boring little life to his big country home and the non-stop business to which he attended. Perhaps it was a bit unfair to judge him that way. "I'm sorry."

"No need to be. I was never much inside the house. I took care of the yard and the job. Alyson took care of the kitchen. That was our way. When she died . . ." Josh's voice trailed off and his eyes went out the window. "Meredith took over when she was old enough, and it was about the same."

Gail could see a trace of pain building in his eyes, and she quickly changed the subject. "The jurors are kind of all over the place, aren't they?"

Josh shrugged. "Don't know that I paid much attention. I've only met a few of them."

"What do you think about Jacob Powell? Does he seem a bit odd to you?"

"What do you mean?" Josh asked as he set his coffee down and leaned back.

"I don't know, there's just something about him. He doesn't take notes and just sort of, I don't know, stares straight ahead."

"You have to know Powell. Most arrogant man I've ever met. Thick with money and full of his own worth. I'm sure he's thinking he's above this kind of thing. Never have liked him."

"I've only met him briefly."

"You spend any time with him?"

"Not really," Gail said. "I did an interview with him for the paper a few weeks ago. Just some input about the bridge tournament and his sponsorship."

"I read that article," Josh said through a cheesy smile. "It was well done. And don't worry about Powell. He strikes me as the kind of man who only cares about himself." The sheriff wiggled uncomfortably in his seat. "What about Diego? What do you think of him?"

"Mr. Lopez?"

"Yeah."

"Oh, he's wonderful. I love the way he scratches under his chin when he thinks someone is lying."

"How do you know he thinks they're lying?"

"Because when he believes them, he nods his head."

"You're sure?"

"Oh, yes." She tilted her head back and scratched at the soft skin under her chin. "Like this. I can see it in his eyes. He's a good judge of character, I think."

"You can tell that by itching and nodding?"

"Sure. Can't you?" She smiled and tapped his hand. She'd caught him off guard with the question and enjoyed her temporary position of power over him. "What about Maggie Johnson?"

"Again, don't know much about her. She's the woman from Frenchglen, right?"

"Yes," Gail answered as she sipped her coffee.

"Frenchglen is about sixty miles south of here. Ever been down there?" Josh asked.

"No."

"Quaint little place. There's about fifteen folks living down there. Other than passing through occasionally, I've not spent much time there. Although I recall having been there for a town hall meeting once, and I distinctly remember meeting Maggie Johnson, but only briefly. She didn't have much to say to me."

Gail thought the town sounded very romantic. Josh described it as a one-horse town famous only for its motel and bird watching. "Mrs. Johnson seems like she's sizing the witnesses up based on some sort of personal scale. She takes a lot of notes and shakes her head a lot! She's driving me nuts with all that head bobbing and the way her hands speak so loudly. It's like she's trying to guide an airplane to park but has no idea what she's doing."

Josh laughed at her joke. "Okay, enough of her. What have you got to say about the witnesses so far?"

"Oh, I don't know. I think there are some holes in the state's case."

"Oh, really?" Josh's demeanor changed suddenly, and she thought he might be offended.

"Yeah, well, I don't want to ruffle any feathers."

"Of course you do. You're a reporter."

"Maybe I should just wait until the story is finished."

The look on Josh's face demonstrated his frustration. She knew how important the case was to him. She knew he'd spent countless hours chasing down leads, hunting the scene for evidence, and interviewing witnesses. To challenge the state was to challenge him, and she didn't want to go down that road.

She checked her watch. "Almost time."

Josh stood from the booth. "Walk you back?"

"Of course."

Josh waved Connie over and asked for the bill. "I'm on right after lunch. Wouldn't want to be late."

The waitress appeared and leaned on the table. "Well, Sheriff," Connie said with her usual spunk, "you gotta be quick around here. Your date already asked for the tab."

Gail smiled at her little coup, and then felt her jaw drop when the waitress handed the bill to the sheriff.

Gail shot the waitress a surprised look. "Hey, you little backstabber."

"Yeah, well, he tips better," Connie shot back with a sneer.

"Oh, you—" Gail caught herself and gave the waitress a look before following the sheriff toward the door.

The walk back to the courthouse was short and quiet. Gail caught Josh watching her, and her heart skipped. In her estimation, he was no ordinary sixty-one-year-old man. His tan, lean muscles gave up a history of hard work and vigorous exercise while his dark hair was only beginning to grey and his lightly wrinkled skin showed few signs of aging. And that was only accounting for the physical attraction she felt toward him. He also had a strong, masculine personality and didn't bend easily, even though his serious side was easily conquered with a touch of humor.

She caught the lawman peeking at his watch and smiled at his sense of punctuality. She suspected he had never been late for anything.

❈ ❈ ❈

If it hadn't been for the stimulating conversation with Gail, Josh would have called lunch depressing, if not intolerable. It wasn't that good, but he'd been hungry and had choked it down. As he stepped into the men's room, it occurred to him that the burger wasn't really that bad. Rather, he was more nervous than he had been in many years. Thinking back, he couldn't even count the number of times he had sat in a witness chair to spew his knowledge and even the occasional mistake. Yet, for some reason he could not explain, the murder of Lisa Martin had him on edge and he dreaded what he knew was coming.

Mike Gordon was shrewd. He would leave no stone unturned, and Josh thought long and hard about his past and what might be dragged out for display. Sure, his relationship with the defendant was strained at times, and it was true that Josh had no love for the man. But he had never acted outside the law. His dealings with James Hodges had always been in response to some wrong the vagrant had committed, and always within the boundaries permitted him. He was quite certain that Mike Gordon would attack him over some baseless accusation, just as he had done with the deputies, and he carefully prepared his temper to cope with just such a possibility.

As he stepped from the men's room, Josh caught Gail in the hall and took her by the arm, leading her to a bench where they sat down. "I need a favor," he said.

Gail smiled and gave him a flirtatious look. "Anything for you, Sheriff."

Josh blushed at her subtle advance before recovering himself. "An old friend of mine, a rancher who lives out by Riley, had himself a rustler."

Gail's eyes burst open with excitement. "You mean like in the Wild West?"

"Yeah, sure, something like that."

"Did they take the whole herd?"

"No, they took one bull, a prized bull—"

"Well," she interrupted, "that doesn't sound like much fun."

Josh stopped her. "This is really serious."

"Sorry," she said.

"I need you to do a story on it. My friend, his name is Russell Ulrich, he lives just down the road from where Nikki Rhodes was murdered."

Gail's excitement returned. "Are you serious? She's on the list, right? I've read the file."

"Yes. Anyway, I want to get the story out, maybe remind people that the bull was taken near the scene of a murder they've forgotten about. Perhaps it will shake something loose."

"Okay, I see where you're going. Can I talk to this Russell fellow, ask him some questions?"

"Of course. He wants his bull back, or to at least be compensated for it, so he wants these people found. More important, I want to see if we can knock some fruit out of the trees."

"I'll write a nice, juicy bit. You'll like it, I promise."

Josh stood up as Carl Franklin approached.

"Sheriff."

"Carl."

"You ready?"

"No, but let's get it over with." He turned to Gail. "I'll talk with you later."

"Sure," she said, "I'll make a call and see if I can get down there right after court."

Josh stood at the bailiff's beckoning call and wondered if anyone else was tired of that particular drudgery. He thought the man was kind of squeaky, like he was talking through his nose.

He grumbled under his breath and snarled when the bailiff said "Be seated." But he waited patiently as Judge Parker looked around the room, asked his usual questions, then turned the floor over to the prosecution for its final witness. Josh approached with his hat in his hand and turned to take the oath. "I do," he said in his baritone.

Carl Franklin stood and turned to the jury. "Sheriff Matthews, would you please tell this court your occupation."

"Yes," Josh said as he cleared his throat. "I am the duly

elected sheriff of Harney County."

"And how long have you been sheriff?"

"I was first elected in 1952 and took office in 1953. So I am in my twenty-eighth year of service."

"So would it be safe to say that you have a lot of experience in matters of the law?"

Josh shrugged. "Yes, it would be safe to say that."

"Are you good at your job, Sheriff?"

Josh wiggled uncomfortably. "I think that question is better asked of the people of Harney County."

"Fair enough," said Franklin. "Considering you're in your eighth cycle, I would say the people are pretty happy with you. So, tell me, Sheriff Matthews, in your own words, what transpired on the morning of May 15 of this year?"

Josh turned to the jury and began. He related the events as he remembered them, from taking the call first thing in the morning, to his drive up the hill, the body, and walking the area looking for evidence. He told of his discussion with Max, his supervision of Jane Smith as she photographed the scene, and a late-afternoon conversation with a trooper from the Oregon state police.

"And, Sheriff, what conclusion did you come to?"

"That Lisa Martin was murdered and we needed to find her killer."

Carl Franklin turned a page in his notebook. "We learned from deputy Shafer that there were other suspects early on in your investigation."

"That is mostly correct," Josh said.

"What do you mean by that, Sheriff Matthews?"

"Well," Josh said as he adjusted his seating position, "there were persons of interest, not suspects."

"Would you please tell this court the difference?"

"Of course. A person of interest is someone who we believe may or may not have important information, or perhaps a slippery alibi. A suspect is someone whom we think may have actually committed the crime."

"And what happened with those 'persons of interest'?"

"We ruled out both of them."

"And who were those people, again?" Carl asked.

"A ranch hand named Sam Reynolds, and Robert Carter."

"And why were they not pursued?"

"Both had sound alibis, and neither had sufficient motive."

"And the accused?"

Josh adjusted in the chair again and glanced at the defendant. "Mr. Hodges had no alibi, ample motive, and irrefutable evidence in his possession."

Carl stepped over to the evidence table and brought back a plastic bag. "Do you recognize this, Sheriff?"

"Yes, I do. That is the knife we found on James Hodges."

"Sheriff Matthews, did you find this knife?"

"Yes."

"Where did you find it?"

"On the defendant, tucked into his pants behind his shirt."

Carl returned the knife and brought forward another bag. "Recognize this?"

"Yes, I do. Deputy Smith found that shirt with James Hodges just after we found the knife. It was in a bag that we found next to James's tent. When we asked who it belonged to, James took responsibility for it."

"Thank you, Sheriff," Carl said as he returned to his seat. "No further questions."

Judge Parker made the usual notes, eyed the courtroom, and then gave Mike Gordon his turn.

"Sheriff Matthews," said Gordon as he looked Josh over.

"Mike," replied Josh with a trace of disgust.

Mike Gordon looked at his notes, and Josh could see a taunting smile on his face.

"Sheriff," Gordon began, "is it possible that Lisa Martin's killer stopped at that turnout, parked his own car there, forced her into her own passenger seat, drove her to the murder scene, got out of the car, killed her, planted the murder weapon in my client's trash can, then drove back down the hill, returned to his own car, and drove away? Is that possible?"

Josh rolled his eyes. "I am not here to speculate, counselor."

"I did not ask you to speculate, Sheriff Matthews. I asked if this scenario would be possible."

Josh thought about his answer for a brief moment, knowing full well that Gordon was trying to trap him. When the answer came, he was proud of himself. "Yes," he said, "it is very possible that James could have done that."

Gordon stared Josh in the eye and seemed surprised that he could come up with such an answer. Then he coughed, rummaged in his notes, and tried again. "Sheriff, perhaps you did not understand the question."

"Oh," Josh interrupted, "I understood it perfectly."

"Sheriff," barked Judge Parker, "please wait for the question."

Josh looked at his old acquaintance and smirked.

Gordon changed the subject. "Sheriff, prior to this case, have you had any run-ins with my client?"

Josh had known the question was coming but wasn't prepared for how far Gordon would take it.

"Objection, Your Honor," Carl Franklin said from his seat. "Relevance."

"Your Honor," said Mike Gordon, "relevance applies here. I intend to show the sheriff's department has been after my client for many years."

"Overruled," Parker said as if bored. "Mr. Gordon, keep it in check."

"Thank you, Your Honor. Now, Sheriff, do you have a personal vendetta against my client?"

Josh did not answer.

"Sheriff," Gordon demanded, "I'm waiting for an answer."

"I don't have one to give you."

Forced by law and character to be an impartial Judge, Parker had no choice but to put his foot down. "Answer the question, Sheriff," he said with a gruff, but respectful, tone.

Josh took a deep breath and held it until his cheeks began to color, then let it out in a long sigh. "I have no love for the man."

"I find it unfathomable that you don't like my client, by your own words, and it just so happens that he is the person you arrested for this crime."

"Objection," Carl Franklin shouted. "The state would like to know if defense's statement is a question or an attack."

"Withdrawn," Gordon said. "I'll rephrase."

And then it happened.

"Sheriff Matthews," Gordon asked, "does my client have a history with anyone in your family? Like, say, your daughter?"

Josh felt his blood boil. It had happened far too long ago, and he would never have guessed Mike Gordon could have discovered it, or even bring it to light. Perhaps James Hodges had mentioned the incident in a conversation, but Josh refused to believe that even he would say anything about it. The actual truth as it happened could not make him look good.

"I'm waiting," Gordon said as he shuffled his feet.

Josh took a deep breath and let fly the answer, knowing he could not let even one moment of dishonesty stain the trial. "Yes," he said.

"Sheriff," asked Gordon, "is it true that your daughter, Meredith Matthews, had a sexual relationship with my client?"

Carl Franklin bolted upright from his desk and slammed both fists on the table. "Objection, Your Honor! Hearsay."

Gordon responded immediately. "Your Honor, I can and will show this court extreme prejudice against my client on the part of the Harney County Sheriff's Department. My client has a right to unearth any and all evidence in his favor, and this line will prove that Sheriff Matthews has a long-standing grudge against Mr. Hodges."

Josh saw the look in Judge Parker's eyes and knew he and himself shared a common position. The truth must be told, even if it might embarrass the sheriff.

"Overruled. Please answer the question, Sheriff."

Josh noted the disgusted tone in Parker's voice, but there was nothing to be done. "Yes," Josh said, "Hodges and my daughter had a sexual relationship for a very short time."

"I see," Gordon said with mocking drama. He turned to the jury for effect, and then continued to pester. "And how did you feel about that?"

"I was not happy."

Gordon's lower lip protruded, and a gleam of happiness sparkled in his eyes. "So, your daughter fell for my client, and you were unhappy. Makes you pretty mad, doesn't it?"

Josh refused to answer.

"Mad enough to, oh, I don't know, overlook evidence?"

"No," Josh barked.

"Maybe look the other way when investigating another suspect?"

"No!"

Mike Gordon took a deep breath as he looked at each pair of eyes in the jury. Josh watched him gloating, and it made him see red, but he kept his tongue in check.

Mike Gordon was not finished. "Sheriff, did you approve of my client's relationship with your daughter?"

"No," Josh said, "I did not."

"Sheriff Matthews," continued Gordon, "there is a young lady named Linda Hollingsworth who lives in Hines. She worked with your daughter and is prepared to give a sworn statement in front of this court that she heard you tell my client that you would see him rot in jail if he ever came near Meredith again. She will testify that you said, and I quote, 'No matter what it takes. I'll put you behind bars if I have to,' end quote." Gordon shuffled his notes and held up a piece of paper. "Miss. Hollingsworth is on the approved witness list. Now, Sheriff, we can hear from you, or we can hear from her. Which is it?"

Josh was trapped and he knew it. The incident had happened not long after Meredith graduated nursing school and was working at the local hospital. And it was true, every word of it. James had gotten cleaned up and met her at the Sawyer, told her stories and conned her. Josh had been hot-blooded angry that James Hodges had taken advantage of his only child, had tricked her to satisfy his selfish desires. She had been torn for weeks about the incident and could scarcely bring herself to tell her father that a man she barely knew had convinced her he would change her world, only to walk away once his urges had been satisfied. Josh Matthews had indeed threatened James should he ever come near Meredith again, and for good reason.

And so he was trapped. Gordon would not let him tell the entire story, as it would cause as much harm to his client as it would to Josh. The only escape Josh could see would be if Carl Franklin had the sense to call for a redirect.

"Your witness would be telling the truth," Josh said, and he said nothing else. Gordon attempted to get him to say it some other way, but Josh kept his answers short. And it didn't matter anyway. The jury was already looking scornfully at him, especially Maggie Johnson whom Josh sensed was damning him to a life in hellfire for raising such faulty children.

When he was finished embarrassing Josh, Gordon returned to his seat, appearing happy that the Harney County sheriff was left squirming.

Carl immediately stood from his table and addressed the judge. "Prosecution wishes to redirect on this line of questioning," he said.

There was the obligatory objection from the defense, but Josh sighed with relief after Judge Parker overruled, and for the next five minutes was given the opportunity to relay the story as it had actually happened. Whether or not it would do any good, he had no idea, but at least all present would understand why he had said what he did.

Feeling like he'd been in a brawl, Josh was excused from the witness stand. All of his pride and ego commanded that he storm through the large double doors at the back of the courtroom, but he restrained his anger and reclaimed his seat next to the sympathetic reporter whose comfort he now desperately needed. Her hand rested on his and he squeezed her dainty fingers.

* * *

"Don't recall it too well," said Russell Ulrich, who sat watching the far distant horizon. "Seems to me Matthews— that's the sheriff, you see—seems to me he was pretty upset about that."

"Can you tell me why?" Gail asked as she crossed her legs to guard herself from the ranchers flitting eyes.

Ulrich fawned over his guest and smiled a crooked, longing smile. "There was a roundup that week. Mustangs was being brought in from all over the valley, and there was a lot of people coming in from places like Boise and Portland. Folks with money. Kids wanting a horse so they could pretend to be cowboys, farmers looking for working stock, ranchers, even some real cowboys out to replace their mount. Real popular thing, that roundup. Mustangs can fetch, oh, four or five hundred dollars for a good one. The mangier ones sometimes go for free, but a real good horse would get a nice bit.

"So, right in the middle of all that, this girl is found right up in them hills, right there." The rancher pointed out to the north above his ranch. "Wasn't anybody up there 'cept the loggers, of course, but it didn't matter. News got to town, and the whole place went bananas. Pretty soon there was reporters and gawkers all up and down the highway. Everybody wanting to see the mountains where the lady was found."

"Didn't you find it strange," Gail asked, "that she was found so far in the hills?"

"Oh, no," Russell said through his stained teeth. "Women was always up in there when the crews was working. Not a lot of women, mind you, but the right kind of women. Or the wrong kind, if you catch my meaning."

Gail averted her eyes and pulled down on her skirt. "I do. Was this woman, Nikki Rhodes, that kind of woman?"

"Darned if I know," Russell said with a spit of tobacco. "Never had myself a hooker, so I wouldn't know the type. But —and you can take this as fact—if there was women up there with those rough types, you can bet your bosom they wasn't the good kind of women."

Gail kept pace with her pencil and, after making a note or two, turned her attention to the rancher's bull. There wasn't much to learn that she hadn't already heard from the sheriff, but she wanted Russell Ulrich to believe he was being interviewed for something that seemed more important to him than a murder from long in his past. She got the details, thanked him, and made for her car, stopping occasionally to take a photograph and admire the crisp, clean air. There was something about the fresh-cut alfalfa that reminded her of the garden her mother kept, and she drew in the pleasant aroma before driving away with the evening sun at her back.

At dinner, Gail watched as Josh squirted ketchup onto his plate and angrily dug into it with his fries. He seemed a bit down-trodden after his testimony, but she knew that his own struggles with Mike Gordon's relentless attack were the least of his worries. Gordon had called Connie as his first witness earlier in the day and pulled out all the stops. At first, he'd made her think he was a friend and showed the court how much she liked James Hodges, even sneaking him an occasional bite out the back door. However, he soon turned on her and had her in tears when she left the stand. Carl Franklin had had to mop things up and present the jury with a rock-solid alibi. Unfortunately, that alibi involved a table of cowboys who'd kept her busy at the diner until well-passed closing time. She had taken a liking to one of the men and taken him home, leaving Connie Newcastle feeling like a tramp before the scornful eyes of the jury.

"Gordon is a fink," Josh said as he stabbed around in the ketchup. "What is he thinking?"

"He's thinking," Gail said, "that he's going to do whatever it takes to get his client an acquittal."

"Well," Josh said with a pale expression, "don't be surprised if he has another of those tricks up his sleeve."

"What is that supposed to mean?" Gail asked through a mouthful of salad.

"We dug pretty deep into Robert Carter's affair with Lisa Martin."

"Deep enough to know that he didn't kill her?"

"Oh, we know he didn't do it. We asked around the office, followed several leads, and tossed them out when they all came to a dead end."

"You're positive they all ended like that? Why would you suggest Gordon had something up his sleeve?"

"An anonymous person mailed an envelope to Carl's office, and he got it this morning while I was on the stand."

"And?" Gail asked with great suspense.

Josh shuffled his feet and gave a nervous laugh. "It held two dozen or so photographs of Robert Carter and Lisa Martin in, well, rather compromising situations. Let's just say his wife will not be happy."

"Sex?" Gail asked in surprise.

"Not the act, but there is nudity."

"His or hers?" she asked with obvious excitement.

"Hers," Josh said. "And a lot of it."

"Oh, dear." Gail laughed. "That's no good."

Josh shook his head. "Lisa Martin showed it all to Robert Carter in the cozy confines of his office with a window wide open. It's almost as if the window was intended to be open, it's that obvious."

Gail sat back and played with an onion ring. Somewhere she had picked up the curious habit of unraveling the deep-fried wonders and presenting the crispy shell to her friends in one piece. Now, in a nostalgic effort, she repeated the nervous trick. "Maybe Mr. Carter was being blackmailed and got desperate. And maybe," she said as she teased at Josh with her fork, "he hired someone to do it."

Josh smiled at her. "We've already pursued that avenue and found nothing. Yes, he and his little sweetheart met in the office supply room and over at the Shady Eight for some fun. But old Carter isn't capable of murder, or murder for hire, although I'm certain Gordon will paint him that way."

"Are you absolutely sure?" Gail was very serious now, and she knew that Josh knew it.

He nodded. "Having an affair and lying about it doesn't shift evidence out of James Hodges's corner."

"Unless Carter planted the evidence," Gail offered.

"You really think that old bird killed his lover and planted the evidence on James?"

"Maybe."

"Listen, Gail," said the sheriff with a stiff tone. "Carter is nice enough, a bit crazy, and feeling old and useless, but the man can't walk ten blocks, let alone a quarter mile up a creek bed at night."

"I don't think it's fair to judge a man's worth by his age. Perhaps—"

"Not Carter. He's just old. I'm surprised he can get his parts to work."

Gail laughed. "His 'parts'?"

"Well, what do you want me to say?"

She laughed harder. "Well, anything but 'parts.'"

Josh's face flushed.

"Why, Josh Matthews," she giggled, "are you embarrassed?"

"Is it that obvious?"

"I think you should take me dancing."

Josh paused at the sudden request. "Talk about changing the subject."

"It's Thursday night. You know what that means?"

"Dare I ask?"

"It's lady's night at The Wagon Wheel."

Josh sighed. "I haven't danced since ..." His eyes wandered

out the window and Gail knew he was thinking about someone else.

"Hey," she said as she touched his hand.

"Yeah. Sorry."

"Josh, it's okay to miss her."

"Miss who?"

"Oh, come on. I haven't known you long, but I know you well enough." Gail squeezed his hand and felt her own loneliness through the look on his face. She didn't sense that he was hurting per se, but that he was lonely and didn't know what to do about it.

Finally, he broke the awkward silence. "I haven't danced since just after the war."

Gail smiled at the open-ended opportunity. "Do you still remember how?"

"Is it like that whole 'riding a bike' thing?"

She smiled and laughed. "I don't know, maybe. I guess we'll find out." She stood from the table and took his hand. "Come on. Dance with me. I promise, no strings. Just dancing."

Gail refused to let the sheriff off, and continued to tug at him until he stood from the booth and followed behind her. Fifteen minutes later, she was leading him into The Wagon Wheel country bar. Tired of him always getting the check, she quickly found a bartender and ordered two drinks—bourbon—and then found a table near the dance floor.

Josh studied the patrons until he seemed satisfied with his surroundings. "Now, give me a minute to get comfortable," he said.

As he pulled out a chair, Gail grabbed his hand and headed for the floor. "Oh, no, you don't."

"Oh, come on. I want to sit and have my drink."

She refused and led him to the dance floor, hooked his shoulder, and followed his unpolished lead. Before the sheriff had had time to finish his first drink, Gail had refreshed his mind and body in the two-step, the three-step, line dancing, and everything in between. City girl or not, she knew the moves, and she whirled and twirled with Josh until nearly one in the morning. When he finally signaled that the end of the evening had come for him, she cut him loose and went home.

Once dressed down into a comfy set of pajamas, Gail found her attention once again consumed by her evidence board with its interconnected tangle of photographs. The board was a mess, and as she wound down for bed, she wrote a new name and placed it beneath Lisa Martin's picture. "Robert Carter," she said. "What are you doing on my board?"

That done, she crawled into bed and turned out the light.

❋ ❋ ❋

Josh scanned the front page for something worth reading and found little. As he thumbed through the pages he stumbled on an op-ed article, hidden away on page 5, written by one Gail Cruz. He sipped his whiskey and started in. "Before I came to Oregon," the article began, "I thought of rustling as something of an outdated crime. In the not too distant past, men of negative report roamed these valleys in search of an easy living, sometimes living off the hard work and sweat of men bigger and better than themselves. Cattle roamed the prairies and were at times an easy target. Men with the proper skill and experience might break off a small number of wayward heifers, herd them to some predetermined location, rebrand them, and sell them cheap on the market. This practice became a pandemic that spread across the untamed West, sometimes stripping entire herds from their rightful owners, and often leading to murder."

Josh smiled at the clever reporter's segue.

"This past week," the story continued, "the age-old art of rustling reared its ugly head within the boundaries of Harney County. Russell Ulrich, a respected and seasoned cattle rancher from Riley woke up one morning last week to find a prized bull missing from his pasture. An investigation, headed by Harney County Sheriff Josh Matthews, discovered that the bull was taken sometime late on the night of June 17 of this year. The fence was smartly cut and patched to mask the theft, but fresh tire tracks gave away the affair. Sheriff Matthews tracked the rustlers into the mountains north of Riley, but lost the trail in an all too familiar place."

Josh set the paper down and poured a second whiskey. "Very nice, Gail," he said, "very nice."

"During that investigation, our good sheriff paused to consider where he stood. In the place where the trail was lost—and just up the hill—lay the scene of a murder that still haunts this county's residents. Unlike the recent murder of Lisa Martin, whose primary suspect is currently standing trial within the halls of the county court house, the murder of Nikki Rhodes still holds no leads. Eleven years' worth of dead ends have led to nothing more than wishful thinking.

"Yet could there be clues revealed as a direct result of this stolen bull? Sheriff Matthews thinks so. He has explained to this reporter in great detail just how much returning to the original murder scene has spurned new ideas through fresh eyes. While the sheriff is unwilling to elaborate on the details, he is convinced that law enforcement is getting closer to the truth.

"The murder of Nikki Rhodes and cattle rustling may not be directly connected, but both are certainly rooted in their past as a means for cowards to express power they do not ordinarily have. To take what they do not own, to harm those who stand in their way, and to force upon the weak a form of cowardice that must be removed from our society if we are to remain free and civilized.

"I have heard some of our citizens call for the removal of our sheriff. This writer does not support such an effort. We must let go of our own pride and help where we can by referring to the sheriff's department any and all knowledge of these crimes. Whether the murder of one of our own or a stolen cow, the difference within the halls of justice amounts to nothing. If you have knowledge of the rustling of Russell Ulrich's prized bull or the murders of Annette Walker, Nikki Rhodes, Gina Bergmann, or Eryn Rogers, please, without delay, contact the Harney County Sheriff's Department and help put an end to this insanity."

Josh laid the paper down and finished his whiskey. He took a deep breath and pulled in the aroma of alfalfa wafting on the wind, then took a drag from the cigar smoldering in his hand. He wasn't certain if the strategy would work, and he hated the idea of lying to the people, even if the lie in question was intended to draw a murderer out of hiding. As he thought about it, he returned to the idea that the same person might have committed some of the earlier murders. That in itself presented a problem that had troubled him years ago. Although he had put it aside for lack of evidence, the possibility existed that a serial killer had been responsible for at least some of these murders, and that killer could not possibly have been James Hodges.

Also on his mind was Connie. While he knew in his heart the waitress was not involved in Lisa Martin's murder, he worried over the effect it would have within the community. After her testimony there'd been a lot of talk that she had as much reason to kill Lisa as anyone, but Carl franklin proved her alibi was rock solid. Still, the intent was to confuse the issue and draw attention away from James Hodges, to place the slightest hint of doubt within the jurors' minds. If doubt existed within the community, then it certainly existed within the jury, and it was beginning to exist in Josh's mind. Something was off, and he couldn't sort it out. If Dusty Stevens was telling the truth, then a man who was a stranger to the campers had passed through their camp in the middle of the night and could very well have placed the knife and clothing into that waste barrel where it was found by the defendant the following morning. In his state of intoxication, James may not have noticed the items were soaked in blood and simply assumed it was grease or some other contaminate to be wiped away on his pants.

Very soon after the arrest of James Hodges, Josh had interviewed Dusty Stevens. If a person never took the time to ask, they would never learn that Stevens was more than just a wayward homeless man. He was bright, articulate, well educated, and kind. He was also habitually high, down on his former employer, NASA, and bitter toward any and all government enterprise. The man, Josh learned, had seen enough wasted tax dollars, heard enough lies, and fought through enough red tape and corruption to leave him feeling as jaded as any individual could feel. Josh also felt a certain trust in him, an honest connection and understanding that the man called Dirt wasn't a liar. That left a bad taste in Josh's mouth. Were Dusty Stevens not a regular marijuana and heroin user, he could have run for any office and won in a landslide. Realizing that was the case, Josh put some cranium time into Dusty's story that a random individual had gone through the camp during the night of the murder.

He sipped at his whiskey and returned his mind to Gail's column. He liked the flow and the feeling behind it, which led him to better understand what was going on inside the woman's head. She was thoughtful and thought provoking, and he knew she was doing her best to help him. The feeling he encountered improved greatly when he remembered his breakfast date with her the next morning.

When the phone suddenly rang Josh rubbed his eyes, because it rang so infrequently that it meant trouble was either brewing or had already been brewed. He lifted himself from the couch and walked to the phone, where he sighed deeply and told himself not to take the call. It rang a fourth time, and Josh's mind flashed back to May 15 when it had brought the news of the accident and then, just a few hours later, of murder. He hated that phone, and he knew that if he picked it up his world would suffer. But duty called, and he knew he must take the call no matter what bad news it brought. On the sixth ring he tugged the receiver from the wall and answered in a voice that must have told the caller he was not in a good mood.

"Wow," said a sweet, melancholy voice on the other end. "That's some way to greet your daughter."

Josh sighed with relief and pulled a chair over from

the dining table. "Sorry, pumpkin," he said with his attitude checked.

"Are you having a bad day?" she asked.

"Very," Josh answered.

"I'm sorry." There was a pause on the other end before Meredith continued. "You know, Dad, you're pretty famous over here in Bend. Seems you've got quite the trial going on."

"Yeah," he said with mixed emotion. "It isn't going so well."

"Oh?" she said. "What happened?"

Josh didn't want to stir up the old wounds, but he had always been honest with his daughter and rarely hid anything from her. She was too precious to leave hanging and worrying over him. "James Hodges is on trial for murder," he said.

"That's what I've heard, Dad. How are you dealing with that?"

"I was on the stand yesterday."

"Why?"

Josh replayed the incident as best he could remember, leaving out not a single detail.

"So," said Meredith with an intellect Josh knew was gleaned from her days watching him work and studying the law books she found on the library shelf, "the defense is trying to show the jury you arrested James because of what he did to me. It's a good tactic."

"Are you serious?" he asked gruffly. "You agree with them?"

"Slow down, Dad. I didn't say I agreed with them. I only said it was a good tactic. It's desperate, but good. Let me guess: the defense attorney found someone to back up the claim?"

"Linda Hollingsworth," Josh said.

"Ha!" cried Meredith, "That cow? What a laugh. Carl Franklin could have buried her beneath a lifetime of perjury. That girl couldn't get the facts straight to save her life." Meredith went on for some minutes about the tactic she would have used—had she been a lawyer, of course.

Josh rubbed his forehead. "Whose child are you anyway?"

There was delightful laughter on the other end of the line. "I'm only the daughter of the best sheriff in the west."

Josh smiled and felt an emotion like homesickness. He missed his only child and wanted badly to reach out and hold her. She had been the crutch on which he walked for so many years that her leaving was like having the air sucked from his lungs. "I'll be through Bend in a couple weeks. I'd love to stop by."

"I'll have the guest room ready for you."

"You don't have to go to any trouble, Pumpkin."

"Oh, Dad, you're so funny. Like I would let you sleep in some dingy hotel."

They spoke like that for nearly an hour, and Josh learned of a recent promotion her husband had received and how much he loved his job at the airport; how Bend was growing and that they were skiing and horseback riding and hiking and loving their lives. They spoke of Melissa Reed and a tear slipped from Josh's eye when he heard Meredith crying. And then he smiled again when she spoke of their efforts to start a family, and more when she told him how much she missed her dad. She loved him, missed him, and couldn't wait to see him . . . and she had to go.

Josh placed the receiver back on the base and hung his head.

NINE

G ail was up with a start, exhausted from too little sleep, showered, dressed, and out the door. She drove through Hines in a fog, unable to wrap her mind around anything. Eventually she arrived at the diner a few minutes early and found the booth empty.

Connie stopped by with coffee. "He said to tell you he'd be over in the park."

Gail looked at Connie. "Any particular reason?"

"Don't know. I'm just the messenger."

"Okay, thanks." Gail took her coffee to go, ignored her hungry stomach, and returned to her car and drove north. The park was less than five minutes away. She found Josh sitting on a bench with his legs crossed, looking stressed. His eyes were bloodshot, and she knew he was not getting enough sleep. "You look terrible," she said as she approached.

"Good. Then I don't look worse than I feel." He shuffled and turned to meet her eyes. "Court's been cancelled for the day."

"Why?"

"Robert Carter has flat-out refused to testify, so Gordon asked for some time. Parker postponed for the day and gave Carter twenty-four hours or risk arrest. I get to give the old man the news."

"Chief Anderson isn't handling that?"

"Nope. This is a county case, and we get to deal with our own trouble. Nick Anderson is not involved in our mess."

"Gordon is going to go after Robert Carter hard, I think," Gail said as she nonchalantly scooted closer to Josh. "I mean, his wife is an old bat—she's mean, selfish, conceited, she won't comfort him or hold his hand or make love to him. So he did what a lot of lonely, older men do. He found a younger woman. Only he wasn't very discreet about it, and public knowledge will be very damning."

"Gordon is going to try to show motive."

"Well, of course he is!" Gail said, shaking her head.

"What he will not do is try to paint Carter as a man who might hire someone."

"That might lead the jury to believe that James is guilty as charged and was hired by Carter to take care of Lisa Martin."

Josh stretched his legs out in front of himself and reached over his head and yawned. "Right. So, he will try to paint Robert Carter as a desperate man who might have taken care of things himself."

"Reasonable doubt?"

"Sure," Josh said. "But Carter has a solid alibi."

Gail let her thoughts wander for a moment. "Problem is James has all the evidence and no motive, and it seems that maybe Carter has all the motive but no evidence."

"Does his wife know about the photos yet?"

"Not yet, but Gordon will show them in court. Then she'll know for sure and there'll be hell to pay. It will ruin him."

"So," Gail said in a suggestive tone, "it's looking like it was a murder for hire?"

"I don't know about that. Anyway, listen, I need to get over to the mill and have a talk with Mr. Carter."

"Mind if I tag along?" Gail asked as she gathered her purse.

"I can't let you interfere."

"I won't be any trouble."

Josh motioned to the truck.

While Gail felt a professional incentive to go with the sheriff, more than that was the opportunity to spend time with him. So, with the window open and a warm June breeze blowing in her hair, she leaned on the old truck's window frame and felt free. Riding with the sheriff felt a bit like riding across the prairie with an old cowboy, always on the lookout for bandits. The smell of the old truck brought back memories of her father, who'd owned a pickup not terribly dissimilar from this one, and it brought a loving smile to Gail's face.

"You okay over there?" Josh asked.

She turned to him and smiled wider. "Yes. I was just thinking that it is a very beautiful day."

"It certainly is."

"Are the summers always like this?"

"Lady, you haven't seen summer yet, but don't you worry. It'll get plenty hot before it's through."

"Well, I can handle this weather."

"Handle it while you can. It's not going to last." Josh turned into the Mill parking lot and stopped in front of the office. "Wait here, would you?"

"I might rummage around a bit," Gail said, almost ignoring the sheriff's request.

"Suit yourself."

Gail stepped from the truck and looked up at the belching smokestack. To the left, the mill stretched into the distance. To the right, there was one mountainous pile of logs after another. Men in jeans and plaid shirts scurried to and fro, each on a mission to complete some task she knew must be far more difficult than whatever she was doing. The mill was a bustling place, and she admired these men and was thankful that their boss had seen fit to invest so much of his time and money to create their jobs. She had met Robert Carter three months prior while doing a story on the area's declining logging industry. He showed her that the rising cost of government contracts, paired with a decline in lumber prices at retail, had pressed the mill, and layoffs were not only happening, but planned for the future. Mr. Carter was insistent that the problems were overblown, but intensifying union strikes and wage demands indicated otherwise. The mill was in decline, and the town was worried.

Adding to those worries was the recent revelation that Robert Carter was having an affair with Lisa Martin. A nice-looking woman had accompanied Carter on the day Gail had interviewed him. She hadn't known it at the time, but that woman was Lisa and she'd been dressed in a manner not terribly conducive to office work. Mr. Carter had introduced her as his personal assistant, but interviews with other employees indicated otherwise. While she did work in the office as a receptionist and answered directly to the office manager, most of her time was spent at Carter's side. Over the course of further interviews Gail had learned that the two were often seen together holding hands or kissing. Robert Carter was seventy-two, a simple fact that led her to believe Lisa Martin saw more in their relationship than charm and good looks. Regardless, the aging man was listed as a hostile witness for the defense, and Gail was smart enough to know it wasn't because he could provide James Hodges with an alibi. What he could do, though, was be coaxed into demonstrating a need for Lisa Martin to disappear.

She also knew Josh Matthews had been thorough in his investigation into the old man's affair with the victim, but there was only so much he could do. Carter's only public dealings were with his contractors and his wife, who was even more of a recluse than her husband, and Gail believed she might be entirely in the dark regarding her husband's affair.

Gail was pondering another possibility when Sheriff Matthews appeared and waved her down. He walked across the parking lot with his head down.

"Well?" she asked.

"We worked it out. He'll testify in two days," Josh said as he opened the passenger door for her.

"So," she said with a smile, "free day?"

Josh stared out over the mountains and frowned. "Wish it were. I'll take you back to your car."

"Shot down again," Gail mumbled to herself.

* * *

Gail entered the *Burns Review* office and sat at her desk. Coffee near to hand, she tapped away on the typewriter, collected notes, and rummaged through her files. It felt to her like all five murders were connected in some way. While there was no evidence on the surface that definitively linked any one to another, she'd finally decided that the similarities among the victims were enough in and of themselves. She just had to find the clue that tied them together. So far, that clue was proving elusive.

She took a paper from the desk and had a quick look at the witness schedule for the day. The first person on the list was the most curious, and she was looking forward to it. Mike Gordon had something no one else had, and he was holding it close to the vest. Gail knew, but could not prove, that Melissa Reed must have seen something that Gordon thought might exonerate James Hodges. But there was no way he could possibly expect the jury to take her word for anything.

Gail gathered her purse and bag and headed outside. For the second day in a row, she was denied breakfast, as the sheriff had once again been forced to cancel last minute. He was never late, but he canceled often. Whatever it was that had come up, she knew it must be important and so took the cancellation without offense. Rather than dwell on it or get her feelings in a knot, she focused on the day's activities and what she thought she could expect from the defense, and from the prosecution's cross examination, which was certain to tear Melissa Reed apart.

These thoughts continued in her head until she found her seat in the courtroom, where she paid attention to the look on Josh's face when the defense called Melissa Reed to the witness stand. As with Connie, Gail had learned that Josh had interviewed Melissa extensively, and yet he still seemed surprised when Gordon put her on the stand. Like everyone else, Gail assumed that Josh believed a jury would never take the young woman seriously and so putting her on the stand would be a waste of time.

Gail had known little about the subpoena, but her own investigation into the accident and Melissa's past revealed no connection between her and any of the players, at least nothing on the surface. Neither Melissa Reed nor her family had any ties to James Hodges, and there was no love lost or gained between them. There were no connections to follow between her and the victim or any of the people at the camp, and there had been no one attending the teenage party who caused any suspicion. It wasn't until Melissa took the oath and sat down that the connection hit Gail. She leaned over to Josh and whispered in his ear. "Gordon is on to something."

"What on earth could that be?" Josh whispered back.

"Melissa was on the road that night. She would have driven past."

Josh gave her a funny look. "I know, Gail, but that kid was so wasted she swore she saw dancing pink bunnies on the road. Gordon can't possibly be that stupid."

"Did you ask her?"

"Did I ask her what?"

Gail shifted closer to the sheriff. "Did you ask her if she saw anything?"

Josh looked surprised at the question. "Of course I did. She has no recollection. She didn't see anything or anyone, at least nothing she could recall while I was speaking with her."

Gail saw the truth in his eyes, but she also knew Gordon had the young woman on the stand for a reason. "Well," she whispered, "when Mike Gordon is finished, Carl is going to crucify her. Regardless of what connection Gordon thinks he's found, Carl is going to have a field day tearing it apart."

Josh nodded and turned to her. "I don't see it going well."

No matter the Assistant DA's intentions, Melissa Reed was Mike Gordon's witness, and within one minute of her taking the stand the jury learned that she had driven by the turnoff where the victim's car was discovered. They also learned that she did so during the late hours of May the fourteenth, or the very early hours of the fifteenth. More important than her driving by was what she claimed to have seen, and it was in this that Gail knew Mike Gordon had discovered a connection that, due to the circumstances, everyone else would refuse to consider. But connected they were.

"So, you did see another car along the highway?" Gordon asked.

Melissa shuffled in the chair. "Yes."

Gail caught Sheriff Matthews out of the corner of her eye and saw the surprise register on his face. Perhaps, because of her condition at the time, she could not recall?

"Can you describe it?" Gordon asked of the young woman.

"I don't . . . I don't know. It was dark and I was . . ."

"You were what?"

"I was kind of drunk."

"Kind of?"

"Yes, I was drunk. But I saw a car. I can still see it in my head, but I don't really know cars."

"Do you remember what color it was?"

"It was dark."

"Yes, you said that, but . . ."

"No, I mean the car. It was dark. Like, black or dark blue, I think." Melissa's eyes darted around the room before momentarily resting on Josh's.

"Did you see the license plate?" Gordon asked.

"No, we went by too fast. I don't remember seeing it."

"Could you identify that car if you saw it again?"

The prosecutor stood from his table. "Objection!"

"What grounds?" Judge Parker demanded.

"Your Honor, Miss Reed has already told this court she doesn't know cars and didn't get a good look at it. The defense is trying to coach a description out of her."

"Oh come, on, Your Honor," Gordon barked, "Miss Reed

saw a vehicle, and it is well within my client's rights to hear any and all testimony that could exonerate him. If the state doesn't want this court to hear exculpatory evidence, no matter the source, then I suggest my client cannot receive a fair trial and this case should be moved to another venue."

"Nice try, counselor." Judge Parker barked as he leaned back and eyeballed Mike Gordon. "Don't take an attitude. You may continue with this line of questioning, but I suggest strongly that you tread carefully. Overruled." The gavel cracked and the counselor went back to the stand.

"Now, Miss Reed," Gordon said as he eyed Carl Franklin, "let me ask this another way. If you saw that car around town again, would you recognize it?"

She shook her head as the wheels spun. "No."

Mike Gordon sighed, and Gail knew he was disappointed. As he walked back toward the table he appeared dejected, as if a great revelation had been proven false.

Then Melissa Reed sat forward and leaned closer to the microphone. "I mean, yes, I think I could."

"What?" Gordon asked as he spun back toward the stand. "What was that?"

"If I close my eyes, and I think about Danny and Todd, I can see it." She was beginning to tear up as the emotion of that evening flooded over her. "It was a long, black car. I don't know what kind, but it had four doors. I think I would know it if I saw it. Or I would at least know what kind."

A long, black car? Gail said to herself. How many long, black cars were there in the county? Or the state, for that matter?

"One additional question, Miss Reed, if you don't mind."

Melissa Reed wiped a stream of tears from her cheeks and nodded. "I don't have anything better to do."

"Of course not. And I am sorry for that. May I ask if you saw any other cars along the road?"

"You mean by the black car?"

"Yes."

"No, there were not."

"So, what you are telling this court is that you saw a long, black car parked at the turnoff to National Forest 2820, but you did not see a gold 1972 Datsun 510 station wagon parked there?"

"No, sir."

"Thank you, Miss Reed. The defense has no further questions."

"Thank you, Counselor," said Judge Parker. "Does the prosecution wish to follow?"

"Yes, Your Honor," Carl Franklin said as he twirled a pencil.

According to her notes, Melissa Reed had received her summons prior to her transfer to the Oregon State Penitentiary. Mike Gordon must have been quick to do the math that placed the teenager so close to the scene, and had certainly spoken with her. Could the DA not see it? Either way she knew what he was going to do.

"Miss Reed," began Carl Franklin, "you recently pled guilty to a host of felonies, did you not?"

Gail looked over at Josh. She knew he was right and the teenager would be massacred on the stand, and she knew it would hurt Josh to see it happen.

"Objection, Your Honor. The witness's record is not on trial here."

"Your Honor," Franklin responded, "the state has no intention to use Miss Reed's record to exclude her testimony. Rather, we intend to show her testimony lacks credibility."

Judge Parker scanned the room and then rested his eyes on the dueling attorneys. "Please approach the bench, both of you."

Gail watched patiently as Carl Franklin and Mike Gordon exchanged words with the hawk-eyed judge. She tried to hear their conversation, but Judge Parker's hand blocked the microphone and she could make nothing out of any of it. Eventually, Gordon and Franklin returned to their respective places and the questioning continued.

"Miss Reed, you recently pleaded guilty to DUI, did you not?"

"Yes, sir."

"Miss Reed," asked Franklin, "just how drunk were you?"

"I don't know. I—"

"Well, I know. I have the toxicology report from the night in question."

"Objection," Mike Gordon shouted, "Miss Reed is not on trial here, Your Honor."

"Overruled, Mr. Gordon."

"Your Honor, I—"

Judge Parker smacked his gavel against the desk. "Sit down, Mr. Gordon."

Gordon returned to his chair as Carl Franklin turned back to the witness.

Through the tears, Melissa answered the question. "I was pretty drunk."

"And you expect these intelligent people," Franklin said while motioning to the jury, "to believe a word you say regarding anything you may or may not have seen?"

"I don't know, I . . ."

"You what?"

"I don't know."

"Of course you don't. You've already told this court you don't remember the details. Also, when questioned by Sheriff Matthews the night of the accident, you said you saw pink bunnies dancing in the moonlight."

"Objection, Your Honor," Gordon cried again. "The state is trying to intimidate the witness and coach her testimony while on the stand."

"Sustained," Parker said. "Mr. Franklin, you are not testifying. The previous line will be stricken from the record."

"Apologies, Your Honor. I submit state's evidence 3-B." Franklin approached the bench, showed the evidence to the judge, then to the defense. With nods all around, he turned back to Melissa Reed. "Recognize this?"

"No, sir."

"This is a copy of the sheriff's report from the early morning of May 15 of this year. Sheriff Matthews documents that, and I quote, 'Melissa was screaming at pink bunnies dancing in the moonlight. She was seriously terrified. I knew she was drunk, but with this outburst I suspected she may have been under the influence of hallucinogenic drugs, perhaps mushrooms or LSD.' End quote. The toxicology report did, in fact, note the presence of LSD in your blood stream, didn't it?"

Melissa fumbled with the document she held and sobbed. "Yes."

"Yes, it did. Knowing that, wouldn't you say it's possible, just possible, that you imagined this 'long, black car'?"

"No, it's not."

"I'm sorry?" Carl said with a surprised tone.

Gail could see from Carl's uncomfortable pose that he was shocked at the girl's answer.

"It isn't possible," Melissa said, "because we didn't drop the acid with the other kids. We did it later on the way home. There was a long, black car there. I remember it. I just can't say what kind it was. That part is fuzzy, but it was there."

Carl turned back to the table and shuffled through the papers in his briefcase. It was clear he didn't know what to do or say, so he took the only route he could.

"Your Honor, the prosecution moves to strike this witness's testimony from the record."

"On what grounds?" the judge demanded.

"Your Honor, Miss Reed was intoxicated and freely admitted to using drugs. Her testimony cannot be trusted."

"Motion denied."

"But, Your Honor—"

"I said motion denied. We'll let the jury decide if her testimony can be trusted or not."

From her perch in the back, Gail couldn't see the look on Mike Gordon's face, but she could tell by the way he patted James Hodges's shoulder that he felt victorious. Whatever path he was on, he had the first real proof that there was more to the story than was visible on the surface.

* * *

Sheriff Josh Matthews was struggling with the revelation he had heard from the courtroom. He had spent over an hour speaking with his young friend and had asked her every question he knew to ask about that night. Everything she could remember was important, and yet she had been able to remember nothing of any importance until Mike Gordon coaxed it from her. In thinking through this, Josh's mind stole him away to that fateful night as he'd taken Melissa Reed into his arms and tried to console her. She'd become hysterical, denying over and over that Danny and Todd Johansen were dead, and she'd demanded to see them. It was soon after that, as he was leading her to the patrol car, that she pulled away from him and screamed into the night. He could see that she was terrified, and he regretted not handcuffing her for her own safety. Even as drunk as she was, she was able to run across the road and hide behind a tree, and then refuse to come back.

Whatever she was on, Josh had never seen anyone react quite like she had. She went on for some time about bunnies, which morphed into dancing bunnies, and then into pink dancing bunnies. He couldn't understand why she was having so much trouble with what he thought must have been cute, furry animals, at least not until the paramedics came over at Chief Anderson's request. They looked her over, shined a light in her eyes to check her pupil response, pinched her under the arm, and spoke loudly to her until a decision was made that she was not overdosing but hallucinating, probably on LSD. She would be fine, but the paramedic reminded Josh that what he thought were cute, fury animals might indeed be terrifying to her. He was instructed to take her to the hospital just in case, have a toxicology test ordered, and allow her to come down under supervision.

That episode had occurred just over a month ago. Although Carl Franklin had been served notice of her subpoena and made it known to Josh, what Mike Gordon intended to do with it had been anyone's guess. No matter, they'd decided. Franklin was well enough prepared to refute anything she said and had enough toxicology evidence in hand to countermand any testimony Gordon could possibly retrieve from her chemically imbalanced memory. There was no way anything could stick with the jury.

But those dancing pink bunnies and the long black car were now playing their dirty tricks in Josh's mind. While he'd been at the hospital that night supervising Melissa's testing and waiting for her parents to arrive, he'd had a conversation with a young doctor who relayed the facts regarding hallucinations, and it had stuck with him, although it did not serve any useful purpose until now. What that doctor told him was that hallucinations could, in fact, be drawn from very recent memory and replayed in radically different ways. Something she'd seen immediately prior to the LSD taking affect could very well have had consequences during the drug's course. Those bunnies might represent something, but even Mike Gordon was entirely unable to lure their true meaning from the young woman's mind. Still, Josh could not discount their meaning. Nor could he discount Melissa's testimony that she'd seen a black car. If that was a fact—if indeed another car had been present—then there was a glaring hole in the investigation that needed patching.

✳ ✳ ✳

Gail was still struggling with Melissa Reed's testimony and trying to sort out whether or not she should take her word for it, or if it should be discounted as Carl Franklin suggested, when Gordon called his next witness.

"Your Honor, the defense calls Dusty Stevens."

From the far back corner of the court a middle-aged man, perhaps fifty-five, stood and slowly worked his way in front of those to his right. He stepped carefully, apologized for his toe stepping, wiggled, shuffled, and stumbled until he was in the aisle. He composed himself, adjusted his pants, and walked through the gated entry to the main floor. He seemed confident, and there was a hint of smugness on his face. He entered the witness stand and turned to the bailiff.

"Do you swear to tell the truth, the whole truth, and nothing but the truth, so help you God?"

"I do," he said.

"Please state your full name for the record."

"My name is Dusty Stevens, but my friends call me Dirt."

"Thank you. Be seated."

Mike Gordon then went to work.

"Mr. Stevens, how are you today?"

Gail thought the question a bit disingenuous.

"I am quite well. How are you?"

Smiles went up around the courtroom and Gail knew that the audience seemed to enjoy the homeless man's polished cordiality.

Mike Gordon joined with the smiling crowd. "I'm fine, thank you," he said. "Mr. Stevens, may I call you Dirt?"

"You seem like a nice enough man. Of course you can."

Gail thought their banter seemed a little too rehearsed, but she still liked it.

"Dirt, would you please tell the jury where you live?"

Dusty looked at the jury, then at his lap. "I am between homes right now."

"So, you're homeless?"

"If you want to put it that way. I mean, right now I'm staying up on Marshall Creek with some friends. We have running water, a toilet of sorts, and we burn our garbage. Why, it's *almost* like home. Food's not too bad, either. We catch squirrel and rabbit, wild hens from time to time. We come into town now and again to beg. Last week we had some fresh fruit and vegetables.

I hadn't had fresh fruit in months until then. Sure was good. A real nice lady down at the mart gave me some money for that. I would like to tell her thanks." Dusty then waved at the back of the court.

Gail caught Josh looking at her with a gruff scowl. "What?" she mouthed at him. "He was hungry." She could feel more eyes on her and could do nothing but smile. The man had been cold, smelled horrible, and looked like he hadn't eaten in a while, so she'd given him ten dollars. At the time, she'd believed he would probably spend it on beer and cigarettes. Dusty's statement was the first confirmation she had that he actually spent it on food, and that knowledge warmed her heart.

"Dirt," Gordon continued, "do you recognize the defendant, James Hodges?"

"Well, sure I do. James is one of my friends. He lives up there with us."

"Have you ever known James to be a violent man?"

"No, sir. I haven't ever had any trouble with him. Although he did tell me he got into some trouble in town for fighting, and I believe him. But in camp, no. He hasn't ever been a hassle to anyone. Friendliest man I've met in a long time."

"Do you understand the crime that James is charged with?"

"Well, I understand the drug charge. I mean, we haven't got much to do sometimes. So we just want to get away for a bit. But that murder charge, that isn't right, man. James wasn't anywhere near that lady."

"How do you know that?"

Dusty shifted forward as if to emphasize his statement. "Because he was with us in camp all night," he said with intense eyes that were focused on Gordon.

"How do you know that?"

"I sleep in the daytime when it's hot. I do my sitting and hunting and whatever at night when it's dark. More critters are out, anyway, and I haven't got the sun beating me down."

"Were you hunting that night?"

"Oh, no, sir. I was sitting under a tree having a little smoke."

"You were getting high?"

Dusty smiled with satisfaction. "Yes, sir. I had a little weed and a couple whiskies, yes."

"I thought you spent your money on food?"

"I do. But Eddy, he had some real nice weed."

"Who is Eddy?"

"Just another one of the boys that lives with us. I don't know his last name."

"Dirt, this next question is very important."

"Okay."

"Did you notice anything out of place on either the night of the fourteenth or very early in the morning on the fifteenth?"

"Yes, sir, I sure did. There was this guy that came wandering through. Now, I'm not sure what time it was exactly, but it wasn't long after midnight."

"Did you recognize this man?"

"No, sir. He was wearing a mask and gloves. He just wandered through like he owned the place. He stood by the trash for a moment, and then he just disappeared back down the draw. Pretty strange if you ask me."

"Do you think this man saw you?"

"Oh, no. I was sitting back in the shadows, and it was dark."

"Did you say anything to him?"

"No, sir."

"Did you notice him place anything in the trash barrel?"

"I didn't pay any attention to that. I was just chilling out, man."

"Did anyone else in your little band go through that barrel?"

"Yes, sir," Dusty said as he focused on the jury.

"Who?"

"Why, James did. The very next morning, he was the first one out of bed."

"And, Dirt, what did James find in that barrel?"

"Not sure exactly. I know he found himself a real nice knife. He said it was sticky, so he wiped it on his pants, rinsed a bit of water over it, and cut us some nice apples."

Once again, Dirt waved at Gail.

She looked at her feet, and then scribbled some notes. She noted that Jacob Powell was staring ahead as usual, Maggie Johnson scribbled and waved her hands about, and Diego Lopez itched beneath his chin.

Mike Gordon admitted a photograph and then approached the witness. "I'm going to show you a photograph. Now, Dirt, do you think that Mr. Hodges is capable of this?" With that, Gordon placed the photograph on the rail in front of Dusty Stevens.

Dusty took the photograph from the rail, looked briefly, and turned away. "No. No way. James would never hurt anyone like that. That's . . . that's . . ." He put his sleeve to his mouth. "No."

"Thank you, Dirt. No further questions, Your Honor."

Carl Franklin waited for the judge's order, and then lit into Dusty Stevens. "Mr. Stevens. Or, uh, should I call you Dirt?"

"No."

Carl seemed caught off guard, and Gail made note of it.

"Why not? I thought you preferred Dirt."

"My friends call me Dirt. You, sir, are not my friend."

Gail turned to the jury box to watch their reactions. Maggie was shaking her head, and Heather Boydega was laughing quietly. The majority of the jurors were sitting motionless while Jacob Powell stared straight ahead with not a trace of emotion, although she did catch him looking at his watch.

"Fair enough, Mr. Stevens," Carl said with a hint of disgust. "You're right, I'm not your friend."

"Good to know."

"Yes, of course. All right, Mr. Stevens. By your own account, you were drinking and smoking a narcotic that the state of Oregon has outlawed due to the known dangers it presents. Is that correct?"

"Well, sir, you are right about that outlawed part, but the dangers you speak of—"

Carl put his hand up to interrupt. "Yes, Mr. Stevens. While I'm sure your science lesson will be very impressive, the facts prove otherwise. What is important here is that you admitted to the use of drugs, and you also admitted you were drunk."

"I never said I was drunk. I said I had a couple whiskies. Takes about ten to get me drunk."

Carl stared at the witness. There was a long pause before he retrieved another piece of paper from his table. "Mr. Stevens, this is a copy of a police report written by Deputy Horace Shaw. Deputy Shaw was with Sheriff Matthews when Mr. Hodges was arrested. Do you remember that?"

"Yeah. Isn't he the fat one?"

Gail noticed Maggie Johnson did not appear to appreciate the comment. She was all business with her pencil, and the blue-gray bun atop her head flopped about as she shushed the others, but her demeanor changed to something that indicated she was disgusted.

"Mr. Stevens," Franklin said, "would you please read this part right here that I have underlined?"

"Sure," Dusty said as he took the paper from the prosecutor. "It says, 'After Sheriff Matthews placed the suspect under arrest, another man in the camp, who identified himself as Dirt, said 'Don't worry, Wiggles, we got your back.'"

"'We got your back,'" Franklin said as he looked at the jury. "Sounds a bit like you and your troop would do or say anything to keep James Hodges out of jail."

"I said that because we were witnesses that James wasn't gone that night. He was with us the whole time."

"I have no further questions for this witness, Your Honor."

Carl stepped away, and the judge called for the evening recess. Gail packed herself up and slipped from the booth, said goodnight to Sheriff Matthews, and left the courtroom. With little to do, she went home to catch up on her sleep.

As court resumed the next day, Mike Gordon once again approached the podium as a man with hope. "Mr. Carter," Gordon asked the old man who now occupied the witness stand, "would you please tell this court your occupation?"

The gray-haired man of seventy-two sat with pride and looked around the room as if waiting for his subjects to bow before him. "Why, I own R. Carter and Sons," he said in a gruff, scratchy voice that indicated his age. "That's the sawmill over in Hines. But you already know that."

Gordon would not be played. "How long have you owned the mill, Mr. Carter?"

"Why, it's been nearly twenty years."

"Is business good?"

"Oh, I don't know," Carter said. "Things are getting pretty tough. Lumber prices are down, folks are worked up over wages. It will all work out, however."

"How are things at home?"

"Objection," demanded the prosecutor, "Your Honor, Mr. Carter's home life is not on trial."

"Your Honor," Mike Gordon, responded, "how can my client receive a fair trial if the prosecution is permitted to disrupt the court and claim some unsubstantiated inconvenience every time I ask a question?"

"Overruled," said the judge. "Mr. Gordon, please continue."

"Thank you, Your Honor."

Judge Parker turned to the witness. "Mr. Carter, please answer the question."

"Of course, Your Honor," said Robert Carter with a look on his face that told Gail he would not be caught in any wrongdoing. "I have nothing to hide. Things at home are as they have always been."

"And how is that?" Gordon demanded.

"Perfectly fine, thank you. I have a wonderful wife, beautiful children, and the most amazing grandchildren you could ever imagine."

"How about the office. How are things there?"

Robert Carter seemed confused. "I thought I already answered that question?" His eyes darted around the room, and he shuffled in the chair. The question was not difficult, but he did not seem to understand that it had not already been asked.

"Mr. Carter, earlier I asked you if business is good."

"Yes, yes, of course. Oh, the office is just fine, just fine, indeed. Thank you for asking."

"Mr. Carter," Gordon asked, "Did Lisa Martin work for you at the sawmill?"

"Why, yes, she did."

"How is the office functioning with her gone?"

"I'm afraid I don't understand."

"It's a simple question, Mr. Carter. How is the office functioning without Lisa?"

"Just what are you insinuating?"

"I wasn't insinuating anything," Gordon said. "But since you brought it up, I may as well ask." Mike Gordon turned to the jury for effect. "Mr. Carter, were you having an affair with Lisa Martin?"

Robert Carter's face turned crimson, and he stood from the witness seat to point accusingly at the defense attorney. "How dare you make such an accusation. I'll not sit here and take this. I am a faithful husband, and an important man in this community."

But Judge Parker would have none of it. "Sit down, Mr. Carter," he demanded.

The mill owner pouted in defiance before returning to the chair.

"Now, if you'll answer the question, please," said the Judge.

"I will not qualify such an accusation."

Judge Parker slammed the gavel against the wood knock. "Mr. Carter, you will answer the question, or I will be forced to find you in contempt."

Carter remained silent until the gavel slammed home again.

"Lisa was a good friend, nothing more," he said with defiance.

"How would you define a 'good friend'?" asked the defense attorney.

Gail noticed Robert Carter looking back into the courtroom. She followed his eyes and saw an older woman, immaculately dressed and shaking her head, and knew she must be Mrs. Carter.

"Like I said. She was merely a friend."

Mike Gordon reached to his table and gathered some items before returning to the podium. "All right, Mr. Carter. I have just a few more questions for you and then we can be done with this." He turned to the judge and spoke with polished efficiency. "Your Honor, I now present defense item 13-B, approved by you to be entered as evidence. Permission to approach the witness?"

Judge Parker took the items from Mike Gordon, studied them intently, and then handed them back. "Granted."

Gordon stepped to the witness stand and laid the items out on the rail in front of the witness. "I'll ask you one more time, Mr. Carter. Were you having an affair with the deceased, Mrs. Lisa Martin?"

Robert Carter looked at the photographs laying face up in front of him and turned his nose to the air. Gail had a pretty good idea what they revealed and knew that they presented a problem not only for Carl Franklin and the state but also for Robert Carter's wife. She glanced at her and wrote in her book, *Yikes!*

Gordon continued his attack. "Mr. Carter, did you and the victim always hold hands in your office?"

There was no answer, and Carter turned his nose away as if a pungent odor were emanating from the rail in front of the witness chair.

"And did you and the victim regularly kiss in the office?"

Still nothing.

"Mr. Carter, are you this close with all your friends? So close that you have a woman pose for you in your office without her clothes on?"

"This is uncalled for," Robert Carter shouted. "It wasn't like that."

"What was it like?" Gordon demanded.

"Lisa was special."

"I'm sure she was, but Lisa is not on trial here. James Hodges is. And for a crime I think you committed."

"Objection!" Carl Franklin shouted from his table. "Your Honor, please."

"Sustained. Mr. Gordon, keep your comments to yourself. The clerk will strike that comment from the record."

"I apologize, Your Honor," Gordon said with counterfeit repentance. "Now, Mr. Carter, how much are you worth?"

"What does that have to do with anything?"

"Just answer the question. How much are you worth?"

"I have no . . . A lot, I suppose. What does that have to do —"

"Mr. Carter, did you hire Lisa Martin for her looks?"

"Objection, Your Honor. Relevance."

"Your Honor," Gordon shouted, "I intend to show that there are other suspects with more believable motives than Mr. Hodges."

"Overruled. Answer the question, please."

Robert Carter shook his head, and Gail knew that Gordon was simply trying to ruffle the old man's feathers. She did not believe Robert Carter could have killed Lisa, but she certainly believed he had something he would prefer the public did not know, and that made the possibility of a murder-for-hire conspiracy even more brazen.

"Your Honor," Gordon pleaded, "please instruct the witness to answer."

"Mr. Carter," the judge barked, "you will answer the question."

Carter pointed an arthritic finger with boldness. "So, what does it matter if an old man wants to look at a pretty girl?" asked the old man with no shame on his face. "How is that your business?"

Gordon continued to press. "Mr. Carter, during my investigation, I learned that Lisa Martin had no appreciable skill set, that she was a poor student, that she had no higher education, and that she was a struggling bartender. Yet she came to work for you and became your overnight 'assistant.'" With those words, Gordon held up his fingers as quotations marks. "So, why, may I ask, did you hire her if for no other reason than her looks?"

"I gave a nice lady a job."

"Yes, you did. But you still have to answer the question."

"It's none of your business."

"Oh, it is very much my business. But I'll get more to the point. Were you sleeping with Lisa Martin or not?"

"No." The old man crossed his legs and arms and looked defiantly away from the jury.

Mike Gordon turned to the judge but said nothing. Rather, he leaned over, swept the photographs into a pile, and, after having received permission, presented them to the jury. "We'll let these intelligent folks decide if you were or not." He spread the photos across the railing in front of the jury box as Gail noted their individual reactions.

There were gasps and awful looks from the jurors. The courtroom filled with hushed murmuring and whispers that sounded like chattering birds. Gail caught Josh looking at her, and the two frowned together. Over in the jury box, Maggie Johnson was scowling. Her pencil was motionless, and her hands were locked in her lap. Jacob Powell even managed something that Gail could call a smile. At that very moment James Hodges could have no better friend than Robert Carter, who sat motionless and expressionless at the witness stand.

"Mr. Carter," Gordon continued, "these photos tell a much different story. I would also remind you that perjury is a felony. So I will ask you one more time. Were you sleeping with Lisa

Martin?"

Carter's chest heaved with an undeniable sigh. His face glowed crimson, and he appeared ready to lunge at Mike Gordon. Still, he was trapped. Gail had only barely seen one of the photographs, but that one alone was enough to destroy the old man. He had nowhere to go. "Yes," he said as he looked at his feet.

And the verbal assault continued. "Did your wife know?" Gordon asked.

"I do not know the answer to that question," he said with his head shaking and his face finally displaying the shame due him.

"Well, now that she does know, do you think she might disown you?"

Carter looked up with clenched lips and glared hard at the defense attorney.

"Objection," cried Carl Franklin, "calls for speculation."

"Sustained."

Gordon reworded the question, and his clever, if not harsh, mind worked around the problem. "Has your wife ever threatened to leave you?"

Carter nodded yes.

"Please," Gordon stated, "let the record show that Mr. Carter has nodded yes." And then he turned back to the struggling old man. "On what grounds did she make these threats?"

"What?" Carter asked.

"On what grounds did your wife say she would leave you?"

Carter again looked at his feet. "If I ever slept with another woman again."

"Again?" Gordon asked with incredulity. "This was not the first time?"

Robert Carter had the look of a man who had let slip a secret better left untold. His eyes darted about the room and he appeared to be looking for rescue, but there was none to be found.

"I see," said Gordon. "Would you, then, consider these

photographs proof that you were sleeping with another woman?" And then he added for effect, "Again?"

Robert Carter nodded dejectedly and again Gordon called for the record to show it.

Then the bomb landed. "Did Lisa Martin ever blackmail you with these photos?"

"Objection!" Franklin yelled.

"On what grounds?" the judge demanded.

Carl Franklin looked around the court before sighing deeply, and sat down. "Retraction, Your Honor," he said as it became clear to all that he had no ground to stand on.

Robert Carter appeared lost in thought. He'd been caught red handed, and there was no getting around it. The pictures were the proof of that, and he had nowhere else to go. "Yes, she did, but I didn't kill her. I would never hurt my Lisa."

A round of stunned whispers went through the courtroom. Silence returned when Judge Parker twice slammed the gavel.

"Where were you on the evening of May 14?" Gordon asked.

"May 14? What's that got to do with me?"

"Where were you?" Gordon asked again.

"I don't recall exactly."

"You don't know where you were, or you won't say where you were?"

"I go to bed very early."

"Of course you do." Gordon turned to his notes and threw one final volley for good measure. "Mr. Carter, who has the money in your family?"

"I do not understand the question."

"You or your wife—who has the money?"

Carter stiffened, looked to the back of the room, and then slumped in his seat. Apparently, he knew the score.

As did Gordon, who appeared to feel confident that the jury had come to the same conclusion. "No further questions, Your Honor."

Gail had known it was coming. The revelation regarding the photos had moved the ball to Gordon's court. The prosecution had to *prove* James' guilt, and they had done a pretty good job of it. However, Gordon had just dropped a very damning case for reasonable doubt, and that there was another suspect whose actions should be considered.

What she didn't see coming was Mrs. Carter storming from the courtroom in a trail of foul language and threats, which drew several whaps of the Judge's gavel before the room returned to silence.

The brush of a hand against Gail's called her from the place she was going in her mind. She looked over and smiled as Josh leaned close to her.

"Paints a foul picture, doesn't it," he whispered.

"Indeed. Are you surprised?"

"A bit. Never thought the old man would stoop to that level."

"I wouldn't know, but he left a big mess for Carl."

"He sure did."

"The jury is divided now."

"Tell me about it later. I've got work to do," Josh said, and then he disappeared through the door.

Carl Franklin stood up and adjusted his pants. Gail would have loved to know what was going on in his mind. She could only guess, but she couldn't be far from the truth.

"Mr. Carter, how old are you?" he asked of the overwhelmed witness.

"Seventy-two."

"Seventy-two. How do you feel—health-wise, I mean?"

"I've been better."

"How's the hip?"

"Hurts, as always."

"How often do you walk?"

"Every day. I walk to the car in the morning. My doctor ordered me to park way out in the lot and walk to the office."

"Go on any hikes or long walks in the woods?"

"No. This old body cannot handle such things. I get tired easily."

"So, would it be fair to say that hiking in the mountains would be a bit difficult for you?"

Carter chewed on his tongue. He was still coming down from an angry place. "I can barely make the walk in from the parking lot. How am I going to hike through the mountains?"

The court rustled with whispers and pointing fingers. Gail noted that Maggie Johnson was shaking her head as she scribbled.

"How is your strength otherwise?"

"I get winded very easily."

"Nothing further, Your Honor," Franklin said.

"Folks," said Judge Parker, "it's four thirty. Rather than run the risk of going past five on a Friday afternoon, I'm going to adjourn for the day. We'll meet back here at nine o'clock on Monday morning. The Twenty-Fourth circuit is adjourned." The gavel slammed home, and Gail leaned back and closed her eyes.

Gail was beginning to understand why Josh's regular table was *the* booth. She walked straight to the diner from court and found the booth empty, so she helped herself and waited patiently for Josh to join her. The view onto the street was a wonder with all of its activity, and it was pleasing to sit back and observe from such a fine vantage point.

When Josh finally joined her and they'd ordered and received their food, she struck up whatever conversation came to her mind. "Boy, Robert Carter sure left a hole in the state's case," she began with a wink, knowing it would get Josh riled up.

"If you say so," he retorted.

"Oh, come on, Josh," she teased. "What, are you worried?" Josh smirked.

"Seriously, though, what do you think?"

"About Carter? He's in a mess."

"You can say that again."

"He's in a mess," Josh said with a joking face.

Gail shook her head and changed the subject. "So, something else is bothering me."

"What's that?"

"Sam Reynolds."

"What about him?"

"I'm a little confused by something he said."

"What did he say that confuses you?"

"Okay, so James went to The Sawyer, sat at the bar, and ordered a beer, right?"

"Right."

"Well, according to someone I spoke to over there that night, Sam Reynolds was sitting at the far end of the bar and was drinking."

"Yes."

"Sam was flirting with Lisa Martin in a noisy bar. The people I talked to all said it's very hard to hear in the evenings with all the conversation and the music. You really have to speak up."

"If that's what they said," Josh said quizzically. "Why does that matter?"

"It matters because Sam Reynolds said he heard James ask Lisa to sleep with him. Or rather, that James demanded Lisa sleep with him."

"Still on track, but what does that have to do with a noisy bar?"

"You see, that's just it. The bar was very noisy. So, how did Reynolds hear James say anything from the other end of the bar?"

"I don't know."

"Josh," Gail said as she tapped his hand, "When Sam Reynolds was on the stand, he had to ask Carl to repeat a question two separate times."

"Are you suggesting Reynolds has bad hearing?"

"Yes, I am. He worked in the mill a few years ago. Did you know that?"

"Yes."

"He was a sawyer, which is ironic, I think. Is it possible his hearing was damaged while he was operating those saws?"

"It sure is. The mill listed him as a sawyer, just like you said, but there is no note in his file about hearing loss."

"Does there have to be?" Gail asked as she took a drink and ate some fries. "Still think he's telling the truth?"

Josh leaned back into the corner and rubbed his head.

"Headache?"

"Yes."

"I'm sorry. You want something for it? I have some aspirin." Gail took the bottle from her purse and placed two pills in his hand. "You see, that's what I'm getting at. Sam tells the story as if he overheard James say something from the other end of a very noisy bar."

Josh swallowed the aspirin and returned to the conversation. "What does Sam Reynolds gain by making it up?"

"His pride," Gail said with a look she hoped would convince the sheriff. "He wants everyone to think Lisa Martin was into him. Hodges was a competitor."

"You really think we men are that shallow?" Josh asked with a harrumph.

"Some men are, yes. Reynolds thinks of himself as a real lady's man. A few of the regulars I spoke with tell me he gets very agitated if anyone steps on his turf. I think he needed an excuse, so he made one up. James may or may not have said anything, but even appearing to flirt with Lisa would have angered Reynolds, and he took it as a challenge. He needed a reason, or he wanted a reason, so he made one up. That's the story he's telling on the stand, because that's the story he's telling everyone he knows."

"So, you think Reynolds is lying. And how does that affect the case?"

"It removes motive. If Reynolds is lying, then James Hodges has no reason to kill Lisa Martin."

"Are you thinking Reynolds did it?" Josh asked with accusing eyes, "Because he has an awfully good alibi?"

"No," Gail said. "I just don't think James had any reason to."

"You would think Gordon would pursue that angle."

"Maybe he didn't see it," Gail said.

"Maybe not, or maybe he did and realized it didn't go anywhere juicy enough to stick. I'm betting Mike Gordon wandered down to the Square Nines, just like we did, and found that Sam Reynolds had the best alibi of the bunch, just like we did, so he decided not to pursue that angle and went with whatever Reynolds wanted to say." Josh nibbled at his food and changed the subject. "How would you say Kipp Martin did on the stand today?"

Gail took a bite out of her burger and chewed slowly, announcing her satisfaction with a soft groan of culinary delight. "I don't know. He seemed a little relieved. I'm not sure what to make of it."

"I find it very strange," Josh said, "that he's so, what's the word, comfortable? Yes, comfortable with her behavior. It's a very unusual relationship."

"I actually wonder if the boy is even his kid."

"What do you mean?"

"He doesn't look very much like him at all. I think one of Lisa's boyfriends got her pregnant."

Josh put his fork down, drank coffee, and leaned back. "Interesting. Do you think Kipp might have known about that, or does he believe the boy is his?"

"I really don't know. Actually I'm surprised Mike Gordon didn't ask those questions."

"Maybe he knows, but didn't ask to save face. Why destroy the relationship between the boy and his father?"

"Maybe Mike Gordon has a heart after all. Or," Gail said in between bites, "maybe Robert Carter is the father, Lisa knew that, and she was attempting to get money from him to take care of his illegitimate child, which would be even more embarrassing for him."

Josh seemed to be pondering the thought. "Maybe. I have

to be honest, though. I cannot believe he would be capable of such a thing. I think he would rather lose everything than kill another human being, let alone pay someone to do it." Josh took a bite and chewed for longer than Gail thought necessary. "Still, Kipp's testimony doesn't add or detract anything. We already knew his wife was sleeping with half the town. The only thing Kipp did was reassure the jury that he stayed around because he loved her and wanted his son to have a home."

"That wouldn't work for me," Gail said. "But who knows, maybe he killed her."

"Seriously?"

"Well, I don't know. Who else could have gotten her up into the mountains? At midnight?"

Gail could tell Josh was thinking about the possibilities, but he shook it off.

"The neighbors put him in his house all night. I'm afraid Hodges isn't getting off with Kipp Martin's help."

"But Kipp does point the finger at Robert Carter," Gail said. "Between the photographs of them together and Kipp's testimony, Mr. Carter looks like he had a lot to hide from his wife. And with the possibility that he could be the boy's father, there are a lot of reasons to look at him. Remember, the wife is the one with the money. If she leaves him, he's broke."

"You're offering up lots of motive, Gail, but no evidence. And I'm still convinced Carter is too frail for the circumstances."

"You know," said Gail, "you mentioned earlier that Robert Carter was too old to walk all the way up that draw to plant evidence in the camp."

"Yeah, I still believe that."

"That tells me you think it's possible that someone else could have."

"Could have? Yes. Did? I don't know. Theories?" Josh asked.

"Well," Gail said as she took Josh's hand, "Connie didn't like Lisa and lured her or kidnapped her. Sam Reynolds was jealous and took out his revenge. Perhaps Robert Carter was afraid of being exposed and hired James Hodges to kill her? Hodges needed money, and he has a history of trouble. So, maybe he did it for the money."

Josh looked at her as if her screws were loose and then smiled. "You need a vacation, young lady."

"Oh," Gail laughed, "I'm hardly young. But I do need a vacation." She patted his hand before returning to her coffee, and drank thoughtfully.

Josh pondered the question. "Either way, right now my gut tells me James is the right man."

"Even with the evidence?" Gail asked as she looked at Josh's hands around his mug. They were rough. His long fingers were wrinkled with age and exertion, but there was tremendous strength in them.

"Yes," he said, "especially with the evidence."

"Well, I have my doubts."

"Do share."

"Well, I've been rummaging through the files you gave me and I'm not so sure."

"Did you find something?"

Gail reached into her bag and produced her paperwork. "We already know all the victims are similar, right?"

"Yes," Josh said with curious eyes.

"Their bodies were found all over the county."

"That is correct. There's no rhyme or reason to it."

"Yes, there is."

"Say that again," Josh said quickly.

"They were all staged."

"What do you mean 'staged'?"

"Look here," Gail said as she scooted to the other side to sit next to the sheriff. She unfolded a county map and laid it out, then placed a few pages on top as a reference. "The first victim was found here, near Steens Mountain."

"That's right." Josh leaned closer and traced his finger on the map. "Next was," he brushed her hand as he traced the map, "right here. Nikki Rhodes was found here, at Buck Spring Creek."

"Right. Then Gina Bergmann all the way back south at the very tip of Malheur Lake."

"Which is a very popular fishing area."

"Was," Gail corrected him.

"And Buck Spring Creek is a popular trail head."

"Exactly."

Josh pulled back. "What do you mean by that?" he asked.

"It's a popular spot."

"So, what?"

Gail referred to the map. "Each of these places is or was a popular spot where someone was bound to be along at any time. I've also spoken to some people who say that the Steens Mountain trailhead is a hugely popular place. Now, see this," she said as she pointed to the map. "There's an old boat ramp there. I talked to some nice old gentlemen who were fishing off the point here. One of those men said he used to have a bait shack down there, and would meet friends there every weekend to fish. But not anymore. He says they don't go there now." She switched files. "Lisa Martin's body was found a quarter mile south of a camp and right where a man hikes every weekend. Eryn Rogers was found just off a busy dirt road right next to a swimming hole in the creek where children were known to swim."

"So, you're saying all these bodies were placed where they would be found?"

"Yes, all of them. Not 'busy' places, like there was a steady flow of cars, but places where someone was likely to stop, maybe to get out and pee or something."

"Or go fishing?"

"Or hunting," Gail said. "The murders were all very bloody and very brutal. No rapes. No visible sign of struggle. As you've said, the killer must have known them. All of them. He lured each one of these women to a predetermined site and left their bodies where it looked like he was hiding them, but he was actually staging them to be found."

Josh sifted through the stack and pulled a different file out. "I can put James Hodges at two of these locations at the time of the murders."

Gail shook her head. "He's too young, Josh. He would have been a little child when Annette Walker was killed. And, come on, does he really strike you as a serial killer?" Gail was serious. She had seen the profiles before, and in her mind none of them looked like Hodges.

"I don't know about that. I only know about evidence. The evidence we have says the right man is on trial as we speak. It points nowhere else. I don't know," he said as he pushed his plate to the edge of the table, "Maybe he's a copycat killer or something like that."

"What's he copying?" Gail demanded, and she knew she had him stumped. She rested her hand on Josh's arm and shoved the files away. "Put all this away. Put all the evidence away. Put it out of your mind. Stop thinking inside your little sheriff's box for a few minutes and look at James Hodges. Only look at him. What do you see?"

"A murderer."

She nodded. "Okay. Well, I see a very scared young man who made bad choices and did some very stupid things when he was a lot younger. He made bad choices all through his life and wound up in the wrong place at the wrong time. Maybe more than once. He's the perfect man to blame, Josh. But I've been watching him in court. He doesn't strike me as the kind of man who would do this." She pulled a photo from the top file. "Why does James Hodges cut a woman's head off? What hatred drives him to do that? And how can a guy who has the shakes as badly as he does make that kind of cut?"

She could see the wheels spinning in Josh's head. Whether or not it would do any good, she hoped at least to get him thinking about things without including James in the picture.

"I'm not a psychologist, Gail. I can only draw my conclusions based on what I know, and I don't know what's going on in the man's head. However, I see your point, which is precisely why I asked for your help. So, here's what we'll do. I'll take you to each and every scene, and you can look around all you want. You ask questions, and I'll answer if I know."

"Okay," she said, "when do we start?"

"In the morning," he answered.

"Where do we start?" Gail asked with fire in her eyes.

"With the first victim. We start with Annette Walker."

TEN

T he old Chevy lumbered up the wash-boarded road through mountains still showing snowpack from a heavy winter. Broken rock and craggy peaks jutted through the snow where the sun's life-giving warmth was winning the war with winter. Ancient peaks stood sentinel against a sky so blue the clouds appeared like cotton balls pinned to a painted wall. It was a forsaken, barren wilderness, beautiful to behold, perilous to travel.

Gail wondered to herself why a killer would choose such a hostile location to perfect his art, and how he could have lured someone, anyone, out here. What forces would have been in play to exercise such a thing? She was convinced they were hunting a serial killer, and that person would have to be a master of planning, having come out here in the middle of spring with no apparent motive and no guarantee a woman would ever arrive for him to prey on.

"What if this guy killed her up here and it was just pure co-incidence?" she asked. "Maybe he was up here freezing his butt off and went a little nuts? Maybe he wanted or needed help and asked her, but she refused him, so he killed her?"

"From the very beginning," Josh said, "I was under the impression that her killer must have known her. Either that, or he kidnapped her. There is a very low likelihood of them having met up here by chance."

"So, just like Lisa Martin?" Gail asked with a hint of sarcasm.

"Perhaps," Josh answered as he did battle with the rutted road.

Gail grabbed for a handhold and released an involuntary squeal as the truck shifted over the muddy road. "He seems crazy to me," she said.

"He stabbed her twenty times, Gail. You'd have to be a little crazy, or very mad, to do that."

"Or maybe both."

The sheriff smiled. "You're always so full of insight."

"Well, I mean, maybe he was hurt or scared and maybe the cold had him a little out of his mind already. Then, you know, he got mad at her because she wouldn't help him, or something like that. He was already nuts and her refusal kind of set him off. He had a knife, and he turned her around and just started stabbing her in the back."

"Twenty times?" the sheriff asked.

"Twenty? Three? What difference does it make?"

"Let's keep the facts straight," Josh said. "What do we know about this case?"

Gail opened her notebook. "The victim's name is Annette Walker. Forty-two years old, brunette. The men who found the body are called Barry Sommers, and I think this says Ian O'Michael, who came up here about ten o'clock in the morning to go snowmobiling and parked at the turnaround. The report says they got out of their truck and walked around behind it to put on their gear. They started across the turnaround for the gate and found the victim lying facedown beneath several inches of fresh snow. Actually, it says Mr. Sommers tripped over the body. There were multiple sets of tire tracks found at the scene, all of which had the same layer of fresh snow, which made their age difficult to determine.

"The body was cold and the autopsy found the murder likely happened on . . ." She paused. " . . . April 12." She looked at the sheriff. "Most likely in the early afternoon." She paused again and stared out the window as they approached the summit road. "The victim had twenty stab wounds to the back. There was no sign of sexual assault. Bruising on the neck indicated the assailant had her in a headlock while he was working her over. The only distinguishing feature found at the scene was a large boulder with an *A* carved on it found near the victim. A rock with an *A*?"

Josh nodded.

"The investigation," Gail continued, "determined the rock was meaningless and nothing more than a coincidence, as there are numerous boulders lining the parking area—all adorned with engraved letters. The report is signed 'Joshua Matthews, Sheriff.'"

Josh groaned as he pulled the truck to a stop in the center of the turnaround. "That's right. The rocks were placed here long before the victim was found, and those markings were already on them. They spell out 'Steens Mountain.' The fool things weigh a thousand pounds apiece." He paused as he killed the engine. "This is the place."

Gail stepped from the truck and breathed in the cold, clean air. She scanned the peaks and the private road up the east side of Steens Mountain. A gate there prevented adventurers continuing any further with their vehicles, but there was no reason for her to go any further than where she stood.

"Right here," Josh said, "under my feet. This is where she was."

"This is such a barren place," Gail said with a shiver. "Why on earth?"

Josh turned to the west. "The rock should be this one. Gail, let me see that photo."

"Say 'please,'" she joked.

"Just . . ." He reached for the picture.

"Hey," she said, "you be nice." She held up the picture and turned so he could see it. Look here." She pointed. "Right in the corner of the picture. See the shape of that rock?"

"Yes. That's the one. And the letter should be there. The snow is covering it."

Gail helped the sheriff brush fresh snow from the boulder. "Well, I'll be. Look at that."

Josh stopped what he was doing and looked at her. "Yeah. That's it."

The stone measured five feet long and two feet high and had a faded *A* etched into the surface facing the turnout. Josh traced the letter with his fingers, then stepped back and took a photograph. "What the hell does this have to do with anything?"

Gail stooped down and ran her fingers across the rough edges. "This wasn't just carved with a pocket knife. These are tool marks."

"Yep. See over here." Josh said as he pointed out another boulder.

She went to where he was and saw what he pointed to. Another rock and another letter. "'*I*.'" She went to the next and dusted the snow from its surface. "This one is *N*."

"It's meaningless," Josh said with frustration. "Like I said, it spells 'Steens Mountain.' They've been here eighteen years."

Gail saw the disappointment on his face and pouted in sympathy. "Well, at least we're leaving no stone unturned. Or at least unread."

Josh cracked a grin, thought a moment as he looked around, and then got himself back on track. "Wait a minute."

"What?"

"The body," Josh said.

"What about it?"

"It was found right here. That's why I took a picture of the rock. This is coming back to me. The body was right here." He stood in front of the stone and faced the mountain. "Her head was this way, to the east. Her feet were pointing straight away from the rock, that way. West."

"Oh, wow, Josh, look at this," Gail said as she held the photo of the body out for him to see. "Look at her arms."

Josh looked at the photograph and seemed to strain his mind to find some meaning in it. "The body was there, right in front of the stone, head down in the snow. The legs were together and formed a mostly straight line with the torso. Both arms are angled away from the body at approximately forty-five degree angles." The sheriff handed the photograph to his companion. "See for yourself."

"It's an arrow," Gail said almost without thinking. "The body is making an arrow."

Suddenly, Josh saw it as clear as the morning sky. "If that's true, then it's pointed right at the stone."

"It's an *A* for 'Annette.'"

"That can't be," Josh said. "If he killed her here, beside a rock bearing her initial, do you know what kind of planning that takes?"

"It means he picked this spot, and then picked the person."

"Or did he pick the person and then pick the spot?"

Gail took another look around. "And you said the stones were here before she was killed?"

Josh nodded. "Put in in sixty-two. She was found in sixty-five."

"No trees," Gail said, "no place to hide. It's cold. Josh, think about it. James Hodges is accused of committing a crime that may be related to this one. He was in grade school in sixty-five. This murder took serious planning, and enough cunning to get her up here. Does it sound like James Hodges could have done this?"

Josh sighed. "Definitely not. But I already knew that."

"And what about these other cases? Was anything ever found there? Like identifying marks or letters?"

"No. Nothing like that, or at least nothing we ever found." Josh blew in his hands and then took Gail's to warm them. "It's getting cold. I think a storm's coming, and we sure don't want to get caught up here if it blows hard." He looked at his watch. "We've been here an hour. Let's get off this mountain."

Gail watched small white flakes whisk by in front of her and stopped walking. "Is that snow?"

"You mean this white stuff falling from the sky?"

She gave him a dirty look. "You're such a brat."

"I have my moments."

"I thought it was June," she asked sarcastically.

"It is June, and we're not exactly at sea level. It can snow up here any time it wants to."

The drive down the hill was slow at best. Fresh snow on the old road made it slick, and Josh took his time.

"It snows in June," Gail said, "yet some guy came all the way up here to kill Annette Walker."

"That's one of the reasons we had such a hard time. Almost any useable evidence was covered in snow."

"Wouldn't it take a truck to get back here?"

"Depends. I've seen this place dry as a bone in May, and I've seen it under three feet of snow in July. That year was an average snow year. I can see that from the pictures. He could have walked in if he wanted to, or come in on a snowmobile, which would free him from using the roads."

"What about this year?"

"We had a good snow year."

"And we were able to get in with no trouble."

"Yes, but it's two months later in the year, and that makes all the difference in the world." The truck slid and Josh corrected. "You okay?"

Gail was gripping the door handle with white knuckles. "Yeah. This is a bit new to me."

"You've never been off-roading?"

"Oh, no. Not my thing."

"Kind of like motorcycles aren't your thing?" Josh teased.

"Yes, just like that." She whooped when a particularly bad slide almost sent the truck into the gutter.

"We'll be okay," Josh reassured her.

"I know. I trust you not to get me killed."

Josh drove carefully, but the road was getting slicker by the minute. Every correction was met by another, and that by sliding toward the ditch on her side or the slope on his. The seatbelt held Gail in place and kept her from sliding forward, but the bench seat had little side support and she slipped back and forth several inches.

"If you grab the handle over your right shoulder, you won't slide around so much."

She did as advised and found she could hold her position. "Thanks," she said with a hint of worry.

"We'll be down out of the snow in a few minutes."

The prediction failed to hold water. The storm continued all the way off the mountain and for several miles on the highway.

"Where did all this come from?" Gail asked.

"No idea. I gave up trying to predict the weather. Every time you think you've got it nailed, it changes and you look like a fool. What I can tell you is that the weather up there can go south in the blink of an eye. These mountains make their own weather. If you're not careful it'll kill you."

"You mean like that slide thing we did back there?"

"Exactly like that."

"It's all right," she said. "I forgive you."

There was another long silence until Josh spoke again. "Could the arrow be a marker? Like 'start here.'"

Gail turned to face him and smiled. "I've seen the other four scenes. No arrows."

"No traditional arrows," Josh corrected her. "Look harder. Maybe we missed something. And I have a plan."

The drive off the mountain and back into Burns took far longer than Josh expected, but they made it back safely, and as Josh dropped Gail at her apartment he took the time to remind her. "Have a good look at those photos."

"I will," she said.

"I'll see you in the office tomorrow morning."

Gail nodded, flashed a smile, and was gone.

* * *

Sheriff Matthews was all business. The previous day's drive with Gail had been nothing less than eye-opening, and he was confident that her theory held enough water to bring the rest of his team up to speed. There was as yet no evidence to support the idea other than the proximity and arrangement of Annette Walker's body, and he was still not entirely convinced. Yes, the letter had been noted all the way back in 1965, but had been written off as coincidence because none of the other crime scenes had ever revealed a similar trait. The Walker scene had been determined to be an anomaly, and nothing more. With these things in mind, he began his staff meeting with an air of trepidation.

"All right, everybody," said Josh, "we're going to reopen investigations into the following." He flipped a large piece of paper over the easel pad and scooted the stand to more closely face his audience of deputies. "Annette Walker, April 12, 1965, stabbed twenty times in the back, no suspect." He flipped the page and repeated the rundown for each of the four remaining victims. When he finished the list he turned to a chalkboard covered in writing and photographs. He pointed to the body of Annette Walker. "Our town reporter has come up with a theory that bears consideration and may lead to the conclusion that we have been dealing with a serial killer."

Max raised his hand and Josh called on him. "You mean you think all these women were killed by the same man?"

"Maybe," Josh answered.

"What about Lisa Martin?"

"We'll be exploring that possibility as well."

Asked Jane, "Is this your idea, Sheriff, or Gail's?"

"Gail's."

"Has she presented evidence?"

"I'll let her answer that question." Josh motioned to the

reporter, who was sitting quietly at the back of the room. "She will fill you in on her idea. However, before we get to that, I want to thank all of you for your hard work over the last several weeks. I know the Martin case has caused all of you a lot of additional workload, but it's about to get worse. I know most of you have had little or no exposure to these cold cases. Max was around in '77, and deputy Shaw goes back to '73, but none of you were here before that. I've never asked any of you to investigate the past. I've either handled it myself or gotten what help I could from OSP. But we need fresh eyes, and now we have a starting point. That said, have any of you looked at the files at all?"

Max and Jane raised their hands.

Said Max, "I've seen them all, but I'll be darned if I can make anything of it."

"Jane?" Josh asked.

"Yes, sir. While I was looking through the evidence, I decided to open the files, but I'm with Max. I do see similarities among the victims, but no calling cards. Unless, of course, we're calling similarities a calling card."

"The similarities can no longer be discounted. So, not a calling card necessarily," Josh said. "But we think we may have one. I'll let Gail hit you with her theory."

Gail approached the front and referenced the photograph of Annette Walker. "Notice the position of the body," she said as she passed the picture around the room. "The position of the arms, legs, and head. What do you see?"

"A lot of blood," Max responded with disgust.

"Her legs are together, and her arms are out," Jane said. "Very typical."

"Yes. And what about this one?" Gail passed around the photograph of another victim.

"Body is straight in a line, right arm is perpendicular." Jane passed the photograph to Max and continued speaking. "I don't see anything that suggests commonality. Serial killers almost always leave their stamp. They want us to know it was the same person, but I don't see anything that indicates it was.

There are no stamps."

Josh interrupted the deputy investigator. "That's correct, Jane. And outside the context, these pictures don't tell us anything interesting at all. However, taken in a different context, they speak much louder. Gail?"

"Yes." Gail pulled a county map down from the ceiling and began pointing at each murder scene. She called out the names, dates, and circumstances of each, and then taped the picture of Annette Walker to its place on the map. "If I place this picture like so, as we would typically view it, we can see there is nothing of interest. Anyone see anything I don't see?"

There were murmurs around the room, but no one spoke out.

Gail took the photo off the map and showed it to everyone. "This is how we would look at this photograph, holding it upright, head at the top. It's natural, right?" She replaced the photograph on the map, but this time oriented it according to the compass. "However, if we arrange this photograph according to the way the body was found on scene, we get this."

There was more whispering, and still nothing of interest from the audience. At least, not until Jane's eyes went wide with understanding.

"The body is arranged like an arrow," she said. "It's pointing at something."

"Very good," Gail said as she high-fived Jane. "That's exactly what it is. What will really blow your mind is what it's pointing at." She took another photograph and showed it around the room.

"It's a rock," Max said.

"Yes, good," said Josh. "Very insightful, Max."

"Well, it is."

Gail broke in, "More important, it's a rock with a message."

"What message?" asked Jane.

"Well, Sheriff Matthews took me up to the Steens Mountain trailhead this morning where we took this photograph of the rock."

"So," Jane said, "she's pointing to her own initial. How long has the letter been there?"

"The engraving was on the stone when it was delivered to the site in 1962," Gail said.

"That's right," Josh said. He held up yet another photo. "I spoke with Alan Dickerson over at Powell Forestry. Jacob Powell donated these stones to the county and oversaw their installation at the trailhead. The company photographer documented the installation as it happened. Every stone up there has a letter engraved on it, and they spell out 'Steens Mountain' when read from the parking lot. They do not appear to have any special meaning other than that. Gail and I were able to identify the exact stone where the body was placed, which was easy because there is only one A in the two words. That the body was exactly in front of this stone was determined to be a coincidence during the initial investigation, but considering we have nothing else to go on, we're going to run with it. For now, look at it as though her body is an arrow that is pointing to a stone engraved with the initial of her first name."

"Sheriff," Jane asked, "you said 'placed.' She didn't die there?"

"Yes, she did. She died in that exact location, but our investigation determined the body was turned over, face down, and the arms and legs were moved. I did not believe it meant anything at the time, but now I think Gail might be on to something."

"So, the arrow is pointing at a rock with an A on it?" Jane asked.

"Yes," Gail and Josh replied simultaneously.

"And you believe the A is for 'Annette'?"

"That's what we think."

"If the killer indeed planned it that way," Jane said, "then premeditation takes on a new meaning."

Gail nodded very obviously. "Yes. The engraving wasn't made by the killer, which means he either planned to use this location in advance, or it's one incredible coincidence."

"With that in mind," Josh said, "we have a new directive. Annette Walker's body was posed in such a way to lead us to a piece of evidence that may provide the killer's calling card. Gail and I will be looking into this matter. In the meantime, the rest of you are going to have to pick up a little bit of my slack in terms of patrols."

There were a few joking boos, and one serious grumble, but the team nodded collectively and Josh knew they were on board.

Max raised his hand. "What about James Hodges?"

"That's out of our hands for now. However, if new evidence proves different, we'll address it at the appropriate time."

"What if he's found guilty?"

"If we unearth anything that could exonerate him, he would get a new trial. But that's for the system to deal with. For now, we have work to do."

✳ ✳ ✳

Judge Parker entered the room and took his seat. The attendees sat down almost in unison and went silent as the two attorneys flipped through their notes in preparation for the day's onslaught.

"Does the defense have anything further?" the judge asked.

"No, Your Honor."

Judge Parker peered at the dueling attorneys over the rim of glasses that otherwise made his eyes seem too large for his head, then scribbled something unseen to all but himself. "Does the state have anything further?"

Carl Franklin stood and adjusted his tie. "No, sir, Your Honor. The state rests."

"Very well. Are both parties prepared to give their closing arguments?"

Counsel on both sides of the room announced their readiness, and Gail made a few final notes. Mike Gordon seemed confident of acquittal, Franklin looked like he hadn't gotten enough sleep last night.

The assistant DA was first to go, so he stood and approached the podium, faced the jury, and entered into a slightly animated final plea for them to hang the man sitting in the seat of the accused. "Ladies and gentlemen, over the past two weeks you have heard testimony from the state and the defense. According to the defense—" Carl pointed at Gordon. "—you are asked to believe that a group of intoxicated teenagers and vagrants, high on everything from alcohol to LSD, were witnesses for the defendant, somehow exonerating him of capital murder by simply imagining ghost men and dancing pink bunnies. Illegal hallucinogenic drugs were in use all over the northern part of our great county. You, as jurors, must weigh that against the actual facts of this case.

"Fact: Mrs. Lisa Martin was found in the woods with her head nearly severed. Fact: the defendant was arrested within a few hundred yards of the murder scene. Fact: the murder weapon was found in the possession of the defendant and on his person. Fact: the victim's cloths were found in the possession of the defendant. Fact: the victim's blood type was found on the defendant's cloths, beneath his fingernails, and on the knife and clothing that was found in his possession. Fact: the defendant was both high on heroin, and was in possession of heroin, when he was taken into custody.

"The burden of proof falls upon the state to prove that the defendant is guilty of murder and possession of a controlled substance. If you believe in ghost men and dancing pink bunnies, then you might decide the evidence should be ignored. However, if you intend to base your verdict on facts, then you will know that you must find the defendant guilty of capital murder and possession. Weigh the evidence and you will know, beyond any reasonable doubt, that there is no other option. The defendant did, in fact, kill Lisa Martin."

Carl returned to his table and sat down. He appeared more confident after delivering his statement, and Gail could tell that he *knew* he was getting a conviction.

Meanwhile, Mike Gordon jostled through some papers on his desk, then leaned over and whispered to his assistant before standing. He straightened his tie, drank water, and stepped from behind the table. There was a clear, deliberate method to his movement.

"Well," he said, "the state has painted a beautiful picture of a murdering, calculating thug, have they not? A simple, homeless man somehow lured a beautiful temptress to his secret lair in the woods where he hacked off her head with an expensive, custom knife using a technique the county medical examiner described as military in nature, even though James has no military service on record. He undressed her body, stole away with her clothes, and 'hid' one quarter of one mile up the creek with a bunch of drunken, stoned vagrants. *And* he kept all of the evidence. We are also to believe the victim parked her car at the bottom of the hill and walked, alone, five miles into the mountains, at midnight and wearing high heels.

"The state would have you believe that my client, James Hodges, is capable of such barbarity. Of course, the state would also hope you buy its story that 'ghost men' and 'dancing pink bunnies' somehow rule out eyewitness testimony proving that there is more to this story than meets the eye. Melissa Reed gains nothing by coming here to testify. There was no plea deal for her. Yet she swore on the Good Book that she saw a black car parked at the turnoff to NFD 2820. Do we suppose that her testimony is moot, even though she also testified that she did not see the victim's car? Or was that also a hallucination? Are we to disregard the testimony of Dusty Stevens simply because he is dirty and smokes pot? What if he is telling the truth, as I believe he is?

"It is the defense's belief that Lisa Martin met one of her lovers along Highway 395. That person got into her car and rode with her to the murder scene. An altercation broke out and he killed her. He then left her body, walked to the vagrant camp, planted the evidence in the trash barrel, and finally drove the victim's car back down the hill and left it there. Eyewitness testimony supports this hypothesis and presents a degree of doubt that must be considered.

"You must also consider the nature of James Hodges and his capacity to commit such a crime, along with his supposed desire to keep evidence of such incriminating capacity as to put him on death row, and then you must ask yourselves what hatred is so powerful as to motivate such an enterprise.

"You heard testimony that James has a debilitating disease that causes uncontrollable shaking, and you must determine how such a perfect cut was made by a man whose hands shake so badly.

"Testimony also showed there were no less than two other people within this community who had ample motive and the means to remove this beautiful, young woman from their lives.

"Ladies and gentlemen of the jury, the state carries the burden to *prove* that James Hodges is guilty beyond *any* reasonable doubt. Examine the evidence, and you will find that the state has done nothing more than conjure up what might have happened, not what actually did happen. Weigh all of these things and you will find that James Hodges is neither capable nor guilty. Ask yourselves, having carefully reviewed all the evidence, do you have reasonable doubt as to James's guilt? If you do, you must find not guilty."

Finished, Mike Gordon clasped his hands and returned to his table.

Judge Parker donned his glasses, rubbed his chin as if in deep thought, and turned to Carl Franklin. "Does the state have any final comments?"

"It does, Your Honor," Franklin said as he returned to the podium. He faced the jury and spoke with animated hands. "Defense claims the people are conjuring what might have happened, yet the state has shown what did happen. It is Mr. Gordon who lays stories out for you, while the state provides you only with the facts. Yes, it is our burden to prove the defendant's guilt. The state has presented its evidence against the defendant, and now it is up to you to weigh that evidence and return a guilty verdict."

Judge Parker lightly rapped the gavel and turned his attention to the jury. He removed a paper from his desk, donned his glasses, and scanned the document one last time before reading it to the jury. "Ladies and gentlemen of the jury," he said with a seriousness that brought complete silence to the room, "you have heard testimony from the state and the defense. Both sides have delivered their arguments, and it is now up to you to decide the defendant's fate. At this time, I will invite the audience to leave the courtroom while I give the jury its instructions. This court is adjourned."

The gavel slammed home, and it was done.

Gail took a deep breath, glanced at the jury and wrote down a final comment, then closed her journal and set it in her bag. The jury was restless, and she knew they were as happy as she to get it over with. Now, it was up to them to decide. She stood for the obligatory ceremony and then she slid from the bench and left the room. It was some time before the attorney's and their teams exited. At last they did, and as it was from the beginning she found herself unable to get a word from Carl Franklin. However, to her surprise, Mike Gordon approached her and extended his hand.

"Ms. Cruz," he said, "I do apologize for my previous coldness. I do hope you understand."

"Of course," Gail said. "You wouldn't want to give anything away, would you?"

"No. I'm afraid these things must be held close to the vest until it is finished."

Gail recognized the opportunity and jumped. "I don't suppose you have time for a few questions?"

"I do, actually. We can sit outside. It's quite nice."

As they went through the doors and onto the terrace, she

began her interrogation. "Clearly you're convinced James is innocent?"

Mike Gordon motioned to a bench near the curb and away from the crowd. "Clearly. My client is being framed, or at the bare minimum was simply in the wrong place at the wrong time."

"Can you tell me why someone might want to frame him?" Gail asked as she sat down.

"I cannot comment on that at this point. However, I am convinced Mrs. Martin was lured to that spot. She didn't walk up there. I mean come on, she was wearing three-inch heels and we're supposed to believe she walked a dirt road in them? I don't buy it. Besides, my client does not own a car."

"How do you feel about the jury buying it?"

"They're smart people. Hopefully, they'll discuss it, at minimum. If they don't, well, James is up the creek, so to speak."

"What about the black car Melissa Reed claimed to see?" Gail asked while scribbling in her notebook.

"Oh, yes. There were tire tracks there, but then there were a thousand tire tracks there. I searched the county registry and there are many thousands of black cars registered in the state. Too many to count, and it would take months to sort that out, time the state refused to grant my client. But—and this is very important—an eyewitness saw a black car where the victim's car should have been at that time. The prosecution refuses to look at that. Carl Franklin won't turn over a single grain of sand because it requires effort. Unfortunately, that also includes your sheriff friend."

Gail considered that comment a hit below the belt, but she shook it off and continued. "What would you have them do?"

"Well, let me tell you. I get it. Melissa Reed was doped up pretty good. But she saw something, and so did Dusty Stevens. You may not know it, but I dropped acid once. I saw a lot of weird things where they shouldn't be, and I saw lots of normal things where they *should* be. Pink bunnies dancing in the sky can be laughed off. But, black cars on the side of the road? I don't believe that was a hallucination.

"And Dusty Stevens? That guy is sharp as a tack. Very smart. If you actually sit down with him and talk to him, you'll find that he isn't imagining things, even when he's high. But you have to take the time. If you just wave him off because he's homeless and smoking pot, then . . ." Gordon shrugged. "He's a wonderfully capable and intelligent person. Did you know he has a doctorate in orbital mechanics?"

Gail shook her head.

"He worked at NASA in some special satellite group. Led a team that tracked them for the military. His wife died from cancer and he couldn't deal with it, so he left the real world and became a vagrant. But, oh, he smokes pot and lives under a tarp, so why take his word for anything?"

"Why didn't that come out during the trial?" she asked.

"Parker wouldn't allow it. He said Mr. Stevens' past is irrelevant. And Melissa Reed—wow, just wow. A straight-A student who is beloved by her teachers, who volunteers at the food warehouse, is an all-around good kid, but chuck her under the bus because she got lit?" Gordon's face was turning crimson. "My client's life hangs on their testimony, and people like Sheriff Matthews, Carl Franklin, Judge Parker—who is supposed to be impartial, by the way—will let the man fry because they live in an ancient world where evidence can only be considered if it's hand-delivered in a gift box.

"And don't even get me started on Robert Carter. The man lied about his affair with the victim. He perjured himself before this court, and nothing is to be done? No charges? That alone demonstrates the trouble James is facing. He's in the wrong place at the wrong time, but he must endure murder charges while the perjuring but wealthy Robert Carter walks away? How many affairs does that man have to have before this community can see through him?"

Gail was struck by Gordon's last comment and attempted to dig further. "When you say 'how many affairs does that man have to have,' do you believe he has had more than the two mentioned?"

"Ms. Cruz, I believe that Robert Carter is a very busy man, if you catch my drift. But, that is all I have for now. Good day."

Gail tried to get in one last question, but Gordon was fast on his feet. Apparently accustomed to making a quick exit, he was too far gone by the time the words even formed in her mouth. She sat there wondering about Gordon's comments until a familiar baritone voice sounded behind her.

"Did you have a nice chat?" Josh asked.

"Yes," she said and changed the subject. "You want to take a drive with me?"

"Where to?" asked Josh.

"I'm not sure I want to say."

"Am I going to like it?"

"I don't know."

"Then let's go. You're car or mine?"

"Yours. My car doesn't like scary roads."

"Have you had lunch?"

"No, but we could get a burger on the way out of town."

"Sounds good." Josh extended his hand and helped her off the bench. "What's on your mind?"

"The trial."

"Still not convinced?"

"Will you like me less if I say no?"

"No."

* * *

Josh sat in silence and wondered why Gail was so quiet as they drove north. When they came to the corner where Melissa Reed and her friends had crashed, she finally spoke up.

"Pull over right here."

Josh slowed and turned the truck off the road and parked in front of the power pole where the Volkswagen Beetle had left an ugly scar. "Why here?" he asked with raised eyebrows.

"No reason. I'm just following my gut." Gail stepped from the truck and looked both directions along the highway. "Why here, indeed?" she said.

"Why not?" Josh asked. "That girl was drunk and high on LSD. This place is as good as any other."

"Well," she asked, "did you know it takes most people about half an hour to feel the effects of LSD?"

"Yes, but why is that important?"

"Think about it, Josh. Melissa said on the stand that she and the boys pulled over just north of where Lisa's car was found. They dropped acid, then continued down the highway."

"So you believe her then, that the effect didn't hit her until they went past the turnout?"

"Perhaps."

"That *could* mean Melissa wasn't hallucinating when they drove past."

"Right," Gail said with a smile.

"But she was still under the influence," Josh said as a reminder.

"But not too drunk to drive a car. Remember, she was barely over the legal limit. She was what? Point-oh-eight-one? As far as Oregon is concerned, she was just slightly over, but enough to call it DUI. Still, she wasn't so incapacitated that she couldn't drive the car. She just couldn't do it safely. But I don't think that's what caused the accident. I think it was the acid that hit her just as they were approaching this corner. She thought she saw something and . . ." She shook her head. "I'm sorry."

Josh waved her off. "It's okay. You may be right. So, they left the party early, say around midnight, right about the time Lisa was being attacked. Melissa was tipsy, but she was coherent enough to keep the car on the road, although maybe she was swerving a bit. They drove down the road a few minutes, pulled over to drop acid, then they drove away and Melissa saw the black car ... just not Lisa's car ..."

"Because Lisa rode with her attacker up to Marshall Creek, and they were in her car."

"Right, but Melissa never thought anything about it until . . ."

"Mike Gordon figured it out and subpoenaed her."

"But she was drugged up, so none of us believed her." Josh slapped the hood of the trunk. "Damn it, Gail."

"Josh, James Hodges is innocent."

Josh looked at her and thought she might see the doubt building in his mind. There was something in her eyes that told him it was all wrong. She might have called it fear, and that might still be the best way to put it. Perhaps he didn't doubt Hodges's guilt or innocence. Rather, he doubted his own investigation, and that scared him.

"It'll be okay," she said. "We'll figure it out together."

"Come on," Josh said, "get in the truck."

Further up the highway they pulled over at the NF 2820 turnout. The truck slid to a stop, and Josh jumped out and walked across the road.

Gail followed. "What are you thinking?"

"This is the view Melissa had while driving by," he said, really thinking about it for the first time.

"Okay. Tell me, please."

Josh turned around and looked across the road. "We found Lisa Martin's car right there where the truck is parked. It was almost exactly in that spot, right in front of the sign, there. If there was a black car, he would have had to park behind her, or he would have blocked the road." Josh walked at a fast clip and stood where he thought the car would have been. "There have been too many cars through here since," He said as he studied the ground. "No way to know."

Gail called to him from across the street. "Let's drive further up the road. See if we can get a feel for where she might have pulled over."

"Yeah. Okay. It's not far," Josh said as he got into the truck with her and pressed the accelerator. "Just right there." Within two minutes they turned left on a paved road. "Technically, this is NFD 31. Up here to the right, see that gravel pile?"

"Yeah."

"That's the spot. The road crew keeps a porta-potty there, so the kids even have a place to pee. This is where they were partying."

"That drive didn't even take two minutes."

"No. They were close. She must have pulled over back there." Josh swung the truck around and stopped. "They go behind the gravel there, and you can't see them from the highway. We busted them up once last year, but they've gotten smart. We caught them once, but not this last time."

"Why not?" Gail asked in a tone that refused to assign blame.

"We were busy. The rodeos, the roundup. That stuff draws a lot of people and it takes all of us to keep the peace. Last thing I need to be worrying about is people's kids out blowing off steam."

Gail seemed to trail off momentarily, and then got herself together and came back to him. "Do you feel guilty about it?"

Josh looked at her. "Every day."

"It wasn't your fault, you know."

"Maybe, maybe not. But it's my county, Gail, and that makes it my responsibility."

Gail sighed and pointed down the road. The old truck shuddered and stopped again, this time at the intersection with the highway.

"Melissa said she pulled over," Josh said. "There's no place to pull over between here and 2820 other than right here."

"Well, she was technically drunk, right?"

"Right."

"So maybe 'pulled over' was really just stopping in the road."

"Maybe they thought the acid would hit them sooner," he said. "Maybe they stopped here and dropped. They waited for maybe ten or fifteen minutes, but nothing happened so they drove away."

"That would make so much sense," Gail said. "They'd never tried it before, right? So, they went to the party and someone gave it to them. They were totally expecting it to happen right away, except it didn't. Perhaps they got impatient and drove off. As they were passing the turnout Melissa saw the car, paid no attention and kept driving down the road. Then fifteen minutes later the acid hit her and she saw, I don't know, whatever she saw and went off the road."

Josh imagined the look on his face mirrored the one on hers. What she was positing is what had likely happened, and they both knew it.

He put the truck in gear and drove back toward the turnout. As the truck crept by, he looked out his window. "At night, maybe they were driving forty, fifty. You'd have a hard time making anything out."

"Or there was just enough moonlight that she saw the car."

Josh sighed deeply and sped down the road. A few minutes later he slammed on the brakes and wheeled around.

"Something still bugging you?" Gail asked.

"Yes."

"Well, I'm just along for the ride."

"This was your idea, remember."

"I do. Kind of fun, huh?"

"I'm not sure I would describe it like that."

Gail giggled. "Hey, you could be doing this alone. Where's the fun in that?"

Josh turned off and continued up the dirt road to the murder scene. "Have you been up here since it happened?"

"Yes. I came up a few weeks ago and took a bunch of pictures."

He pulled over and got out. "I've been over this area twice. Jane's been over it three times. Max twice."

"Find anything useful?" Gail asked.

"Just a footprint."

"And you found all this evidence on James Hodges, who was upstream from here?"

"Yes."

"That makes no sense."

"I'll play along," Josh said, "and assume that James didn't kill Lisa Martin. Let's assume Melissa and Dusty are telling the truth. Now, why would you plant all of the evidence in the camp north of here? Why not destroy it?"

Gail sat deep in thought before responding. "I would bet that, if it was James, he was high and confused. When he figured it out, he stumbled across the creek, turned north, and went back to the camp."

"That's assuming James did it. I thought we were assuming he didn't."

"Fair enough. You're right. Let's change the rules, then," Gail said, "and make the assumption that James was framed, or at least someone in the camp was."

"Okay. Then the murderer met Lisa down at the turnout. He got into the car with her and they came up here to do whatever they were doing. Why they had to come up here, I have no idea."

"Because the murderer wanted someone to find the body and he knew there were people up here. He wanted it to be close to the camp."

"That means he scouted the area ahead of time."

"Could it have been Harry Grey?" she asked.

"No," Josh shook his head. "I've known Harry too long. He has no reasonable alibi, but he also has zero motive."

"Who knew the area better than him?"

"No one. Or maybe the logging crews."

"What about someone who knew him? Someone that Harry talked to about this place?"

"That's possible. We asked him those questions, and he had nothing to give us."

"Okay, we're thinking outside the box here."

"Are you saying that I'm stuck inside a box?"

Gail did not want to hurt him and shuddered at the insinuation. "I don't know, Josh, but we wouldn't be here if we kept the status quo. Something isn't right, and we're not going to find it unless we try a different tack."

"You're right. I took the obvious path. I'd like to think I did it right, but I seem to have missed something."

"You did." She reached over and touched his hand. "We've all missed something."

Josh stood silent before pointing up the draw. "The footprint was up there, plain as day when we saw it."

"So, why there?"

"I don't know for sure, but now that I think about it I only found that one print, and it was nearly perfect."

"And it was pointing upstream?" she asked.

"Yes. It was so good I had to ask myself if it was planted."

"As a diversion?"

"Maybe, but the print never slowed us down. In fact it sped us up. I mean, it pointed right to James! He just … just fell in our laps with all the evidence on him," Josh said as he turned toward the tall pine where the body had been found. "Let's go."

"What is it?"

"Remember the way Annette Walker's body was posed?"

"Yes, like an arrow."

"Right."

"Yes," Gail said, "of course."

"Remember how you decided that Lisa's body might have been posed, too."

"Yes," Gail said, "but it's different."

"Look here," he said pointing to the scene. "The body was there, right behind this tree. The creek is right behind it." He reached into Gail's bag to remove the case file. "Now," he said as he produced a photograph of the victim's body, "look at her body."

Gail examined the photo. "What are you seeing?"

"Look at her body. What does it look like?"

"Her body is straight," Gail said as she held the photograph, "with one arm mostly at her side and one stretched out perpendicular, like she's pointing. Except she's not pointing. Her hand is making a fist."

"If her index finger had been extended," Josh said, "we would have followed that line of thinking. But it wasn't. Like you said, her hand was curled in a fist, so it didn't dawn on me until you brought it up."

"Annette is posed like an arrow," said Gail. "Body, straight, arms at forty-five degrees. Lisa is different. So, if she's pointing, what's she pointing at? And what is she pointing with?"

Josh scanned the forest in the direction of the extended arm, to the south and slightly west. There was nothing there other than trees, sage and grass. And the road sign.

The road sign.

"I'll be a stuck badger," he said as he stared across the road. It took a full minute of silence for the reality of the discovery to set in, but it was there now, as plain as day. He started back toward the pickup and stopped at the intersection.

Gail followed behind him. "What is it?"

"The road sign," he answered. "Look at it."

"I don't see anything. It just says 'NFD 3935.'"

"Correct you are, Gail," Josh said as he reached out and touched the wood post. "Powell Forestry placed these signs so his loggers wouldn't get lost. They're all over the place out here. So many roads, it's a confusing mess. Every intersection, just like this one, his guys stuck a sign in the ground. Every one of them was identical. All shaped like a cross, and all painted bright green."

"Josh, I hate to tell you this, but that sign isn't shaped like a cross."

"No," Josh said as he stroked his fingers across a stripe of recently exposed wood. "It is not. The cross bar has been moved. Every intersection out here," he said, "has a sign just like this one. When you come out of wherever you are, you meet the road, and a sign tells you what road you've found. They've been up here for at least ten years."

"Then this one was definitely here when Lisa Martin was murdered?"

"Definitely," said Josh as he produced one of the many photographs included in the file. "Look here. Jane took this photo May 15 from right over there. You can see it was like this on that day, which means it was changed before Lisa was killed, or *immediately* after."

"So, someone moved the cross bar to the top of the post and over a bit. Why does that mean anything?"

Josh turned to face her and winked. "Think outside the box, Gail." He turned and quickly walked the twenty-five yards back to the tree where the victim's body was found. "Lie down," he said, "on your back, head facing that way."

Gail did as Josh said and rested her butt gently on the soft earth.

"Lie in a straight line with your left hand out."

She did as he said.

"Gail, you are now lying exactly as the victim was found. Her head was cut off back to the spine and laying on the ground but looking in the direction her arm is pointing. So, you can now look at the sign from her perspective and tell me what you see."

Gail turned her head and followed the line of her arm. She could just make out the brightly painted sign off in the distance through the grass and sage. From her slightly upside down perspective it was obvious, and when Josh's discovery dawned on her, she sat bolt upright. "It's an *L*," she said, her mouth agape. "It's upside down, but it is definitely an *L*, and it stands for 'Lisa.'" Gail jumped to her feet in a flash, threw her arms around Josh's neck, and kissed him.

Gail was still very fresh on Josh's mind. It had been thirty-five years since he last kissed a woman, and until recently the feeling had been lost entirely from his memory. For three and a half decades he put work before pleasure. However, this past month he'd found himself getting close to the reporter, and she wasn't resisting. In fact, she was moving faster than he thought comfortable. Being a big-city girl, he thought she might be accustomed to the rapid advances of men more cavalier than himself and had seemed taken aback that he was so old-school. Still, his character came first, and that character included a deep respect for women, especially women he liked. They were not to be treated like cattle, or a paper sack to be tossed in the wastebasket once its purpose was served. He was a slow mover, in it for the long haul, and sorting out whether or not Gail was rowing the same boat was taking some time.

Josh had known his wife, Alyson, for six months before they shared their first kiss. They'd been married barely six months before the army called, and he had spent nearly three years apart from her as World War II raged across Africa and Europe. He'd returned home to a daughter and a million horrible memories, but Alyson was patient and caring and held him through the sleepless nights and loved him and made him feel like the man she knew he was. Those memories were not just etched into his mind, they were a part of who he was.

Now, for the first time since that fateful day, Josh felt something had to give. His strong belief that Alyson was the only woman he could ever love was being undermined by the sultry New Jersey temptress who now occupied much of his private thinking.

After the wonderful, passionate kiss she'd laid on him and from which he could not force himself to escape, she seemed motivated to go further.

"You have to let go," she had told him. "That's so far in the past, Josh. You can't let yourself be captive to it. Don't you want to love again? Don't you want to feel a woman's arms around you? Don't you want to watch the sun go down with someone beside you?"

Josh knew Gail was thinking of more than just a few moments with the sunset. There was a yearning inside her, something she was warring with as much as he was. She had been hurt, too, but did not want to spend her nights alone any more than he did. He liked her, and knew she liked him. Her spontaneous kiss was proof of that. But that kiss had ended as quickly as it began, and neither had spoken a word of it since, despite what's she'd said to him about letting go. Yet it weighed on his mind. Her lips were like honey and reminded him of the simple pleasures only a woman could provide. He had not felt it since the day his beloved wife had died, and now that he had tasted a woman's lips again, he wanted more. But he could not bring himself to press Gail. She was too sweet, too kind, and too beautiful for pushing. He would bide his time and let things happen as God and time intended.

Now, with the trial over, Josh had ample time to spare for other things. Although he was putting a great deal of that time into Gail and her theory, he had other business to tend to as well. There were speeding tickets to be written, break-ins to be investigated, the occasional teenage disturbance to be broken up, old ladies with flat tires, and ranchers concerned that someone was eyeballing their cattle. Even with his deputies taking on the majority of that, there was still paperwork to be done, employees looked after, and meetings attended.

Josh tried to throw himself into these things, but he could barely get his mind wrapped around them. The discovery of a clue he had missed was stuck fresh in the front of his mind, implanted right next to the reporter's soft, feminine curves. It seemed impossible that someone would go to such trouble, and there was a piece of him that could not be brought to believe he had seen what his own eyes saw. The revelation was tearing at him and his deep, personal conviction that James Hodges was indeed Lisa Martin's killer. Perhaps Mike Gordon was right. Perhaps Hodges's unwanted involvement with his daughter was clouding his judgment. Perhaps, also, Robert Carter had hired the vagrant to do his dirty work and a number of circumstances had placed coincidence directly into the puzzle.

He would have acted immediately under different circumstances. He would have gone straight to Carl Franklin and Judge Parker to reveal what he and Gail had found. But it was scarcely evidence strong enough to be used to stall the trial, much less strong enough to win an appeal should Hodges be found guilty. The sign was subtle, and anyone could have done it. Before Josh could fully commit, there would have to be additional evidence. There had to be more.

The morning sky was lost in brown fog and leaves as a warm summer wind blew from the west, bringing with it a million tiny flies, grasshoppers, and a hail of street garbage. A crowd of desperate souls rushed the doors with hands guarding eyes and mouths while three deputies herded stragglers to safety.

"You want the truth?" Josh said over the wind.

"I'd prefer that," Gail said as she stopped and leaned against the building.

"All right. If you have to know, the county just hasn't got the resources to handle this kind of thing. You already know we've had five of these things. Each time, I got the call. We looked into it, dug around, did everything we could. We collected evidence as best we could, followed every lead we could, and hung our heads when it went dry. Every time it's happened, the trail has gone cold almost immediately. I've never had the manpower, the budget, or the smarts to follow it all the way to the end. So, we've always turned things over to the state police."

"But you didn't do that this time?"

"No."

"So, the previous cases aren't even technically under your control?"

"Yes and no. OSP has them, but they cannot stop us from continuing our investigation."

"And they've found nothing?"

"Nothing," he said. "All the state's resources and men and smarts haven't gotten any closer than we ever did."

"So, what was different this time?" Gail asked as she stroked Josh's arm.

Josh took her hand in his. "This time we had evidence laid out right in front of us. It couldn't have happened any easier."

"Do you think maybe the killer wants to get caught?"

"I don't know what to think," Josh said. "What I do know is you're the first person to come along and challenge our thinking. You make me feel like we've done a pretty poor job, you know, asking all the wrong questions, looking in all the wrong places. For the first time in fifteen years I feel like there's something more we can do."

"Then do you still think James Hodges killed Lisa?"

"Honestly, no. But if we have a serial killer on our hands —and at this point I'm pretty much convinced we do—then we're better off if that person believes we're entirely focused on Hodges."

Gail stopped and leaned against her car, still holding Josh's hand. "I'm going to tell you something," she said, "and I want you to consider it."

"Okay," Josh said as he caught Gail's eyes.

Gail pulled herself close to the lawman and pressed her lips to his.

"I thought you were going to tell me something," he said with surprise.

"I just did," she said as she winked and entered the court-house.

* * *

Inside, there was a feeling of completion. After three days of deliberation, the jury had reached its verdict. The defense said it was good news, the prosecution the opposite. For all who had been agonized by the slow progress, relief was on the way.

"All rise!" called the bailiff.

Three days away from the uncomfortable benches. Three days away from the bickering and back-and-forth warfare. Three days without the sound of the gavel slamming its wooden block.

Three days.

Gail flipped through her notes and settled on a blank page. She had penned an article every day since the trial began and kept her readers up to speed on the court's goings-on. She told them about the attitudes, the deceit, and the indifference. Each character had his or her day in court and then their fifteen seconds of fame on the pages of the *Burns Review*. Over the last three days she'd summarized the trial and offered her own opinions.

Now, with the trial in its final day, Judge Parker claimed his throne as the masses stood out of respect. "I understand the jury has reached a verdict?" the judge said with a sour look.

Jacob Powell rose from his seat. "Yes, Your Honor. The jury has reached a verdict."

"Bailiff, please bring the verdict to the bench."

The bailiff stood, straightened his suit, took the paper from Jacob Powell, and presented it to the judge. A deep, foreboding silence filled the room as the judge scanned the document before handing it back to the bailiff.

Judge Parker removed his eyeglasses and rubbed his head. "The defendant will please stand while the jury foreman reads the verdict."

The bailiff returned the document to Jacob Powell.

Powell cleared his throat and spoke as clearly as any professional speaker. "Regarding the charge of possession of a controlled substance, we the jury find the defendant guilty as charged."

Whispers filled the courtroom and the tension built. Gail knew Hodges couldn't get off on that one. She looked at Maggie Johnson and watched as she used a handkerchief to dry her eyes. She seemed a much different person. Throughout the trial she'd been animated and alert, but now she seemed sad and conquered, as if she had lost a great battle.

Powell continued. "Regarding the charge of murder in the first degree, we the jury find the defendant, James Hodges, not guilty."

Gail felt her jaw drop. She made some quick notes and

fumbled back through the pages. There was great celebration throughout one side of the court. She caught Mike Gordon's eye for only a second, and he seemed elated. James Hodges fell into the arms of Gordon's assistant and sobbed uncontrollably. His hands shook, his legs shook. If anyone in the room was relieved, it was he.

Judge Parker called for silence and waited until the room quieted down. "Very well," he said. "The defendant will be taken into custody. We will meet back here one week from today for sentencing on the possession charge. We thank the jury for your service. You are excused. This court is adjourned."

The gavel landed one last time, and it was over. People stood and shook hands while others filed away into the hall. In the past, Gail would have rushed to interview the attorneys, but this day she could not pull herself from where she stood.

The soothing voice of Sheriff Matthews sounded beside her. "Are you okay?" he asked.

She turned to Josh and smiled a weak smile. "I don't even know what to say."

He sat and touched her arm. "We put these things in the hands of the citizens to decide. It's a heavy burden."

"What will happen to James now?"

Josh sighed. "We'll come back on Thursday next and the judge will sentence him. Knowing Parker as well as I do he'll go pretty heavy on the possession charge. As far as the murder charge, James is not guilty, which means I have work to do."

With that thought firmly in her head, Gail snuck out of the building and braved a furious wind down to the diner. She found the booth occupied and snuck into another, then pulled a file from her purse.

She opened a map and laid a photograph on top of it, then removed another folder and spread its contents over the table. With eyes closed and hands in her lap she imagined the crime scene and tried to orient herself. Steens Mountain stood in front of her to the left, the ridge straight ahead. The half circle of large stones nearly surrounded her, and the body lay at her feet.

Gail opened her eyes and picked up the photograph. When the sheriff had first arrived on the scene back in 1965, he'd taped off the area and dusted the snow from the body. The woman lay in perfect contrast to the gleaming cold surrounding her, legs together, arms at forty-five degrees to her torso, face straight down in the snow. The killer had tidied up the area and left without a trace.

"What are you telling us?" she asked of no one.

The door jingled, and an older woman came into the diner. Gail scraped the pile of documents into the folder and slid it aside as the woman sat down across from her.

"Am I late?" she asked.

"No, not at all. Thank you so much for coming. Would you like coffee?"

"Oh, no, I don't touch that vile poison. Hot tea, please."

Connie came and went and Gail pulled out the familiar notebook. "Do you mind?" she asked.

"No. You write whatever you want."

"Okay. So, it's all over. Was it difficult for you?"

The old woman shuffled in her seat, a smug, defeated look upon her face. "Yes."

"I'm sorry. You know, I was watching you during the trial. You're very, what's the word? Busy?"

"I fidget a lot. It's a nervous habit."

"I see. I try to figure out what people are thinking by watching their habits. In poker it's called a 'tell.' Players watch each other and try to sort out whether or not they're bluffing by watching body-language cues that give away their thoughts."

"I don't gamble."

"No, no, but you still have tells. I caught onto them, and I'm a bit curious."

"Oh?" Asked the sour woman. "And just what are my tells?"

"Well," Gail said as she thrust up her hands, "you do this with your hands when you're frustrated or things are moving along too quickly." She made another motion. "You do this

223

when you don't believe someone is telling the truth, and then you do this when you think they are."

The woman frowned and looked into her lap. "Is this what you wanted to talk to me about, my body language? Was I embarrassing to you?"

"No, not at all. None of those things are bad. It's just who you are."

"Then what do you want?"

"I wanted to talk to you about the jury's decision."

"Shouldn't you be talking to that Jacob Powell fellow? He's the foreman."

"Nah." Gail waved her off. "Who wants to talk to that stiff?"

The woman appeared to smile and rested her hands on the table.

"Actually, Maggie, it felt to me like you were struggling."

"I wasn't."

"But you voted not guilty."

"I know, but I never wanted to. That man is a murderer, I'm quite certain of it."

"You never wanted to?"

"Listen, Ms. Cruz, the rest of the jury, they all wanted to accept the testimony of Melissa Reed and that Dirt fellow. Now, I don't prescribe to drug use, you see, and those two people contradicted the official evidence. And the way that poor woman died, I just can't get it out of my head." Maggie Johnson finished her tea and stood to go. "I've been away from my home for over two weeks, and I'd like to get back."

Gail followed her out the door. "Maggie, there's something I need to ask you."

The frustrated woman stopped and turned. "Okay, but then I'm going home."

Gail nodded. "If you thought James was the killer, why did you vote not guilty? I need to know that. The people need to know."

The old woman seemed to drift away. A minute passed,

then another.

Gail reached out and touched the woman lightly on the shoulder.

"I'm so stupid," Maggie said.

"What?" Gail asked in her firm, feminine way.

"I thought I knew what I was supposed to do in there, but that man made me feel so stupid."

"What man?"

"Powell," Maggie snapped as she pulled away. "I said James was guilty, and he said I was nothing but a stupid old woman who was going to put an innocent man in prison. I was ashamed, so I voted with everyone else. I feel terrible because I did not stand up for Lisa Martin." Maggie shook her head and dabbed at her eyes with a tissue. "Now, if you don't mind, I would very much like to go home."

Maggie Johnson fought against the wind to open the door of her car, and then turned to Gail. "I've never felt so weak," she said.

As the woman drove away, Gail returned to the diner and messed with her hair. She quietly laid her papers back out on the table, stared at them for several minutes, then laid her head down and wondered what to think of the news.

* * *

"Have a look over here," Josh said.

Gail turned to the sheriff and moved to the other side of the road where he was standing.

"I can't recall exactly, but I think James was set up right about here." He pointed to a shady spot behind the haystack. "His tent was about here, I think. James was sitting on a bucket washing his socks over an old milk can. Oddly enough he didn't seem to know we were around. He was surprised when we walked up on him."

"Can you see the murder scene from here?"

"Yes. Come here." Josh stepped out onto the dirt road and pointed to the east. "Down there. We'll drive back down there in a few minutes. See there, where the road goes through the trees."

"Yes."

"Just to the right of there, down near the creek. The man who found her was the farmer that owned this land at the time. He's since sold and moved on, but the farm hasn't changed a lick."

"And it's just hay? Do they do anything else out here?"

"Just hay, and logging up Calamity Creek Road here, about five miles or so. Not much else to do out here."

Gail stood and walked to the truck. "It doesn't make any sense." She got in and waited for the sheriff.

Josh turned the engine over and put the old truck in gear with a grind.

Gail winced. "Missed that one."

"You think?"

She laughed and patted his hand. "Drive on yonder, Sheriff."

Josh smiled and drove the quarter mile back down the dirt road to the bridge over Wolf Creek. When he got out, he looked over the area. It hadn't changed much. The desert still controlled the land for miles, punctuated only by the distant stands of juniper and pine at the ridges, and by the green grass along the banks of the creek. Josh went to the familiar place and looked down at the murky water as it flowed lazily from a culvert. "Got that photograph?" he asked.

Gail removed the picture from the folder and handed it to him.

"Amazing how much the details change in seven years. The grass is different, and that big shrub wasn't here."

Gail walked closer to the creek and tried to imagine the body lying among the reeds and thistle. "Can I see that?"

Josh handed her the photo.

"So, her head was in the water?"

"Yeah, but look. Only the crown of her head was. I always

thought he meant to dump her in the creek and missed. Now, with your theory, I'm not so sure. I think she was staged, like you said."

"The question is how does she fit into the puzzle?"

"You tell me. Her body was not arranged with any kind of pointing appendages. She's just . . ." Josh thought for a moment. "She's just straight as an . . ."

"Arrow?" Gail interrupted.

Josh took the photograph from Gail and held it out in front of him, trying to align it with the current terrain. The alignment of the body pointed into a grove of trees. "Unbelievable," he said.

"We need to have a look over there."

"I think you might be right," Josh said as he studied the darkness amongst the grove.

"Annette Walker is an arrowhead, Lisa Martin is pointing, Eryn Rogers looks like a straight line."

"If the killer is thinking that far in advance—" Josh replied.

Gail cut him off. "In order for him to finish whatever he started, he'd have to be certain he could not be caught. Ever. Not *would* not, but *could* not. He couldn't ever leave a trace of evidence that would lead investigators back to him."

"Well, we've never found anything," Josh said, "so his plan is working."

Gail looked out over the southwestern horizon. "Serial killers leave a calling card to identify themselves, maybe even to tell a story. This guy is way beyond that."

"Annette Walker's body pointed to a rock with the letter *A* on it," said Josh, "and Lisa Martin's to a sign shaped like an *L*. If this guy is truly that consistent—"

"Then there will be something over there that has an *E* on it," Gail interrupted again. Before he had time to respond, she was up the bank and running across the bridge. "It's over here," she said, pointing over her shoulder.

Josh was only a few steps behind her when she veered

off the road and plowed into a stand of tall, leafy weeds. She stopped immediately and cried out in pain as Josh took her around the waist and hoisted her from the wretched plants. He hauled her out and sat her on a boulder.

"Are you all right?" he asked as he crouched down in front of her.

She nodded and rubbed at the inflamed bumps on her arms. "What on Earth is that?" she asked with a wince.

"Stinging Nettle," he said. "I saw you jump in there and thought you must be mad, but then it occurred to me that you've probably never seen it before. Sorry, I should have said something."

"It's okay. I'm all right. It just stings."

Josh nodded. "Yeah, thus the name."

She smiled at him and leaned in for a kiss, then turned her attention back to the stand of trees. "In there," she said. "Come on. We have to find a way in."

"I have one. Be right back." Josh hurriedly walked back to the truck and returned with a machete. "A man can never have too many tools," he said with a smile.

It took fifteen minutes to clear a path into the thicket with Gail following at a safe distance behind. Once the route was clear, she stepped in front of him and walked to the tree she had spotted from the opposite side of the creek.

"Here," she said, "have a look at this."

Josh stepped up beside her and ran his fingers around a circle carved into the trunk of an old tree. Inside the circle, the barely visible scar of an *E* was etched into the aged bark. Folds of growth wrapped over the edge of the ring, nearly burying the letter.

"It's old," she said. "Look at how much the bark has grown around it."

"So, do you think he carved it, or was it here before the murder?"

"I have no idea," Gail said. "He placed Annette where a letter had been for many years, but he changed a sign where Lisa was found, so he clearly sometimes makes the environment and the victim fit together organically."

"This is insane," Josh said. "We never saw this. I recall scouring this area thoroughly, but this escaped us."

"More important," said Gail as she took Josh's hand, "we've found his calling card."

* * *

The sun had fallen beyond the horizon and the roar of bubbling fountains and bottle rockets streaking across the sky delighted children who raced to and fro with sparklers streaming tiny lights of diverse colors. Bloomers and snakes and black cats popped and whizzed while adults battled for control of their offspring. A shrill eruption sounded across the parking lot, followed by laughter as a group of pranking teens took cover behind parked cars and tossed firecrackers at the feet of unsuspecting passersby.

Josh leaned back on a blanket to stare at the sky overhead. He didn't much care for the activities of the teenagers, but he was off duty, and unless they got out of hand he would leave them be. Their rambunctious shenanigans were of little harm, although from habit he kept an eye out for any turn toward the worse.

"It's a beautiful night," said Gail as she took Josh's hand in her own. "I can't remember a Fourth like this."

"It's quieter here," Josh said.

"Well, if you can call this quiet," she remarked with a gentle nudge to his ribs.

"Last year we got rained on."

"Seriously?" Gail asked with a humored look.

"Yeah, just as the kids were getting started. Quite the downpour, actually."

"That's too bad."

"I went home. I was here by myself anyway, so nobody

missed me."

"Not even your deputies?" she asked.

"Well, maybe a little bit. If I recall, Max did say something the next day."

"Tonight you have to stay until it's over."

"If you say so. Got nothing else to do."

"This is nice," Gail said as she placed a soft peck on his cheek. He was enjoying that feeling when she suddenly sat bolt upright, her eyes wide. He barely had time to register her actions before she gasped out. "It's a word. It's definitely a word!"

"What are you talking about?" Josh asked as he sat up to meet her.

"I'm sorry." She stood up, fumbling for her things. "I have to go."

Josh looked up at her as she began to back toward her car. "What's the matter?" he asked.

"It isn't their names," she said. "He's spelling something."

"What are you talking about?" he demanded again.

"The letters," she said. "It's a message, like he's spelling something. I have to go look at my notes right now."

Josh watched her go with a great deal of surprise and concern. He had no idea what she was talking about, although he understood what she meant. "A word?" he said to himself as he stood to follow her. "What word?" He went through the victims' names in his mind and tried to piece them together. When he got to her car, he knocked on her window.

She rolled it down and leaned toward him. "'Angel,'" she said in explanation, guessing rightly that he wasn't going to let her leave without an explanation. "He's spelling 'Angel.'"

"How do you know?" Josh demanded.

She recited their names in order, and then spelled it out for him. "I can see it now as plain as day." Then she turned over the engine and winced as she fought with the transmission. "We need to get to Nikki Rhodes and Gina Bergmann. We have to see those sites as soon as we can."

Josh placed his hand over hers as it rested on the windowsill. "I'm leaving for Salem this week, Gail."

"I know that, but we're really close on this. I can feel it."

"The other two sites are at opposite ends of the valley. I'm not sure there will be time before I leave."

"Make time," Gail demanded as she ground into reverse and started backing. "I'll talk to you later!"

Before Josh could say another word, the Mustang was spitting gravel from the rear tires and Gail was off like a shot. He stood there a moment longer, just long enough to decide there was no way in hell he wasn't going to follow her and continue the train of thought. The hypothesis she'd landed on was too incredible to set aside.

He loped to his truck and turned the engine over, found first gear, and sped from the parking lot focused on catching the feisty reporter. She was already far enough ahead of him and had caught the lights in her favor. He slowed for a red, looked both ways, and thought about running the light, but reminded himself that there was plenty of time.

When he arrived at her apartment in Hines, he sat in the truck for several minutes second-guessing his move. Perhaps he was pushing her a bit too much. Maybe she'd wanted this time alone to gather her ideas together, to sift through the photos and files on her own, letting her thought processes decode what her brain was telling her. After all, she hadn't invited him to come with her.

He breathed deeply, let it out, and breathed again. He needed to right his own mind and let himself think over her statement that the killer was spelling a word. Again, he wandered down through the names of the five victims . . . and it made sense. The first letter of their names, when taken in order, spelled the word *Angel*. But he couldn't get his mind around it, the forethought that would have had to go into it. Could it be a coincidence? He thought not. It seemed far too obvious now. But that obviousness could only be recognized now that Lisa Martin had been found dead. Prior to that moment, the rest of the letters would have made no sense.

Giving up, Josh stepped from the truck and went to the apartment door. He knocked gently, and then louder when there was no reply. A minute passed, and then another. He knocked again. He breathed, looked at his watch, breathed again. He was knocking louder when the door opened and Gail stood before him—disheveled, he thought, and perhaps a bit less dressed than usual. Not that she wasn't dressed, but more buttons were loose than he could remember her leaving open in the past. She was breathing heavily, and her face shone with passion and excitement, and Josh caught himself looking at her partially exposed bra. He averted his eyes and focused them on hers, then reached out and took her cheek in his hand.

"Are you all right?" he asked.

She nodded and leaned into him, and Josh slipped his hands around the small of her waist.

ELEVEN

G ail looked at herself in a hand mirror and wondered what Josh thought of her. The previous night he had suddenly appeared at her door while she was changing into her lounge clothes. Her shirt had been half unbuttoned and her bra exposed, and she'd been flush with the excitement of her new theory, and when she'd seen him through the peephole, she'd opened the door without even thinking about her appearance. As the strong, masculine sheriff held her in his embrace, she'd felt herself melting and known she would not ask him to leave. She'd let him hold her and kiss her and nuzzle her neck and shivered when his hot breath whispered gently into her ear. His body felt warm against her, and she'd wanted nothing more than to continue on into the night, to feel her hands explore his muscular frame while his caressed every inch of her aching body.

But there had also been something in his embrace that made her feel uncomfortable, and so she had pulled away from him. She had not wanted to hurt him, and so she did so as nonchalantly as possible, but his reaction had shown her it was the right choice. Josh had looked around the room as though he were in some kind of trouble, smiled politely, and then apologized for coming on to her so strongly. He was out of practice with women, he was moving too fast, he was sorry.

She'd shaken her head and folded her arms across her chest. "No, Josh," she'd said with passion still flowing through her. "It was really nice. Thank you, actually. I needed that."

He'd smiled warmly, taken her back into his arms, and held her close. She'd stayed like that for several minutes and then moved to the couch, where he'd sat with her until very late, drinking wine and talking about the war and sharing his fears with her and his concern about the speed their relationship was developing. He was honest in his perception that she wanted him, but that he was struggling to let go of a past so far away that her entry into his life seemed only minutes ago. He'd gently pressed her about her marriage and the way it had gone bad, then confided that he'd never been so completely mad about a woman as he was about her. He'd opened up to her and explained why he had never fallen again, that he felt guilty for Alyson's death and could not allow himself to love again. He was terrified of losing Gail the way he had lost his wife.

The night had ended with him remaining true to his character. He'd politely excused himself, gave her a firm, warm embrace and a kiss so gentle that it melted her heart, and then he quietly left her to herself.

The following morning her duties called to her, and she went through the normal morning routine as best she could, ate her toast, and drank a cup of coffee. She then took a shower, got dressed, and left the apartment, but not before looking over the notes she and Josh had scribbled together and taped to the board.

At the office, she got her mind back into the present and continued typing. "Harney County has not had to endure so much strife as it has this year. The heartbreaking news that a tragic accident took the lives of two of our young people has left us mourning and wondering. Then came the murder of Lisa Martin, a local wife and mother, and the shocking evidence that she was having an affair with Robert Carter, the longtime owner of R. Carter and Sons sawmill. We have endured hard times, but in these events we have all learned that we can and will endure even harder times ahead."

Gail stood from her office chair and looked through the dusty window out onto the highway as it coursed through town, past restaurants and the food mart and filling stations. Cars lumbered along, and she wondered who they were. Were they residents? Passersby? Where were they going and what were they doing? A black Mercedes Benz passed, and she wondered if that was the car Melissa Reed had sworn she saw the night Lisa Martin was killed.

"What we learned during the course of James Hodges's trial," she continued back at the typewriter, "is that evidence, no matter how convincing, is sometimes ignored due to our own human frailties. Or perhaps *ignorance* is the better word. Evidence is sometimes discarded because the individual who presents it is seen as someone with poor character, or someone we cannot and should not trust, even if they are absolutely telling the truth."

She looked at her watch and decided she could not make the noon deadline, so she left the office and went to her car. As was her routine, she put on the seatbelt, pressed her foot against the brake, brought the transmission into neutral, and turned the starter. The Mustang coughed to life and she put it in gear. Or at least she tried to. Instead, the transmission caught, then ground like so many nails in a blender, and then caught again. She lurched forward until the car stalled. Grumbling, she repeated the process and got the car into gear, then drove up the road to the diner.

* * *

Josh Matthews was happy about the change occurring in his life. While still struggling to come to terms with the likelihood that he had arrested the wrong man, he was especially excited to have Gail seated beside him in the old truck. Rather than sitting way over by the door as she had been doing, he found her planted on the bench seat next to him with the stick shift directly between her knees. Although shifting gears had suddenly become far more challenging considering his desire to touch her slender legs, he was managing through it whilst keeping his hands to himself. And the smell of her sweet perfume was just strong enough to overcome the age and masculinity of the truck's interior. It was intoxicating.

"When did you talk to this guy?" Josh asked.

"I think it was right at the end of May," Gail said, "or the beginning of June. I could look in my notes."

"Doesn't need to be exact. I was just curious."

"I spoke to him and he said he and his buddy used to fish off the dock."

"That's right," Josh said. "Too bad too. The old man was a bit of a fixture down here on Sundays. He and his buddy sold bait out of a little shack."

Josh turned right onto Narrows Princeton Road and followed it as it wound its way along the southern shore of Malheur Lake. They drove for fifteen minutes before the old truck squeaked to a halt near the boat ramp.

Josh stepped from the truck and strained to hear over the roar of the wind. He barely had time to catch his hat as a gust came up and blew dust and dirt in a vortex around him. "The water's low," he said with raised voice to overpower the wind. "She was found right over there."

Gail followed Josh's pointed arm to a muddy spot of water just east of the boat ramp.

"She was tied to a stake just far enough up on the shore that she didn't wash away with the rising water. Usually does that in the spring and reaches peak in late May or June."

Gail produced the file and rummaged through the photographs. "There isn't a very good picture that shows how the body was in relation to the compass."

"Sure, there is," Josh said.

"Then help me see it," Gail responded, "because I don't."

Josh pointed out over the lake. "That's north," he said.

She shrugged.

"We took the photos from the shore, right where we're standing."

He watched the realization dawn on her face. "I see. So, the bottom of the picture is south?"

"Yes."

"Her legs are spread apart, but her arms are tied together. Her body is in a straight line and her legs represent the tail of the arrow, and they're pointing . . ." She paused to look at the few features the lake had to offer, ". . . that way." Gail aligned the photo and clipped it into her journal. "But I don't see anything. I'm guessing the marker is probably under water."

"Maybe," Josh said, "maybe not. Let's have a look around."

"I don't know. If the pattern follows, her body should be aligned with the letter, and that means it's behind us somewhere."

Josh looked over Gail's shoulders and took them in her hands. The surface of the lake was windblown, and wavelets scoured the bank beneath his boots. Prairie grass wafted as the stiff breeze tossed it about, and the softness of Gail's hair tickled at his chin.

"You see anything?" she asked.

"Not a thing. The water is too murky." Josh turned for the truck. "If he left his card under water, it will be very hard to find it before the levels drop closer to August. This could be a temporary setback."

"It has to be here," Gail insisted. "He left everything to be found. There's no way he wasn't thinking about this very possibility."

Josh turned to her and tried to set her mind at ease. "We found her in late June. The water was as high as it was going to get, and she was right at the edge of the lake."

Gail turned and faced out over the cloudy water again. "Is there more or less water this year?" she asked.

"Less, but not by much."

Josh watched as Gail kicked at the dirt and rocks at the

lake's edge. "This is frustrating. There's nothing out here."

With nothing left to see, Josh walked Gail to the Chevy and held the door for her. She thanked him, and he found his way to the other side. He put the truck in gear and spun the wheel in a hard left, but the truck wouldn't make the turn in one shot, so he pulled as close to the fence across the road as he dared—and slammed on the brakes, not breathing, silent and motionless as he stared ahead. When he looked at Gail he knew she was seeing exactly what he did, and they smiled at each other.

Back at the office, Josh leaned in his chair and kicked his tired feet up on the corner of the desk. It had been one of those weeks, one full of stress and revelation. He was close. *They* were close. He reminded himself that nothing he could call new evidence had been discovered that was of his own design. Rather, it was Gail's tireless effort, her enduring sense of adventure and exploration that had led them both to this point.

Josh reached across his desk and took a photograph in his hand, freshly developed and still smelling of fixer. He held it up and stared at it for a seeming eternity. Had the other letters not been found, this one would never have stood out—and still might be considered too much of a coincidence to even possibly be true. Yet there it was, as plain as the others and hidden so thoroughly from sight that no one would ever give it a second glance.

The license plate had been nailed to a fencepost some years before—many long years ago—along with a multitude of others. A collection, of sorts, that stretched for miles along an old rancher's fence line. It was that rancher's hobby—collecting license plates—and he had hundreds of them, or perhaps thousands, with one nailed to each fencepost surrounding a thousand acres of prime grazing land. But this one was unique. It was a plate from Georgia, and the single, stamped letter read simply *G*. Whether it was a vanity plate, a souvenir, or a gag did not matter. It was there. Every other plate within a hundred yards contained the customary seven-character signature of an

American license plate. Only this one was different, and the fact it matched a strange and hidden profile told Josh he now had four of the five murders linked to the same killer, whoever that might be.

Names ran through his head. Sam Reynolds and James Hodges and Robert Carter. Even the name of his favorite waitress was stuck in there, eager to pop out from time to time and tease at his intellect. James *could* be Lisa Martin's killer, and his name *could* stand the test against Eryn Rogers, but he was too young for the other three. Sam Reynolds had a rock-solid alibi for Lisa Martin, but he was old enough, strong enough, and lady's-man enough for another three, but still too young to be a possible suspect in the case of Annette Walker. Connie was crazy in her mind more often than not and could display a rotten temper if pushed hard enough, but he could not see the woman who wouldn't even kill a kitchen mouse having the fortitude to kill another human being. And that left only Robert Carter. Granted, Josh did not believe him capable of killing in his old age, but a quick check of the available facts left him with no alibi on the night of Lisa Martin's death, and none at the time Eryn Rogers had been murdered. Those three other victims had been found at times when Carter was unaccounted for, having taken "business trips" with no itinerary. And, now, along with the revelation of his affair with one of the victims, further investigation conducted by Jane Smith had revealed that Robert Carter was no stranger to loose women. In fact, there was evidence that he had had multiple affairs, and a number of those women had worked for the mill owner around the office.

Josh was contemplating these things when the sweating, fatigued figure of his favorite reporter practically fell through his door and into the chair in front of the desk. She had been crying, her face was a mess of mascara and tears, and her clothes were soaked with perspiration.

"What happened to you?" he asked with gentle concern.

"My car won't go into gear," she said with feminine emotion.

"Just take it over to Lipton," Josh said with a smirk.

"I did," Gail said with an obvious flair of dissatisfaction. "Apparently there's a recall, but the parts won't be in for three weeks."

"Sounds to me like someone is going to be walking a lot."

Gail looked at him with slightly crossed eyes. "Oh, you think this is funny, do you?"

Josh smiled at her. "I'll take you anywhere you need to go, Gail. Just say the word."

"Okay," she said, "how about you take me up to Buck Spring Creek."

"Buck Spring Creek?" Josh asked. "That's where Nikki Rhodes was found."

She shot her finger at him and winked. "Yep. When can we go?"

"I have patrol tomorrow, then I'm going over to Salem to see Melissa, and I have patrol when I get back, so it might be a few days."

"What about right now?"

Josh shook his head. "I'm sorry, Gail. I've got so much to do, and I'm getting behind on paperwork."

She leaned forward in the chair and eyed him through watery lashes. "I'm sorry if I'm taking too much of your time."

Josh squeezed her hand and reassured her. "It's not on you. I have responsibilities." He thought for a moment and then decided it was time to tell her. "In fact, it's getting to be too much and, actually, I've decided to retire."

Gail pulled back from him in shock. "Are you serious?"

"Yes. Listen, I'm sixty-two this year. I've been at this for twenty-eight years without so much as a two-day vacation. I need to take a break from it."

"When?" she asked.

Josh leaned back and crossed his hands behind his head. "Soon. I haven't decided on an exact date, but I just haven't got the energy to do this anymore. Besides, I thought maybe we could spend a little more time together. I have very little time for you unless I give this job less, and I can't afford to give the job less."

Gail focused her eyes on his. "You don't have to do this for me," she said.

"I've been thinking about this for a year or so. You coming along has only made me think a little harder."

Gail stood from her chair, walked around the desk and sat in his lap. She gently pressed her lips to his, moaned softly, and held herself against him. "What about the case?" she asked.

"We're very close. If we haven't got it buttoned up before I leave, I'll turn it over to Jane."

"Not Max?"

"No. He's a great deputy, he'll be a fine interim sheriff, and I think he'll make a great sheriff if he can get elected, but Jane is better suited to the investigation. Her brain works differently. Max is a better administrator, and you have to have that skill to do this."

"It will all work out," said Gail. "I have faith in you."

Josh pressed his lips to hers. "Thank you. For everything."

She hugged him tight and then pulled away.

"If you need anything," he said as he eyed her from head to toe, "just holler."

Gail gave him a final hug and left the office.

Sheriff Matthews emptied his pockets and placed his effects in a tray, including the .45-caliber revolver he carried as a sidearm, and waited patiently for the guard to inventory the items and place them in a sealed bag. Josh then stepped through a metal detector and posed for the mandatory pat down.

"What brings you to our neck of the woods, Sheriff?" asked the guard, who was merely making small talk.

"Visiting a friend."

"Wow," said the guard, "a sheriff with friends in the slammer."

Josh gave the guard a look. "Where to?"

"This way, sir." The guard led the way down a hall and

through a locked door, then another and another. "In here, sir. She'll be in shortly."

Josh found a seat in the middle of the room, crossed his legs, and placed a fast food sack on the table. The room was forty feet on a side with high, barred windows and doors at either end. Five tables were occupied by a combination of visitors and prisoners in orange jumpsuits. It was a cold, stale environment, uninviting to the inexperienced.

The door at the far end of the room opened, and a guard stepped through. Behind her, a young blonde girl in orange walked with her head held high and her eyes full of joy. Josh stood as she rushed to him and thrust her arms around his waist, holding her for several minutes without exchanging a word, and then sat next to her at the table.

"How are you doing, kiddo?"

Melissa Reed smiled, and Josh could tell she was hiding her loneliness and pain.

"I'm okay. It's nice to have a visitor."

"Have your parents been out to see you?"

She looked at her hands with shamed expression. "No."

"You've been here nearly a month, and they haven't come to see you?"

"No, sir," she said with a definite and respectful tone.

Josh sank in his seat. "I'll fix that when I get back. I—"

"No," she interrupted. "Please, I don't want them here if they don't want to be here."

"They shouldn't treat you like that."

"No, but this is what they need right now."

"Still." Josh said as he took her hand. "You deserve better than that. It takes a lot of courage to admit your mistakes and accept responsibility for them."

"I think I did it mostly for the Johansens. I couldn't put them through a trial just to spare myself."

"You did the right thing."

"I hope so."

"Listen, Melissa, you did. Judge Parker went easy on you

because you admitted your guilt. Had you plead not guilty, the evidence would have crushed you and Parker would have swung the hammer hard."

"How hard?"

"He would have likely given you the same sentence, but extended your parole eligibility to five or more years."

"Ouch."

"For each conviction, concurrently," Josh warned with a stern face. "You would be in here ten years before there was any chance to get out."

"Double ouch," she said through clenched teeth.

"Yes. So, instead you're eligible for parole in a year. You mind your business, and you'll be out of here before you know it."

"Yes, sir."

"Am I going to hear anything bad about you?" Josh asked.

Melissa laughed nervously. "No, sir."

"Good girl."

She pulled the paper bag toward her. "Is this for me?"

"Yes. Thought you'd like a burger."

"It smells really good."

"I got one for each of us. Thought we could have lunch together."

"We haven't done that in a long time," said Melissa, and Josh knew she was right.

"No, and that's my fault. I should have done more."

"Sheriff, please don't take any of the blame for what happened. This is my burden." Melissa then changed the subject. "How's Miss Meredith these days?"

"Oh, I suppose she's fine. I stopped to see her yesterday morning on the way over. She said to tell you hello and that she loves you."

"I miss her."

"She misses you too. And she has it on her schedule to come see you as soon as she can get away."

Melissa smiled at the news. "And how is your murder case

going?"

Josh paused and looked at the windows. The panes were frosted, and he couldn't see out. "James was found not guilty."

"Oh. Is that good or bad?"

"I'm not sure."

"I thought that would be good," Melissa said as she patted his hand.

He squeezed hers in his and held it to his mouth and kissed her fingers. "Not so much. Unfortunately, some things are keeping me up at night."

"Is my black car one of them?"

"Yes," Josh said, surprised at her intuition.

"Is that why you came to see me?"

"I came to see you because I love you."

Melissa smiled from ear to ear. "But you need something from me."

"Yes, I do." Josh said. He was uncomfortable asking his young friend questions she had already been asked over and over again, but he had to know what she had so far been unable to remember. His being there had been planned long before any revelation of black cars came about, but being there now presented an opportunity he could not pass by.

"I think about that car a lot," she said with cold, reaching eyes.

"Melissa," Josh pleaded, "I need you to tell me exactly what you saw."

"I did that in court, but no one believed me."

"Well, I know someone who does, and I trust her."

"Do you like her?" Melissa asked with an inquisitive smile.

"What?"

"Do you like her? It's that reporter lady, right?"

Josh sighed.

"It's okay, Sheriff. You have my permission to fall in love."

Josh laughed. "Oh, is that what you think it is?"

"It's in your eyes. I can read you like a book."

He sighed again.

"What's her name? Gloria, or something?"

"Gail, since you have to know."

"I do. I have to know. There's not much romance in here, you know. Besides, you've been alone long enough. It's time for you to share your life with someone special."

"Okay, okay," Josh said to curb her incessant picking. "Yes, I like her. You happy now?"

Melissa giggled playfully. "I'm happy for you."

"Thanks, kiddo. Now, let's talk about that car."

"Yeah, okay." Melissa adjusted her chair to be closer to his. "So, like I said, the boys and I stopped to do this acid stuff."

"You stopped before you turned onto the highway, didn't you?"

"Yes. How did you know?"

"Gail and I drove up there to try and figure it out. It's the only place you could have stopped and not been on the road."

"Cool. Yeah. So, we left the gravel pit and stopped right before we turned onto the highway. A guy at the party gave us these little pieces of paper and said we just had to lick them, so we did. We waited a few minutes, but nothing happened, so we started down the road. I actually felt pretty good. I was drunk, I think, but I didn't feel like I wasn't in control. I was a little fuzzy, but I was wide-awake and we were laughing. At first, when I saw the car, I thought it was way down the road, but the more I've thought about it the more I realize that it was just around the corner, like a couple football fields."

"That's right," Josh said. "About a quarter mile south."

"Yeah. Well, it was right before midnight when we left. I think Todd said it was eleven forty-five, and I was supposed to be home by midnight."

"On a school night?"

"No, it wasn't a school night. We had parent-teacher conferences the next day, and there was no school. The guys who planned it were way ahead of you, Sheriff."

Josh felt a sudden, overwhelming embarrassment, and

the look on his face must have been obvious to Melissa.

"I guess now you know what to look for on the schedule, huh?" she asked with a teasing smile.

"I guess so. I wondered why you kids were doing that on a school night. Now I know." Josh shook his head and made a mental note to hang the school calendar in his office.

"So," she continued, "we drove by that turnout and I saw a black car there. For a long time I wondered why I even noticed it, but I did. At first, I couldn't remember what it was, but then a few weeks ago I did."

"So, you remember?" Josh asked.

"Yes."

"And?"

"It was a Mercedes."

"A black Mercedes?"

"I'm not positive it was black. It could have been dark blue or something. It had four doors, like the one Mr. Powell has. I remember the brake lights glittering off the car after we drove by. I was starting to feel funny, so I stepped on the brakes, and my brake lights reflected off all this chrome that was on the Mercedes. A little while later is when I saw all these pink bunnies dancing around. I think that's why I swerved. I thought I was going to hit one and I ... I went off the road." Tears welled in Melissa's eyes and she stopped talking.

Just then, a guard approached from the visitor's entrance. "Sir, five minutes," he said.

Josh moved to put his arm around her. She leaned into his body and sobbed against his chest. As she cried, a thought went through his head regarding something the young woman had just said to him. *Like the one Mr. Powell has,* he said to himself.

"Melissa," he said suddenly, "you said that Mr. Powell has a Mercedes like the one you saw?"

"Yes, sir," she said.

"Jacob Powell?"

"Yes, sir."

"How do you know he has one like that?" Josh asked with

a stern voice.

Melissa sat up and wiped her eyes. "Dad works for him, remember? We go to all his barbecues. He keeps it in the garage, and I saw it one day when I was getting soft drinks out of a fridge he has in the garage."

"Time's up, sir," came the guard's voice again. "Sorry." The guard stood by until Josh rose from the seat.

Josh squeezed Melissa's hand and kissed her fingers. "I'll come see you again next month, okay?"

She nodded and accepted a hug from the sheriff and then followed her escort back through the door at the far end of the room.

The guard escorted Josh back the way he had come in, and as soon as he was certain Melissa could no longer hear him he turned to the uniformed officer. "You have a phone I can use?" he asked with urgency.

"Yes, sir. In the office, right there."

"Thanks," said Josh as he stepped into the small room and dialed frantically.

A woman's voice picked up on the other end. "Harney County Sheriff's Office."

"Linda," Josh said with excited voice, "I need your help with a car."

Josh left the prison in a rush and started the old truck. He found his way onto the Highway back to Bend and began winding his way through the mountains. He was rounding Detroit Lake when things began to fall into place. There was one name he would never have entertained, would never have investigated, and at first he dismissed it as too outrageous. As he drove, though, his brain went to work, and the details began to emerge. He found himself needing to pull over to process his thoughts. Why would Jacob Powell's name strike him so hard? After all, Robert Carter owned a black Mercedes, too. It was a mark of their success, a status symbol that told the little people to watch out.

But as the details came together in Josh's head, he began to recognize the reality of the situation. It was Powell who had donated the stones at the Steens Mountain trailhead, the road signs at Marshall Creek, and the boat ramp on the southern end of Malheur Lake. He had replaced the culvert at Wolf Creek after a flood, and he'd built the water tower at Buck Spring Creek. He had been present at all five murder scenes at some point in time, and he was not only familiar with all of them but had contributed in some way to each of the clues Gail and Josh had found. That he owned a Black four-door Mercedes could not be coincidental.

Josh dug into his knowledge of the man and could see it all as plain as day. Jacob Curtiss Powell had taken himself a wife some years ago, long prior to the discovery of Annette Walker's body. He'd met her at a Las Vegas strip club and been immediately smitten with her. So much so that he married her that weekend in a backroom marriage parlor, and then brought her home to Burns, Oregon, where she soon recognized her place as someone important within the upper crust. She'd borne Powell a son who became his pride and joy, a wonderful young boy who had his father's dark hair and piercing gray eyes. But things in the Powell household were not as perfect and rosy as they seemed. Mrs. Powell had taken to the bottle and begun sleeping around. One evening, in a fit of rage, Powell cursed her to her face. He was mean and harsh and empty hearted, and he'd swung and struck her with the back of his hand so hard it knocked two teeth from her jaw.

In a vengeful act, Jacob Powell's wife had taken their son and a .38 Special and ended first the boy's life and then her own.

Josh had believed Mrs. Powell to be a two-timing, pathetic excuse of a woman, and her actions were inexcusable. He'd tried for many months to help Jacob Powell find some solace in his life. Alas, it was a fruitless effort, and Powell had slipped into solitude, pouring every waking minute of his life into growing his company.

Now, as Josh sat on the side of the road and remembered

that chain of events, the deceased wife of Jacob Powell came back into his mind, and he remembered her name.

Angela.

In Las Vegas, her stage name had been Angel.

Which begged the question: if the murderer was Powell, was he spelling *Angel*, or was he spelling *Angela*? If the latter, then he was not yet finished.

The truck threw a stream of gravel off the right tire as Josh hit the accelerator hard. His radio in hand, he called desperately for anyone who might be listening, but the canyon he was in had cut the signal and there was no response. He switched from channel 9 to 19 and called for any and all truckers, but none answered. He needed a telephone, and badly.

❋ ❋ ❋

"Hey, hon, need a refill?" Connie asked as she strolled by the booth.

"No, thanks, Connie," Gail said as she spread a series of photographs across the table and arranged them chronologically. "I've had enough of that stuff to keep me up for a week."

"Suit yourself," said the waitress, who then turned to a group of men whose appearance suggested they had just come off a logging crew. "Well, bless my heart," she said as she wiggled her hips. "Look at these handsome devils."

Gail smiled and tried to ignore the waitress's silly efforts at tip wrangling and went back to her task, staring at the pictures of five women no longer alive. There was little rhyme or reason to the ages of the victims, but they were certainly similar in appearance.

She laid more photographs out side by side with her own written victim profiles. Many of the pictures were fading, and some were blotchy or yellowed. There were images of flora and fauna, taped-off areas around trees and grass, bodies in grotesque conditions. There were boot prints, car tracks, keys, jewelry, purses, and weapons of various forms, rocks, logs, shrubs, and creeks. Many of the photographs were recent, and three of them had been taken just recently when their respective letters were discovered. She knew with little doubt that the letters were the calling card of the killer, and the *only* card he left. She knew he had spelled out a name, but she had no idea what the significance of that name was.

She set the three more recent photos off to the side and continued through the pile. After ten minutes of attention-sapped staring, an old, yellowed photo caught her eye. The victim's body lay in the foreground, her clothes torn and stained with blood. The body lay in a mostly straight line, with both arms at her sides parallel to one leg. The other leg protruded at a grotesque angle to her torso. Which meant—

Gail held the photo in better light and squinted. What she saw could not possibly be real. Or could it?

The photograph depicted Nikki Rhodes. Her body lay situated in just such a manner that her bent leg pointed directly at the water tank on the hill just above her. Two vertical supports held the tank aloft, and an angled strut connected the top of the western leg with the bottom of the eastern. When seen together from the perspective Gail had in front of her, the supports formed a very large and plain-as-day letter *N*. The tank sat atop this base, large and proud, as the decaying body of Nikki Rhodes lay cold and pale beneath it.

So, now she had them all. All five bodies had exactly one thing in common. There was just one key that tied all of the victims to a common killer. And with Hodges exonerated, who could it be?

"Carter," she said to herself.

With a commotion that disrupted the gaggle of loggers with whom Connie was still flirting, Gail shuffled all of her papers and photographs back into her bag and made for the exit without even thinking to pay her tab. Connie called to her, but Gail ignored the plea. When the waitress followed her out the door, she merely waved and yelled that she'd be back later. She practically ran toward the office and cursed that it was so far away, pausing only when an approaching car forced her to stop at a crosswalk.

Before she could continue, a firm, masculine voice called to her. She stopped in her tracks. Her mind was racing, and she needed to get her thoughts in order, but she was in such a hurry that she forgot herself and turned toward the voice. She instantly recognized who had stopped her.

"Mr. Powell," she said to the man in the car before her, "could I trouble you for a ride. It's very important."

The man with the piercing gray eyes smiled and invited her in.

✳ ✳ ✳

Sheriff Matthews stormed through the door with such force that the jingling bells above slammed against the wall. He looked around the dining room. Several rough, tired men stopped eating and turned to look at him, then went back to their meals. "Connie?" Josh yelled.

The waitress appeared from the kitchen and hurried toward the sheriff. "Everything okay, hon? You seem—"

"Have you seen Gail?" he demanded.

She was shocked at his tone, and Josh knew she saw the look in his eyes. "Well, sure. She was in here earlier working on that case you two been worrying over. You just missed her. She left about ten minutes ago."

"Did she say where she was going?"

"No. And she didn't pay, Sheriff. Just run out of here like something was on fire."

Josh pondered the situation momentarily, and then looked toward the booth. "Did she leave with anyone?" he demanded. But Connie had returned to her men, and Josh had to yell to get her attention. "Connie!"

The waitress turned back to him. "What?" she said in a

tone that indicated she was busy.

"Did Gail leave with anyone?" His tone now was more forceful.

"No, she was here alone." She turned back to her job but then paused as if remembering. "Wait. I did see her get into a car with someone."

"Who?" Josh barked.

"I don't know. I didn't see who was inside."

"What kind of car?" asked Josh.

"A real nice Mercedes."

"What color?"

"The car?" Connie said with a confused look.

"Yes, Connie," Josh said impatiently, "the car. What color was it?"

"Black."

Josh's heart stopped and he felt the air rush from his nostrils.

He rushed back through the door, found the truck, and got on the radio. "Linda," he said, "Have you found Max and Jane? I want that APB on Powell's car covered right now. I don't care what else they're doing."

"Yes, Sheriff," Linda said. "Max is on his way back from Wagontire, and Jane is here in the office."

"Get Jane in a cruiser and send her up to Powell's home. I want eyes on him. Tell her not to approach."

"Yes, sir."

"And tell Max to meet me there."

Josh slammed the mike into the receiver and started the engine with a roar. A few minutes later and he pulled into the *Burns Review* parking lot. Gail's car was not there, and it took him a moment to remember that she was on foot.

When he went through the door, the paper's owner looked up from whatever task she was doing and scowled.

"Sheriff," she said cooly, "what may I do for you?"

"I'm looking for Gail. It's important."

"Abigail?" Sandi asked. "What would you want with her?"

"Abigail." Josh said incredulously. "I mean Gail Cruz?"

"Well, yes, Sheriff."

"Gail is Abigail?"

"Did you not know that?" Sandi asked with a bit of smugness. "Well, we are on a more formal basis around here. Why, when we first spoke over the phone she identified herself as Abigail Cruz. I've called her that ever since."

Josh was stunned. If Gail's full name was Abigail, that meant her name began with A rather than G. He immediately knew what that meant, and he struggled to hold his frame from collapsing.

"Sandi," he said in a pleading tone, "I need your help. Gail is in imminent danger, and her life depends on us finding her immediately."

The look on Sandi's face told the story of her relationship with her new reporter. Josh could read that look and he saw the compassion the old woman felt for Gail. Her countenance fell, but she went into action. "What can I do?" she asked.

Josh knew his only chance involved predicting the killer's next move, and that meant knowing exactly where he was going. Anything less and Gail would die. "Sandi, can you think of any place in the valley where the letter A exists in some form? It would have to be a place where Jacob Powell has done some form of work."

The old woman leaned against her desk and thought for too long, but Josh had to remain patient, and his struggle with the task shown through.

"Nothing comes to mind, Sheriff. I am sorry. What does it mean?"

"It means," Josh said fiercely, "that Gail might be dead before this day is over."

"Sheriff!" Sandi exclaimed. "You cannot possibly believe that anyone would hurt that wonderful lady!"

The look Josh gave would have melted steel, but he had no more time to concern himself with Sandi's approval. If she had nothing to offer, he must move on.

And then, as he was leaving, Sandi called to him from the door. She spoke softly, almost apologetically, relaying the thought that had just come to her. And Josh knew where to go.

* * *

Gail sat motionless as the car went past the cemetery and on down the highway to the east. To her left, Jacob Powell sat quietly, his dark eyes staring straight ahead, his left hand cradling a handgun that she could not reach. His face was cold and emotionless, and he breathed so softly that he seemed almost dead.

"What do you want with me?" she asked through quivering lips.

"I want to show you something," he said as cold as ice.

"What do you want to show me?"

"My wife," was the heartless reply.

"What do you need me for?"

"I need you to finish what I have started."

"What have you started?" she asked.

"You will see soon enough, Ms. Cruz. When we have arrived, you will see."

Gail turned her head away and knew if she did nothing she was going to be killed. Whatever it took, she had to find a way to free herself from this. She could open the door and throw herself from the car, but they were traveling fifty-five miles per hour, and the impact would certainly harm her gravely, if not kill her outright. She could wait for the car to stop somewhere, but the gun he held was pointed at her, and she feared he would not hesitate to use it.

About halfway down the straight leading out of town to the east, Powell slowed the car and turned north onto Rattlesnake Road.

"We have been logging up here for thirteen years," he said. "We have been cutting road the entire time, and they extend into the furthest reaches of the forest. It is so easy to get lost. Fortunately for you, many logging truck drivers use this road every day, so it won't be long before they find you."

"Are you just going to leave me on the road?" Gail asked, already knowing the answer.

"No, not on the road. But close."

"Why are you doing this? How do I fit into your plan? What have I done?"

"You," Powell explained as if he bore no responsibility in the matter, "are simply perfect. You will fit nicely."

"People will have seen me get in the car with you. They'll talk."

"Of course they will. I am counting on it."

"But why?" Gail demanded.

"Because it is time for Mr. Carter to pay for his crimes, and I shall reveal all to the world. I have collected evidence against him for years, and now I must show the world who he is. Then he will suffer as I once did."

Gail recognized that Powell intended to monologue, and she used that moment to make her move, swinging her fist at Powell's face in a powerful backhand. The impact was sudden, but the effect was not as she intended. His cold eyes narrowed, and he shrugged off the blow, reacting quickly with a swift backhand of his own that caught Gail square across her left eye and threw her toward the side window. Her head struck with tremendous force and throbbed immediately on both sides, and she screamed in pain and fear. But before she could raise her hand to her eye, the fist struck again, and she knew she could not overpower a man so strong as Powell. His years logging had gained him an immensely powerful build, and his sinewy muscles swung his arms like battering rams. Gail was helpless. Her only hope lay in her capacity to flee from him once the car stopped.

They drove on for many miles, penetrating the dense forest and diving deeper and deeper into the unknown. Gail had scarcely been off a paved road in her life, and not until her forays with Josh had dirt roads passed beneath her.

With one good eye, she watched out the window for any sign of help, and thought it might arrive as they came upon a logging truck coming down the hill. She prepared herself to scream, but Powell held the gun toward her belly and she held her breath as the throbbing worsened around her swelling left eye. The log truck passed with nothing but a friendly look from the driver.

Another ten minutes passed before Powell turned off onto another road. Gail saw the road sign, NFD 2810, and recognized the crossed sign as described by Josh. She wondered if Powell would mark her with such a thing. A tear rode down her cheek as she thought about the sheriff. He was such a good, kind man, and this murdering maniac had been outsmarting him for all these years. It pained her to know that she would be at the center of the next investigation, and she hoped he would know what to do.

Finally, the car came to a stop. Immediately she grabbed the door handle and pushed, but it was locked. She fumbled with the latch, pulled desperately at it with her thumbs as Powell's backhand returned to her already swollen face. It didn't matter. She continued to pry at the little knob until it finally released and she fell through the open door and ran from the car.

She was having a difficult time seeing, and her head still throbbed from the impact with the window, but she ran ahead and into a thicket where she found cover behind a tree and paused to catch her breath. The sound of a snapping twig jolted her, and she turned to run—

She was stopped cold as Jacob Powell's blade sank into her abdomen.

Searing pain coursed through her as her body, loaded with adrenaline, began to fight the intrusion. She looked up at the hellish gray eyes, frozen in painful madness. At first Powell only sneered at her. Then his expression gave way to a sickening smile as he slowly withdrew the knife from her guts.

"Welcome to my little collection, Abigail Cruz," he said.

Gail sank to her knees.

"A pretty girl like you shouldn't be taking rides with strangers," Jacob snarled as he stooped down and gripped her jowls. The pain was so intense that Gail could only respond with tears. Blood began to trickle from her mouth. The salty, iron taste of it told her she was going to die in this place.

Jacob Powell rose and lifted her with a single hand clenched tightly about her jaw. He lifted the knife to strike her again, and all Gail could do was look up at him and feel sorry for the man. Somehow he seemed to sense it. His face turned crimson, and he brought the knife down.

Gail closed her eyes and waited for the blow to land. In the spilt second of time she knew she had remaining, she allowed her body to relax and wished she had told Josh she had fallen in love with him. The timing had never seemed to be right, and now she regretted not having the courage to just come out and tell him. The calm, handsome face of Sheriff Matthews filled her mind and stayed there, and she imagined his strong arms holding her.

But, the blow did not land. Rather, Powell jerked, and Gail opened her eyes. Powell's own eyes stared down at her. His mouth agape with a stream of blood and brain matter pouring from his temple, Jacob Powell dropped to the ground in a heap. A split second later the crack of a gun echoed up the draw and the sound of heavy footsteps smashing through the brush peeled away at the silence.

"Gail?" a familiar voice called. "Gail?" The voice was panicked, urgent. She knew the name that went with it, but couldn't get it to form on her lips. She listened intently, but she could only hear the sound of rushed footsteps crashing through brush and a sound like blowing leaves. Then sticks cracking and rocks sliding in loose dirt.

"Gail?" came the booming voice.

"I'm here," she said through the pain.

Suddenly, Josh's face appeared above her. He looked over her and pressed his hand against her abdomen. The pain was excruciating, and she called out in agony.

"I'm sorry," he breathed as he took her in his arms. "I'm sorry. Let's get you out of here."

"It was Powell," she muttered.

"I know," Josh said. "I know."

"I thought it was Carter ..."

"It's okay, sweetheart. I've got you!"

* * *

Josh Matthews grimaced as his back rebelled under the weight of his reporter. She was slender and delicate, yet her limp body felt like an overflowing sack of grain as he plowed his way through the dense brush. He tried keeping to the trail and forced his way through the thicket while struggling to hold Gail's head above a tangle of thorns. Using strength he did not remember having, he pushed forward even as the spikes and nettles scraped across his arms with agonizing consequences. A few seconds of this and he finally plowed a path and was on the road back to the truck.

He glanced angrily at the Mercedes as he yanked the truck's passenger door open. "Sweetheart," he said with the passion that had been building ever since he first laid eyes on her, "I'm going to get you to the hospital, but it will hurt a little. I'm really sorry about that."

Gail found his eyes and tried to smile. "It already hurts."

"Okay," Josh said as he slammed the door and raced to the other side. His foot was to the floor the moment the old V8 sputtered to life. With engine roaring and wheels chewing into the wash-boarded dirt road, he reached over with one hand and gently eased Gail's head to his lap. "Lay down here," he said, "so I can get some pressure on that wound." With her head in his lap, he pressed firmly against the oozing cut just above her belly button. He choked back his anguish and struggled to set aside the eerie feeling of déjà vu.

He desperately needed to get on the radio and call for help, but the wound was bleeding badly, and he couldn't bring himself to take his hand away. With another stroke of daring, he took the wheel between his knees and reached across his lap to take the radio with his left hand, flip the call switch, and send out a panicked request for assistance. As before in the canyons west of Bend, there was no answer. His heart sank, and he felt his eyes tearing up.

The road was rutted and felt like driving over an accordion, and the old truck skidded around every corner like a drifting track car. "Sorry," he said, fighting to keep his voice calm.

When Gail failed to respond, Josh looked down and patted her cheek with a bloody hand. "Wake up, woman. Please, wake up!" He slapped harder, and her eyes opened, if only slightly.

"Am I gonna die?" she asked through blood-stained teeth.

"Hell no, sweetheart," Josh said with restrained panic. "I'm not losing another one like this. Hell, no!"

Finally off the mountain and onto pavement, he pushed the truck beyond its limit, its body shuddering and shaking as he broke eighty on a long straight, mashing the brakes to the floor in the corners. With the g-forces pushing and pulling across the bench seat, Gail slid back and forth, leaving a bloody streak on the seat. Josh took his hand away from the wound and a plume of darkening blood spewed forth.

He regained the radio and made his demands. "This is Matthews. I need an ambulance on the way! Gail's hurt very bad."

"Roger that," Linda's voice said on the other end. "We need to know where you are."

"I just turned onto 20 from Rattlesnake Road. Heading west toward town."

"Roger that, Sheriff. How is she?"

"She's bad, Linda. Very bad. Deep knife wound to the abdomen."

"You get the guy?"

"Yes."

"Do we need to send an ambulance up there?"

"No. He needs Don Jackson."

"Roger that."

As he rounded the corner toward town, the flashing of sirens greeted the old truck as Josh skidded to a stop in the middle of the highway. He was out in a flash and to the passenger side as an ambulance and cruiser pulled alongside and turned around. Josh took Gail's limp body into his arms and laid her gently on a gurney as two paramedics went to work with needles and tubes.

"We've got it from here, Sheriff. We'll take good care of her."

Josh choked back his fear and turned to his deputies. He was crying, but fighting hard to keep his composure. "You two get up on that hill. You'll find Powell's body up there where King Mountain Road comes down onto 2810. Where that old log dump is at. Know where I'm talking about?"

"I do," Max said.

Jane seemed surprised by all she was hearing. "You said he was shot?"

"Yeah. The bastard is dead. Get on up there and get it roped off. You'll find him in the thickets between a big rock and the creek. You can't miss the rock. It has a big letter A on it in red paint. It's right at the turnoff."

"You got it, boss," said Max. "Now, you get on down the road and catch that ambulance."

"Max," Josh said as he looked back toward the hills, "I have to go. You get on up there and finish this."

"Sheriff," Max interrupted, "Jane and I have this. You go on now. Gail needs you. We've got it, okay?" He leaned forward and pushed Josh toward the truck. "You go."

Josh looked at his protégé and smiled, then wiped his eyes and got into the truck. His deputies waved him off, and Josh pressed the accelerator. The ambulance had already disappeared into town, but he knew where it was going.

TWELVE

J osh leaned back on the uncomfortable couch and closed his eyes. He thought back over his life, from the childhood years when he'd wanted to join the army, the war years as he fought alongside his buddies all across Africa and Italy, then into France and beyond. He remembered the fear as bullets streaked past and shells rained down from above. He remembered the joy upon seeing his beloved Alyson for the first time in so many long, lonely months, and the time they'd shared before their daughter came into the world. He remembered the uncontrollable horror when Alyson had fallen down that awful ravine and the sickening sound she'd made when he pulled her from the log upon which she was impaled. And the anguish that tore through him when she stopped breathing and he knew she was gone from his life.

All those horrible, dreadful memories paled in comparison to what he felt right then as Gail lay on an operating table fighting for her life. He loved her. He knew that now, and he loved her more deeply than he had ever loved before. Whatever hidden power she had over him, he gave in to it completely. He was desperate for her to live. He could not lose her as he had lost Alyson. As the emotions overcame him, Josh rubbed his forehead and fought against the moisture building once again in his eyes.

He was too tired to think about recent events and too overcome with emotion to sleep, so all he could do was lie back and worry. He had no idea how much time had gone by, but the sound of footsteps brought him upright as he scanned the room for some unseen dread.

"Sheriff," came a strange voice.

Josh rubbed his eyes and yawned. "Yes," he said.

A woman came into focus, and he recognized her as a nurse he had met many times before. "You can see her now."

"How long has it been?" he asked.

"You've been out all night. She's waking from the anesthesia, and the doctor says you can go in, but you have to be quiet. She won't be able to talk for about six hours, but you can sit with her."

"That . . ." He took a breath. "That's great. How's she doing?"

"Well, she made it through, so that's good. She'll be in pain, but we'll manage that throughout the day. Make sure you wash your hands, okay?"

Overwhelmed, Josh could only nod as he followed the nurse down the hall. He entered the ICU behind her and followed her lead at the wash station, then went to a small room off to one side and gazed down at the miserable state of Gail's condition. She lay on her back with a breathing tube in her mouth and taped to her cheeks, an IV dangling from her left arm, and two collection bottles hanging from the side of her bed. She looked cold and miserable. Her left eye was swollen and badly bruised, her nose was lacerated across the bridge, and there was a nasty bump on her right temple.

"She has a catheter to manage urine," said the nurse, "and the other one is drainage from the site. She'll keep both bottles for a few days. Once she can get out of bed and walk around, we'll take them out."

Josh nodded that he understood, although he could barely remember what the nurse had said.

"Remember, she's not supposed to talk for a while, so you

just sit in here and mind your business."

Josh looked at Gail and frowned at the pain he knew she must be feeling. She was hurting, and her breathing was shallow, even with the assistance of the breathing tube and the whir of the machine pumping air through it. Very gently, he took her hand in his and pulled a chair to the edge of the bed.

"We got him," he said.

Gail opened her good eye and slowly eased her head into a single nod, then closed her eye again while lightly squeezing his hand.

"You were right," said Josh. "You were right about all of it."

She squeezed again.

Josh sighed deeply and laid his head on her forearm as if seeking her forgiveness. She had been right, and were it not for Sandi, a woman who regularly scorned him, she would not be alive.

"It was Sandi," he said as he looked up at her swollen face. "She told me where you would be. She knew the place. Three years ago Powell donated that place as a snowmobile-parking site. He had these big clearings all over where the skidders dragged in the logs, then loaded them onto trucks to haul to the mill. He owned seven of them, all designated with a letter. That one was site A. Sandi said it's where her husband worked for years until he died. She would sometimes take him lunch up there and eat with him. Made him feel a little less disconnected with the long hours. They sat behind this big rock and listened to the creek. So, when I asked her if she knew a place connected to Powell with a letter A somewhere nearby, she knew it had to be the place. Turns out she was right." He took a breath, considering the alternative. "Thank God she was right."

Gail again opened her eye and Josh saw a twinkle in there and knew she was with him. He knew she would be okay.

Time passed slowly and Josh had never been quite so bored, yet he refused to leave Gail's side. Max shuffled in and out to carry instructions to the office, as well as to request a warrant to raid Jacob Powell's residence. He returned only thirty minutes later with a note from Judge Parker. "Burn the place down" it said. Josh smiled and knew what that meant. The warrant covered the entire property, and his deputies were free to dig up whatever needed unearthing. There were no restrictions.

Finally, the doctor came for a visit and determined the breathing tube should be removed. "Could you give us some privacy?" he asked.

Josh left the room and paced the hall for nearly an hour as the medical staff did what needed to be done. When he was invited back in the request for silence remained. Besides, Gail was high on morphine and resting. Four more hours passed before Max returned again, this time seeking permission to begin the raid.

"No," Josh said. "You've got a car out there?"

"Two," Max answered.

"Wait until I have a chance to talk with this awesome lady. Then I'm going out with you."

"Yes, sir."

"Jane," Josh reminded Max. "I want her there."

"She's ready."

Rustling came from the bed, and Josh turned to see Gail's eyes locked on him. "Hello," he said.

"Hi," she said back. Her voice was raspy, but she refused to let it stop her. "How's my favorite lawman?"

Josh stood to be next to her. "I'm fine," he said.

Max started out of the room, but Gail stopped him. "Max," she whispered as she waved him over. She reached up and took his hand, and he bent down and kissed her on the cheek.

"Get better," he said. "We miss you out there."

Gail smiled and Max left.

The brief conversations had sapped her strength and she closed her eyes to rest. Another hour passed before she was finally able to talk.

"Want to know something funny?" Josh asked her.

"Oh, do tell," she said, then coughed and grimaced.

Josh slid closer and took her cheek in his hand. "Are you hurting?"

She nodded. "Yes."

"I'm sorry, I—"

"Josh." She reached up and touched his hand. "It's not your fault."

"I know. I just don't like to see you hurting."

"Maybe you could kiss it better?" She managed a wink.

Josh smiled and laughed. "I think I could help with that." He leaned down and gently pressed his lips to hers and held her for a full minute.

"Now," she asked, "what was this funny thing you were talking about?"

"Ah, yes," he said as he adjusted himself on the bed so he didn't put pressure on her. "Do you remember Melissa Reed's testimony?"

"Yes."

"Remember when Carl reminded her that she saw dancing pink bunnies?"

"I remember."

"I thought she was seeing things, too. Honestly, I never would have thought anything else about it until I saw Powell's car."

Gail strained to sit up and squinted at him. "Do tell," she said.

Josh leaned into her and gently pushed her head back against the pillow. "You stay put, young lady. I would prefer you heal."

She sighed deeply, and again the pain revealed itself in her expression.

"Do you need something for that?"

"No. It's okay. The doctor says I can have more, but it makes me feel funny. Besides, I want to see your handsome face. Now, the pink bunnies. What gives?"

"This is going to sound silly."

"What?"

"This big, long car . . ."

"The black Mercedes. Yeah, I know. I rode in it."

"Yes," Josh chuckled lovingly, "I know. Well, on the back bumper, on either side of the license plate, there are pink Playboy bunny stickers."

"Say what?" Gail asked with a pained smile.

"You heard me. Here's the funny part. There's no way Melissa would remember seeing that."

"Then how could she have known?" Gail asked.

"The only thing I can figure is that when she stepped on the brakes when they went by, the brake lights lit the back of the Mercedes very briefly and she saw those bunnies. They're reflective, you see, so they kind of flare when light strikes them. Even if she can't *remember* seeing them, her brain stored the image, and that's exactly what she saw when the LSD hit her."

"Dancing pink bunnies."

Josh smiled. "How's that for evidence?"

Gail started laughing. "I bet that's a real head scratcher for Carl."

Josh joined her in laughter. "I'm sure it is. Always remember, dancing pink bunnies are not admissible."

"Oh, I will." Gail's soft laughter filled the room until a grimace revealed her pain. "It hurts," she said.

"I'll get the nurse." Josh found the staffer and then returned. "She'll be in in a minute." He took Gail's hand and stroked her cheek. "You're so beautiful."

"Oh," she sighed, "you like a frumpy hospital girl, do you?"

"I'll admit you've looked better."

"Ha!" she chortled.

A nurse finally entered the room with a needle and plunged it into the IV. "This should help." She straightened a few things, wrote something in the chart, smiled, and left the room.

"Thanks," Gail said and closed her eyes. "Wow," she said, "that's so nice."

Josh kissed her lips, her forehead, and her nose, and then left the room. She'd be sleeping for a while. And regardless of his love's situation, he still had work to do.

Sheriff Matthews stood by as Jane took a key from her pocket, slid it into the bronze lock of Jacob Powell's front entrance, and pushed the oak door open. It was massive—Josh guessed it weighed two hundred pounds or more—yet it opened with a smooth, silent swing until it stopped against a rubber pad protruding from the wall. Josh stepped through the door and gasped at the unrestrained splendor on display. The entry was twenty feet high and dominated by a crystal chandelier aglow with a hundred yellow lights. The entry led the party into a great room of pine logs and walnut furniture, floor to ceiling drapes, and plush carpet. In an adjacent room, a table set for fourteen appeared to be made from a single slab of pine, delicately finished with lacquer a quarter-inch thick and surrounded by generously cushioned chairs of matching wood. Silver-plated utensils, fine china settings, and sterling shakers adorned the surface, all neatly set atop silken placemats.

"This guy lived like a king," Josh said.

"Yeah, you ain't kidding," Max said from a different vantage point. "The man knew how to spend his money."

"Have a look at this, Sheriff," Jane said as she opened a glass-top case.

Josh stepped over and looked into the case. Upon a velvet liner, a collection of firearms lay in all their menacing glory. "Wow," he said, "would you look at that Colt. Beautiful."

"Might want to take that one home with you," Jane said with a smile. "Don't you think?"

The sheriff whistled. "Don't I wish, but the people might not take too kindly to their sheriff swiping guns from a criminal's home."

Josh ran his fingers over the guns before closing the case, and then walked through the living room, tapping the furniture with his flashlight and looking at the stunning artwork hanging on the walls. He tested the couch, dug through a random drawer or two, then hunted through the kitchen, even opening the refrigerator and noting the man liked thick rib eye steaks, beer, and ketchup.

"Jane?" came Max's voice from another room. "Come in here, please."

Josh caught Jane's eyebrows rising and accompanied her to where Max stood at the opening of a narrow door that led down into a darkened basement. "Who wants to go down the creepy stairs first?" he asked.

"Aren't men supposed to be the valiant, chivalrous ones?" Jane chided.

Max smiled, flipped the light switch, and started down the stairs.

At the bottom, they turned a corner and stepped into a room eerily lit with old-fashioned wall lamps. The walls were red velvet, the floor dark-stained wood, the ceiling the same. A desk with a green-shaded lamp stood against one wall and a file cabinet against the opposite.

Max decided to test the desk and seated himself at the fine leather chair. Josh motioned to the uncountable articles, photographs, maps, and charts attached to the walls. "He was a busy fellow, don't you think?"

Jane stared in silence while Max walked from wall to wall, marveling at the detail and organization spread over the velvet coverings.

"Sheriff, are you seeing this?" Jane asked.

"I'm seeing it," Josh said, "but I don't believe what I'm seeing. This just can't be what it looks like. These articles date back twenty years, Jane." Josh pointed at a newspaper clipping dated in the mid-sixties. "This one recounts the day his wife killed their son and herself. That was in sixty-three. It says, 'Marcus Powell, the nine-year-old son of entrepreneur Jacob Powell, was killed on Monday. Authorities have determined that the child's mother, Angela Powell, shot the boy before turning the gun on herself. No motive has been given."

Jane pointed to a series of photographs held to a corkboard with small pins. "Annette Walker, Nikki Rhodes, Gina Bergmann, Eryn Rogers, Lisa Martin. They all look a lot like his wife."

Max came around and scanned the pictures. "Hard to believe there are five such similar-looking women in the world let alone one county of eight thousand people."

"I don't know," Jane said, "there are a lot of brunettes on the planet."

"Here," said Josh, pointing at a pile of material. "This is what we're looking for."

Jane stood beside him and took the top paper, which was a list of names, locations, and letter codes. "A, N, G, E, L, A," she read. "All the victims' first names, and all in order. That last one would be Gail. Or should I say Abigail? Where they were killed, how, when. This is amazing."

"I can't even conceive of that kind of forethought to take a human life," Josh said.

"And he took five," added Max.

"He was sick," said Jane as she studied a series of recent articles from the *Burns Review*. "Gail is definitely not on his list, so I think she must have been more of a last-minute decision, because she was maybe getting in the way. Look at this." She pointed at several lines underlined in red.

"We were getting close," observed Josh. "Gail sorted out the last bit a little too late."

"Yes. She even theorized that one of Burns's wealthy residents was the culprit. She was definitely onto something, and he must have adjusted his plans in order to get rid of her."

"He almost did."

"You cut it pretty close, Sheriff," Jane said. "A few more seconds and she'd be gone."

"I wonder if he planned to wait two or three more years, but Gail unwittingly became an easy target for him to finish his little game."

"I think so," Jane said. "Otherwise, why would he risk another investigation so soon?"

"Desperation." Max said.

"I don't know if I would call it desperation, or even a momentary lack of reason."

"Something triggered him," Josh said. "I'm guessing something Gail wrote got under his skin, and he decided to do something about it. How convenient he must have thought it that her name began with an A."

"Listen to this," said Jane as she held up a fading page from a journal. "It's a poem penned by Mr. Jacob Curtis Powell.

Alone in the night, mystery keep
Watch over my shadow, but cannot see
Sheriff and minions, blind and deaf
Chasing for nothing, lost in the dark.

"Wow," she said. "That's pretty dark. Poking fun at Sheriff Matthews like that . . . Just wow." And she smiled at her humor.

Said Max, "The sheriff put a bullet in the man's temple with an old .45 from twenty yards. So, I guess he got the last laugh, right?"

Jane smiled at the thought. "Wish I'd been there to see it. Oh, here's a laugher. Check this out. This is the article Gail wrote after the trial. He wrote 'stupid, stupid, stupid' and circled Sheriff Matthew's picture. Sheriff, it's like he was toying with you and loving that he was driving you mad."

"Things have a way of working full circle," Josh said as he turned from the desk and hunted the walls, this time looking behind each page, each article and photo. There was nothing left to see. To the last minute, Jacob Powell had kept the truth of his handiwork from the authorities and played the part of innocent businessman and duty-bound jurist to perfection. The only mistake Josh could determine he had made was driving a car with pink bunnies on the bumper. He could never have foreseen Melissa Reed's drug-induced hallucination leading directly to his own death.

Josh turned to leave the room and stood at the base of the stairs waiting on his deputies. From some random bit of morbid curiosity, Jane turned to a shelf and opened a file, removed a photograph . . . and stood speechless.

"What is it?" Josh asked.

Jane turned the photograph so Josh could see it. "Only Robert Carter standing with who I presume is Annette Walker."

Josh took the photo and studied it. "I do believe that is her, but it makes no sense."

"It does now," Jane said as she produced another photo from the file. "Have a look at this."

Josh took a small stack of photographs from Jane and scanned through them. All had a common theme. "All five victims," he said, "and they're all with Robert Carter."

"So that's the tie-in?" Jane asked with an amazed look upon her face. "Carter was having affairs with all of them?"

"And they went unnoticed before Lisa Martin."

Josh decided the photographs could not be interpreted any differently. Each victim, at some point in the past, had been seen with Robert Carter in a situation he would certainly not want revealed to his wife.

When Josh flipped to the last photograph, it suddenly made sense.

"Powell's wife was having an affair with Robert Carter?" Josh asked with stunned emotion.

Max stood speechless while Jane produced yet more photographs, all witness to the fact that Robert Carter had indeed had an affair with the killer's wife. "It seems Mr. Carter was a little busier than he let on."

Josh could only shake his head. "Carter's mill made Powell rich, and the whole time Carter was doing the man's wife. Unbelievable." He thought back to his limited knowledge of the Powell family and then remembered the big fight they'd had a few weeks before Angela Powell had killed her son and herself. "They fought about it. Then she shot her own son and shot herself through the base of her chin."

"Do you think," Jane asked, "that Powell arranged all of this to get even with Carter?"

Josh thought about the question. "Perhaps. So why frame Hodges?"

"I don't think he did," Jane said with an all-knowing smile. "I think he planted the stuff hoping any one of those men would find it."

"But why?" Max asked.

"To buy time, maybe," Jane said. "After all, he still had one more letter. Clearly it was all part of his plan. It's weird, for sure. But we have what we need. This room will convict Powell."

"You can say that again," said Max.

Josh took a last look around the room and went back up the stairs. One final thing needed doing before he went back into town. He went to Jacob Powell's refrigerator and pulled three bottles of beer from the six-pack he had spied earlier. "Now, don't any of you say a word of this to anyone."

They shook their heads.

Josh opened the beers and passed them around. He held his up and smiled a pained smile. "I've sent a letter to the commissioner announcing my retirement effective September 1."

He expected a different response than the one he got. Jane was the first to step forward. She put her arms around his neck, leaned up, and kissed him on the cheek, then whispered congratulations in his ear.

When Jane had had her fill and backed away, Max reached out his hand and gripped Josh's with a firm, triumphant squeeze. "We got this guy, my friend. We got him! And good luck to you."

Josh smiled at his deputies. "Max, I'm recommending you as interim sheriff until the next election. I have faith in you, son. You'll do well."

Max nodded. "Thanks for cleaning this mess up, first," he said with a chuckle.

"I had to finish it," Josh said. "Gail and I had to finish it."

* * *

The sun shone brightly on the horizon, and a mystical purple-red glow began to creep across the sky just as it had countless evenings before. Butterflies danced in the air, and misty clouds shimmered across the distant waves as a soft, salted breeze blew across a white sand beach. The rush of wind and the rumble of the big V-twin shattered the advancing twilight as dashed yellow lines drifted past in the rearview mirror.

"You okay back there?" Josh yelled over his shoulder.

Gail's arms drew tighter around his waist. "I'm doing just fantastic," she called back. "Can this thing go any faster?"

"You bet she can. Hang on." Josh twisted the throttle and the old Harley thundered forward. The power and the vibration and the wind gave him a thrill he hadn't felt in a very long time, surpassed only by the eager passion of the beautiful woman clinging to him.

"I can't believe we're doing this," Gail yelled over the roar of the engine.

Josh reached down and rested his hand on her thigh and warmth he hadn't felt in so many years rushed through his body. He stroked her leg and squeezed and felt the firmness of her, and he was happy.

Gail followed with her own hand and intermingled her fingers with his as the sparkle of wedding rings shown in the setting sun. She leaned harder into him and nuzzled his neck. "This seat could do with a little padding," she said into his ear.

Josh smiled into the wind. "Where's the adventure in that?"

She laughed and laid her head against his shoulder.

Josh maneuvered the bike around the curves and watched as the hills and beaches of the Pacific Ocean slipped past. He loved it all: the sound, the smell, and the rumble of the exhaust thudding against his ears. And the feel of his wife's soft, feminine curves pressed against his back. With her, he was finally free to roam, free to play, and free to love again.

And they rode on as the distant, glowing sun sank out of sight.

273

Kenneth Scherer has a lifelong fascination with writing and the perils of war. He enjoys backpacking in the Idaho mountains and endlessly dreaming up the next great story. In *Honor*, his first novel, he explores love, loyalty, and the intricate complexities and horrors of warfare. In his second novel, *Redemption*, he told the very personal story of his own son wrapped around a host of fictional characters. Now, in a collaborative effort with his good friend Theodore Bohlman, *The Sixth Angel: A Murder Mystery* comes to life. Kenneth lives in Boise, Idaho, with his wife, Heather, and daughter, Jessyka.

* * *

Theodore Bohlman was born March 12th 1943 to Dr. Ivan and Lola Bohlman in College Place, Washington. He received his education in a parochial school system from grade 1 thru medical school at Loma Linda University. Having grown up in a physician's family, it was always assumed he would become a doctor, and he was privileged to practice medicine for over 30 years in the discipline of gastroenterology. Now long retired, he fills his day with activities that interest him such as woodworking, photography, drone flying, golf, fishing, and travel. He is happily married to his wife, Susanna, has 3 wonderful children, and 6 grandchildren. Theodore resides in Meridian, Idaho.

Made in the USA
Middletown, DE
29 February 2020

85563623R00168